Say It Ain't So

Say It Ain't So

La Jill Hunt

URBAN
Renaissance

www.urbanbooks.net

Urban Books, LLC
78 East Industry Court
Deer Park, NY 11729

Say It Ain't So Copyright © 2009 La Jill Hunt

ISBN 13: 978-1-60162-324-9
ISBN 10: 1-60162-324-0

First Mass Market Printing November 2011
First Trade Paperback Printing November 2009
Printed in the United States of America

10 9 8 7 6 5 4 3 2 1

This is a work of fiction. Any references or similarities to actual events, real people, living, or dead, or to real locales are intended to give the novel a sense of reality. Any similarity in other names, characters, places, and incidents is entirely coincidental.

Distributed by Kensington Publishing Corp.
Submit Wholesale Orders to:
Kensington Publishing Corp.
C/O Penguin Group (USA) Inc.
Attention: Order Processing
405 Murray Hill Parkway
East Rutherford, NJ 07073-2316
Phone: 1-800-526-0275
Fax: 1-800-227-9604

In Loving memory of my big brother, Troy V. Lee. For all of the love, laughs, and joy you brought into our lives. I will make sure the secret recipe for your Cheese burger Macaroni Hamburger Helper remains a legacy with our family, LOL. I miss you, Troy!!

R.I.P. my friend!

Acknowledgments

Without a doubt, and as always, I thank God for opportunity, talent, patience, and sustenance.

To Alyx, Kam, and Ken, you know Mommy loves you, even though I snap every now and then, LOL.

To my family, for all of the love and support! Welcome baby Karissa aka Apple and baby Kaiden aka Cheeto. And welcome to the fam Chante Jones Hunt and Ken Moore.

My BFF's for life: Joycelyn Ward, Shantel Spencer, Saundra White, Yvette Lewis, Jana James, Roxanne Elmore, Tonya Kabia, Toye Farrar, Norell Smith, and Torrence Oxendine. After all of these years, it's good to know you still have my back!

To The Breakfast Crew—My NEW BFF's, LOL. Chenay Cuffee (girl, you are def my ride or die road dawg who keeps me laughing), Monteal Cuffee (you are the glue that holds the crew together), Monica Simon (the fashionista glam diva who loves us enough to "waste" an outfit) and Anisha Holmes (the only one of us with any sense). I love you guys so much and I don't know what I would do without our weekly "talks."

To Pastor K. W. Brown, Elder Valerie Brown, and the Mt. Lebanon Missionary Baptist Church Family, thanks for loving, supporting, and praying for me, even in my absence. The prodigal child will be home soon. Believe that.

To my VZ BFF's: Omedia Cutler, Milly Avent, Angela Burleigh, Pamela Carrington, Robin LeBron, Yolanda Stanislaus (and John, LOL), Cherie Johnson, Ross Cooper aka Mosaic, and Chris CTY Young. You know I love you guys!

To my literary fam who stays in my corner and continue showing me love: Dwayne S. Joseph (man, you are truly my brother), Nakea Murray (for all of your hard core advice), Portia Cannon (my agent and cheerleader!) Robilyn Heath, Thomas Long, K'Wan, Kevin Elliott, Erick S. Gray, Nikki Turner, Tiffany L. Smith, Brandon McCalla, and Karen Q. Miller.

To Carl and Martha Weber and the Urban Books staff, thank you for all that you do.

To my Navy College Crew: Leslie Dickey (my on-the-job therapist), Tamara James (my personal fashion police), Tommy Hale (for listening to me talk ALL DAY LONG, lol), Rebecca Ludwig (the "token white chick" girlfriend), Bill Rogers (who stole my desk), Anissa Walker, Lowell Bellard (and no, I didn't write this book on company time!), Ray (one Ray, not Ray-Ray, or Blue Ray) Samson, Hugo (GOOD MORNING!) Roman, Rosnette (I'm at the Exchange) Hayes, Mr. Byrd (the new GRANDPA) and Robert (The Rev) Jones.

To the fans, the readers, the bookstores, and the supporters—thank you, thank you, thank you! Please hit me up at **MsLajaka@AOL.com** or on Facebook.

Prologue

"The cream always rises to the top, ladies. Don't ever forget that!" Paisley called out as she seductively moved her body off the floor and kneeled in front of the empty chair. The sounds of Prince's "Darling Nikki" blared from the speakers and she swerved to the beat. "More! More! More! Make him want you, ladies! Come on!"

Her eyes closed as she imagined her lover seated in the chair, and she moved her body in a way that she knew would please him. She glanced into the mirror at the group of twenty women mimicking the movements she had been teaching them, each with a chair of their own in front of them. They were a varied group, from the twenty-one-year-old, pencil-thin blonde, to the full-figured, fifty-year-old Asian grandmother, to the small-framed African American business woman. Each student had paid an extra fifty dollars for tonight's sold-out, two-hour "Flavor of the Month" class, where they learned a sexy dance number Paisley choreographed.

Dressed in men's dress shirts and ties, the women let Paisley know by the intensity of their facial expressions that they were trying to perfect each step of the exotic lap dance routine. As the music pounded louder and guitar sounds pumped in the air, Paisley opened her shirt and tossed her head around and around, her long hair whipping across her face. The song ended, and she could hear the relief of her students as they all sighed, groaned, and applauded at the same time.

"Now that was a workout!" one student gasped.

"Naw, the workout is when I get home tonight and demonstrate for my man!" another laughed.

Paisley laughed, "That's right. Use what you got, ladies, and I have given you a lot tonight!"

"Indeed, you have," the older lady told her. "I told my doctor that coming here was so much better than the boring physical therapy he prescribed for me. And my mobility has improved so much."

"Believe me, I look forward to coming to The Playground every week. I wish I could come more, but my schedule just won't let me," the black woman, who Paisley knew was a real estate agent, added.

The other ladies nodded in agreement as they wiped beads of perspiration from their faces and foreheads. The moment made Paisley proud. She knew that opening a studio like hers was a risk, one she almost hadn't taken, but seeing the smiles on her students' faces and hearing the excitement in their voices let her know that she had made the right decision. After graduating with her degree in physical therapy and finding no satisfaction working in a confined clinical setting, she had decided to purchase the old dance studio she passed daily and transform it into an erotic fitness center for women. She coupled her medical training with her talent, her extensive experience as a video vixen, and her dance training, and the result was a hit that she named "The Playground." Paisley's classes were all about teaching women how to embrace being sexy—how to move, look, and feel sexy. She felt that all women were beautiful regardless of age, shape, size, or weight, and she instilled that confidence into all of her Playground members. Her studio was more successful than she ever could have imagined, and was now the "it" place for women.

Paisley's BlackBerry chimed. She looked at her watch and announced, "All right, ladies. Same time next month, unless you're scheduled for regular classes this week!"

"Bye, Paisley!"

The women all hugged her as they left. Picking up her phone, she walked over to the stereo and turned it off. Smiling, she redialed the last number.

"Too busy shaking your ass to take my call?" the deep voice asked.

"Now, is that any way for a man of God to be talking?" She laughed.

"Yeah, if he's trying to get in contact with you and he knows you're too busy shaking your ass to come to the phone. And don't go there with that man of God crap. God knows my heart and my flaws. No man is perfect."

"Boy, someone is having a bad day," Paisley said. "And for your information, I was finishing up my class!"

"Oh, so you were too busy teaching other women how to shake their asses to answer the phone."

"Whatever!"

It had been a while since they had talked. Nearly four months. They would check in with each other weekly via text messaging, but their verbal conversations were few and far between. It was just one of the downsides to their friendship, but she had gotten used to it. He was busy and so was she. The more successful they both became, the less they were available.

"How are things going? I read the article they did on you in *Jet*. You know I was so proud," she told him.

"Thanks," he replied. "I saw you in *XXL Magazine* a few months back. You're looking better than ever."

Paisley was surprised. She wondered if he'd had to sneak a peak in the grocery store. *Who are you kidding? You know he doesn't go to the grocery store. He would get mobbed by the fans. Hmm, maybe he glanced at it while waiting at the airport. They sell XXL in the terminals. It doesn't matter. The important thing is that he saw it and he thinks you look good.*

"Thanks. That means a lot coming from you," she said.

"I really need to talk."

Something in his voice made her uneasy. She could sense the distress. "What's up? Talk to me."

"Are you done for the night?"

"Yeah. I have a meeting later with Diesel," she said, referring to her friend and business partner, "but you know I got time for you. What's going on?"

"Let's go to Charley's."

"Huh? When did you even get into town? How long are you here for?" The words came out of her mouth so fast that it sounded like one long sentence. The thought of seeing him excited her. It had been almost a year since they had met face-to-face. The last time they had seen each other was backstage at the BET Awards. She was about to go on stage as a lead dancer for the Outkast performance, and he had just received an award for Gospel Album of the Year.

"Congratulations," she said, and smiled as he walked by.

"Thank you, beautiful lady," he said, leaning over and gently touching her hand. The moment was brief, but meaningful. Later that night, he left her a message on her voice mail telling her how wonderful it was seeing her. She still had the message saved. Now, here he was, out of nowhere, telling her to meet him, *and wanting to meet at a bar at that. Something's up, and it must be big.*

"No one knows I'm here. I just landed and I'm getting a rental car. Catch a cab and meet me there in twenty minutes," he said, and hung up the phone before she could object. Paisley gathered up her towel and tried to think. Twenty minutes didn't even give her time to shower and change. *Well, my being late won't make him any more pissed at the world than he already is,* she thought as she smiled and rushed to get ready.

An hour later, all eyes were on her as she made her way through the mixed crowd of college students, cowboy hats, and surfer dudes to the back of the club where, to her pleasure, she found him sitting. At any other place they would be worried that someone would recognize them, but not at Charley's; most of the customers were so drunk that they probably wouldn't recognize their own parents if they walked in the joint.

"I knew you were gonna be late," he said as he stood up. He still looked the same: tall and lean, cocoa brown complexion with deep-set, mysterious eyes. They were dressed alike, both wearing jeans and white shirts. His black leather jacket was on the back of his seat, while she had hers on.

She rushed into his arms, elated to finally be able to hug him. The familiar scent of Kenneth Cole Black filled her nostrils. His arms held her tight and he almost crushed her body into his. It was a struggle holding back the tears of joy that were threatening to emerge. Instead, she blinked them back and her eyes rested on the table. She saw the glass holding the dark liquor.

"Whoa! I know this drink ain't yours," she said, releasing herself from his grasp.

"It's been that kind of week," he told her as they sat down. The telltale signs of weariness were in his expression and she couldn't resist reaching over and touching his handsome face.

"Must be, for you to sneak down here to see me," she said as she smiled. "Drinking, cursing. What's going on?"

"Everything," he told her. "I don't even know where to begin."

"Start at the beginning," Paisley told him. She eased her jacket off and turned to place it on the back of her chair. She could feel someone's eyes on her, and turned to see a guy staring. His eyes went from her breasts to her face, then he quickly turned away. She was used to the attention and ignored him, turning her focus back to the conversation. "Things can't be that bad. Every time I turn on the radio, I hear 'You Are'."

"Crazy, isn't it? I can't believe it myself." He laughed shortly.

"What's crazy about it, the fact that it's being played on all the stations now, not just the gospel ones?" She laughed.

"Well, yeah, plus it's a song I wrote about you! You still got that letter I wrote all those years ago?"

"As a matter of fact, I do," she confessed. It was tucked right in her top drawer, along with the rest of the letters and poems he wrote her that eventually became hit songs. She couldn't help but feel flattered that she was his muse. "But having a platinum album and a number one single is a good thing, right?"

"You know what, Paisley? I really don't know. It's all beginning to be so damn much. Sometimes, I feel like such a fraud. This whole image thing, you know it's not really me," he said. "I'm not some perfect saint like people think I am, you know that."

"No one says you have to be perfect. You're human just like everyone else," she replied.

"Naw, I'm the Prince of Praise, the Gospel Godson, the Singing Sensation . . ."

"You're right, and those are all things to be proud of, but you're also you. You're putting these expectations on yourself, and you don't have to," she interrupted him. *There's no way I'm going to let him have a pity party on me. I am not the one. He has too much to be thankful for, and he's too blessed to even go there.* She was determined to go word for word, and they both knew she could out talk the best of them.

"Did I mention that I *hate* my wife? I hate being around her. I hate that I have to look at her. I extended my tour a month and a half because I didn't want to go home," he said, and stared. Paisley didn't have a response for that one. All these years, she knew how he felt, but he never said anything, so neither did she. It wasn't her place. He had chosen to say "I do" all those years ago; no one had made him. He picked up his glass, swallowed the liquor in one gulp, and told her, "I can't do this anymore. I want a divorce."

Paisley sat speechless, not knowing what to say. He seemed to be relieved, and smiled.

"Would you like another?"

The voice seemed to come out of nowhere and startled her. She looked up and saw a waitress in a Charley's sweatshirt standing next to the table.

"Pais, you want a drink?" he asked.

"No, no thank you," she answered.

"You can bring me another one," he told the waitress. "Jack on the rocks."

"Coming right up." The girl smiled and rushed off to get his drink.

"Say something," he told her.

"What do you want me to say?" Paisley shrugged.

"Hell, I don't know. Say what you're feeling. What are you thinking?"

I'm thinking that you're out of your damn mind. I'm thinking that you shoulda thought about all this nine fucking years ago when I told you marrying her ass was a bad idea. I'm thinking that if you think I'm going to just say "okay" and we're going to live happily ever after, you've got it twisted!

Instead of sharing what she was thinking, Paisley just said, "I think you should pray before you do anything."

"Oh, come on! What the hell is that? I fly all the way here, risk everything to come and meet you, pour my heart and soul out and all you can come up with is 'I think you should pray'?" His voice was full of frustration.

"What do you want me to say? You know that divorcing your wife for no reason would be career suicide right now. You also know that there's not a snowball's chance in hell that you and I would be able to just pick up where we left off before your ass decided to get married. You didn't like her when you were dating her!" Paisley shook her head. The waitress brought his drink to the table and he reached into his pocket and gave her a fifty.

"I'll be right back with your change." She smiled.

"Naw, you're good," he mumbled.

"You sure?" she asked, looking at Paisley for confirmation.

Paisley nodded and told her, "Yes, thank you."

He picked up the glass, again swallowing the entire drink, his eyes never leaving Paisley. The tension now between them was thick, and she wondered what was next.

"Now what?" she asked.

"Well, I guess now I take you home and go back to the hotel, unless you wanna join me?" He smiled.

"You know that's not happening." She smiled back. For a split second, she considered joining him. She still wanted him; wanted to feel him inside her once again. Feel his lips on hers, his tongue tasting her very being. Have him satisfy her like only he could. Make love to him like they had done many nights, many years ago, before he stood before God and everyone else and vowed to love, honor, and cherish a woman he knew he couldn't stand.

They stood up and put their coats on, then walked hand in hand out into the chilly January night. Being the true gentleman that he was, he opened the car door and they got into the rented Lincoln. He turned the radio station as they waited for the car to warm up, and both of them laughed when they heard his voice singing "You Are." He pulled out of the parking lot and as she listened to the words of the song, her song, Paisley again considered going back to his hotel room.

No one would ever know. You can be his and he can be yours, just for tonight. Just like old times. No harm, no foul. Just go. You are Pais-

ley Lawrence, the Sensual Seductress. Be the fantasy you know he wants. The one you once were. The one you'll always be.

Paisley looked over at him and he took her hand into his. She loved him. He was her friend, *still the best of friends after all this time.* He needed her. She wanted to be there for him.

"I love you," he said.

"I love you too," she replied.

The glare of beaming headlights caused both of them to look ahead. He leaned on the horn and she closed her eyes as she braced herself for the impact she knew was coming. Tires screeched and pain seared through her body as her world faded to black.

Chapter 1

"Tell him I'll call him later. I don't have time to meet. I have a family emergency. Scooter has everything else under control. If you need anything, just call him."

For a moment, Paisley thought she was dreaming about her friend, Diesel. But as she struggled to open her eyes, she realized that it wasn't a dream and he was standing in front of her, talking into his cell phone. She blinked, trying to focus. Pain radiated through her body like ripples of fire, causing her to instantly squeeze her eyes shut and moan.

"Paisley, hey, it's okay." She heard Diesel's baritone voice.

"Oh, God," she whispered, struggling to breathe.

"Let me get a nurse," Diesel told her.

"Nurse?" She tried to think, but she was in too much pain.

Moments later, he returned with a small brunette who smiled at her as she fumbled with the IV that, she now noticed, was running into her arm.

"This will take the edge off some of the pain, Ms. Lawrence. I just need to get some quick vitals on you."

"What the hell happened to me?" Paisley's voice cracked as she strained to talk.

"You were in an accident, Paisley. A bad one, too. You're lucky to still be with us, girl," Diesel smiled and gently touched her face.

Paisley suddenly felt light-headed. The pain subsided and she fought the drowsiness. "An accident? What the hell? Is my truck totaled?"

"Paisley, you weren't driving." Diesel glanced over at the nurse who was watching the blood pressure monitor, which was squeezing Paisley's arm.

"Ahhh." Paisley grimaced.

"I'm sorry." The nurse gave her a sympathetic look.

"This is crazy, Diesel. What are you talking about? I don't know what's going on," Paisley told him.

"It happened late last night, Paisley. The car you were riding in had a head-on collision." Diesel sighed. "I'm just glad you're all right. Man, we were worried."

"You didn't have to do that." Paisley could feel herself dozing off. She looked over at Diesel. He was truly one of her best friends, more like a brother. They met during her "wild days" when she was seventeen, living on her own and trying to make ends meet by tending bar in a strip club called Shorty's. He convinced her to enter a sexy swimsuit contest he and his friend, Scooter, were having at a club near the college. She won the contest five weeks in a row, then he helped her land her first role in a rap video and their beautiful friendship was born.

"Ms. Lawrence, the doctor will be here shortly to check on you. Buzz me if you need anything," the nurse said.

"Thanks." Paisley's eyes closed and she nodded her head.

"Is she awake?"

Okay, whatever that nurse put in my IV is making me hallucinate, for real, Paisley thought. She turned her head and, sure enough, walking through the door was Seymone Davis. It had been almost a year since Paisley had seen the woman she at one time had considered her best friend.

"Yeah, she's talking," Diesel answered.

Seymone leaned over and whispered, "Paisley, can you hear me?"

"Yes, Seymone. What the hell are you doing here? Diesel, I know you didn't call her." Paisley gave him an ugly look.

"No, actually, she called me." Diesel shrugged.

"And she called me. You would think that you would be a little nicer to your friend considering she was the name listed as your next of kin rather than me, and I'm your own mother."

At the sound of her mother's voice, Paisley knew one of two things had to be taking place. Either she had died and was truly in hell, or God, with his warped sense of humor, had allowed her to survive the car accident and was about to make her life a living hell. The pain she was feeling let her know that she was far from dead, and although she was truly shocked to see Seymone, she prayed that the image of Emma Jean Lawrence standing before her was a result of the drugs the nurse had just given her. Diesel's phone rang, breaking the silence that seemed to engulf the room.

"I gotta take this call," he said, and rushed out the door.

"Uh, I'm gonna run down to the cafeteria," Seymone quietly said. Paisley gave her a threatening look, which she pretended to ignore. "You need anything, Paisley?"

"No, Seymone, thanks. You've done more than enough."

"I'll bring you some coffee back, Mrs. Lawrence," Seymone said to Paisley's mother.

"Thanks, honey. I certainly appreciate that," Mrs. Lawrence said.

"It's no problem." Seymone smiled and eased out of the room.

When the hell did they become BFFs, she wondered. Suddenly realizing that she was alone with her mother, Paisley closed her eyes and prayed that she would fall asleep and wake up from the dreaded nightmare she seemed to be living at that moment.

Seymone

Paisley Janelle Lawrence has got to be the most arrogant, selfish, self-centered creature God ever created. I guarantee that if the tables were turned and it was she who had gotten a call at two o'clock in the morning telling her that I had been in a car accident, you'd better believe her reaction woulda been, "And?" But, did I do that? No, my dumb ass dropped everything and rushed to her bedside. For the past two days, I've been worrying, crying, praying; trying to survive off of little to no sleep and stale-ass hospital coffee. This is some straight bull . . . Why am I even here? Here I am, trying to do the right thing and this is the thanks I get.

Bobby, her fiancé, told her that she was crazy for rushing to be here. He told her that Paisley was going to hurt her feelings and it was a waste of time and money. Money, like they had to worry about money. The fastest running back in the NFL, he had just gotten traded to the Falcons, and signed major endorsement deals with Nike and Frito-Lay. Not that she was broke. The hundred and thirty to a hundred and fifty grand she was making a year wasn't anywhere near what he made. But then again, since dating him, she wasn't working as much, at his request. It was as if he could sense her thinking about him; she looked down at her vibrating cell phone.

"Hey, baby," she sighed as she answered it.

"When are you bringing your ass back home?"

Chapter 2

Heavenly Father, thank you for sparing my life . . . for watching over me and allowing me to live. I know that by letting me survive this, you have more for me to do, more work for me to accomplish; my purpose and will for my life has yet to be fulfilled—and I swear, God, I don't have a problem with that, I'm grateful for another chance—but, God, you know I do have a problem with this woman. I need for you to deliver me from Emma Jean and her mouth . . . Remove her from this hospital room so I can stop faking sleep and find out what the hell is going on . . . In Jesus' name I pray . . . Amen

"Come on, *Diva*, I know you hear me. Open your eyes and flash that Lawrence smile for me."

Paisley opened her eyes halfway. The antiseptic smell of the hospital room made her stomach turn and the constant sound of the beeping heart monitor beside her was annoying. She opened her eyes wider and saw Chester, her first cousin, standing over her, grinning.

"It's okay, girl. The witch is outside talking to your dad and the doctor. You're safe," Chester whispered.

"Make her leave," Paisley whined. "Why is she even here?"

"She's here because you almost died and she's your mother. Don't go there. And you know her ass isn't going anywhere until you're well." Chester sighed. "How are you feeling? You look better than you did yesterday, that's for sure. I ain't mad though, I got to look at that cutie pie, Diesel, all night long. Whooo, that boy is fine!"

"Don't go there. You know that will never happen." Paisley smirked. "My neck and chest are killing me."

"You got some chemical burns when the air bag deployed, Pais. And you broke your wrist, too," he said. "You're pretty banged up, but you're gonna be fine. Nothing a little TLC won't fix."

Having Chester there instantly made Paisley feel better. Standing at only five three, he was dressed as impeccably as always in a white linen shirt, tight True Religion jeans, and his signature black cowboy boots. What truly made her cousin an unforgettable persona to anyone with whom he came into contact, outside of his obvious homosexuality, was the bright orange afro he wore.

"I still don't understand what happened," Paisley told him, rubbing her hand across her forehead.

"Honey," Chester said, taking a deep breath, "if you don't know, then no one knows. I mean, you wouldn't believe how much commotion this situation has caused. It's a media frenzy, Paisley."

"Okay, but I don't understand why." Paisley frowned.

The door opened and her mother walked in. "I would like to understand why as well, Paisley. So would your father, your friends, and a whole lot of other people. So why don't you start explaining."

"Explaining what, Ma?" Paisley closed her eyes again.

"No, no, you will not. Open your eyes," her mother demanded.

"Emma Jean, let the girl rest," her father's voice said gently.

"She's rested, Gordon. She's done nothing but sleep for the past three days. And it seems mighty funny that she can be wide awake, holding entire conversations, until I'm in the room. Now, the doctors have said she's going to be fine. And I think we deserve some answers." her mother told him. "All these reporters and camera people trying to get in here."

"Mama, please." Paisley tried to wish her mother away, but it didn't work.

"Paisley, please," her mother imitated her.

"EJ, please," Chester added.

Paisley knew things were about to get intense. Her mother and Chester, who was her nephew, never got along. When Paisley got caught skipping school in the eighth grade, her mother blamed Chester. When she and her friends snuck away to the New Edition concert, her mother blamed Chester. When she and her boyfriend got caught kissing in the garage when she was fifteen, her mother blamed Chester. And when, finally, she could no longer take living under her parents' roof and she ran away from home, her mother blamed Chester.

"Okay, Mama. I'll explain." Paisley was frustrated. "What is it that you wanna know?"

"Hell, I wanna know the same thing everyone else wants to know." Her mother folded her arms and took a step back.

Paisley was confused. She looked at her father, Chester, and Seymone, who had eased into the room. Even though they looked sympathetic, she could also tell by the looks on their faces that they were waiting on answers too.

"And what does everyone want to know?" Paisley asked.

"What the hell were you doing leaving a bar with Warren Cobb?"

Suddenly, memories of the accident came flashing before her. Warren, Charley's, holding hands, leaving. They had been together when the accident happened. He had been driving.

"Oh, God, Warren," Paisley gasped. "Where is he? Is he all right?"

"He's still unconscious, Paisley," Seymone told her. Paisley couldn't stop her tears from falling as she realized how the situation had to look. After all, none of them even knew that she and Warren were friends.

"I need to go see him." Paisley struggled to sit up, but the pain in her chest quickly stopped her.

"It's okay, honey." Chester rushed over and comforted her. She buried her face into his shoulder and cried.

"Is it true, Paisley? Were you having an affair with this man?" her mother demanded. "My God, he's a minister!"

"Emma Jean, come on now, that's enough," her father told her.

"Why, Paisley? When does it stop? Do you know how hard it is being your mother? To see my daughter prancing, her body practically naked on videos and magazine covers. To have my one and only child's claim to fame be the Sensual

Seductress of the entertainment industry. And then, you go and open up a 'studio,' saying that you're 'teaching' the art of seduction. Yeah, that's really something for me to be proud of. Warren Cobb! A married minister!"

"Mama, it's not like that," Paisley sobbed.

"Is there no limit to how low you will go?" Tears were streaming down her mother's face and she could hear the hurt in her voice.

"EJ, leave her alone," Chester hissed.

"There you go, always defending her." Paisley's mother shook her head. "That's why she turned out the way she did. Because of you."

Chester looked into Paisley's face and gave her what they called that famous Lawrence smile. Paisley couldn't help but smile back. They listened as her mother continued her tirade.

"Chester, from the time she was born, you, Gordon, and my sister were always dressing her up, calling her beautiful, and telling her she was better than everyone else. You made her think that she was this untouchable creature, and little did you know. I told you back then that you were creating a monster. This is all your fault!"

"Well, Emma Jean," Chester said as he smiled, "that's the greatest compliment anyone has ever given me. I'm actually proud of the way Paisley turned out. She's beautiful, smart, successful, famous, rich, and—most of all— *glamorous!* Women look at her and want to be her, including you!"

"Okay, now that's enough," Paisley's father admonished them. "Now is not the time nor place for all this bickering. Paisley, you know I've never judged you or what you've done, that's between you and the good Lord. And whatever happened between you and Warren Cobb is between you and the good Lord as well. All I care about is your well-being and your safety. All this other mess is just that, mess."

"Thanks, Daddy." Paisley sniffled as she touched her father's hand.

"Now, there's one thing I want you to tell me," he continued.

"Yes, Daddy?" She waited for her father's request.

"What can we do to help you get better?"

She looked at her mother scowling and then into her father's loving face. She never understood how a man so gentle and kind-hearted could stay married to a woman so controlling and surly. It made no sense. She knew her father was willing to do anything to help her, so she did what she had to do.

"Leave," she told him. "Get yourselves out of the middle of this mess and take her with you."

"What do you mean, 'take her with you'?" her mother asked. "You have got to be the most selfish, self-centered person I have ever known."

"Mama, you said yourself that it's crazy. I know there are reporters everywhere, hanging around here, hounding y'all. That's the last thing you and Daddy need. I'm fine," Paisley tried to reason with her mother.

"And you know she's in good hands with me," Chester said, nodding. "And although you don't approve of me, you know I'll make sure she's taken care of."

"And I'm here for her too," Seymone spoke up. For a moment, Paisley had forgotten that she was even there. "I can stay with her as long as she needs me."

"See, Emma Jean, she's got plenty of folks to take care of her. And if our not being here helps lessen the stress, then maybe we should just go."

"Thanks, Daddy." Paisley was glad her father understood.

"But she hasn't even been released from the hospital, Gordon," her mother told him.

"Emma Jean, Paisley has been on her own since she was seventeen-years-old. She's been grown a long time." Her father laughed. "I'm sure she's gonna be fine."

"Ain't that the truth," Chester said under his breath.

"Stop," Paisley warned him.

Later that night, her father came in to say good-bye, alone.

"Daddy, you know I didn't . . ."

"I know you didn't, sweet cheeks." Her dad smiled.

"But having Mama here makes things so much harder." she told him. "I mean, you know, she's my mother and I love her but I just can't be around her, not right now, not with all of this going on."

"Believe me, I understand. But we love you, and I know you're gonna have to deal with all this, your way. You call me if you need anything, you understand?"

"Yes, Daddy." She smiled.

"And Paisley, next time they need next of kin, have them call me."

"Yes, Daddy."

"And one more thing."

"Yes, Daddy?"

"I'm so proud of you. Every video, every magazine cover, every calendar, every TV show, I see you and I think 'that's my Paisley.' Chester is right, you are a success and don't ever let anyone make you feel bad about anything you do." Her father kissed her forehead and walked out of the room.

For what felt like the hundredth time that day, Paisley cried. She cried for the years she spent away from home in order to be away from her mother, the time it caused her to be away from her father, and the fact that despite the mistakes she made, and the road in life she chose, his love was unconditional.

Chapter 3

"You okay, Pais?" Paisley nodded. Seymone reached over and passed her a Kleenex, and she blew her nose. "Thanks."

"You need me to get anything?"

"No, I'm fine," Paisley told her, lying back on the bed. "You don't have to spend the night. I'll be fine."

"I wanna stay. It's okay," Seymone said.

"I'm sure your fiancé has something to say about that," Paisley commented.

"Bobby is fine with me being here. He knows you were in an accident," Seymone answered. "Don't start tripping."

"I'm not tripping. I'm just telling you up front that I know how your man is and I don't need to feel like I'm distracting you from your relationship." Paisley shrugged.

"You're not distracting me from anything. If I didn't wanna be here, then I wouldn't be here," Seymone snapped. "Dammit, Paisley, you would think you would be a little more humble considering . . ."

"Considering what?" Paisley's voice got louder.

"Divas, divas," Chester hissed as he walked into the room, "let's get ourselves under control here! We got enough people talking about us without giving them something else to add to the stories."

Paisley glared at Seymone. "I was just telling Seymone she didn't have to feel obligated to be here, that's all, and she got defensive."

"Oh, Paisley, shut up. You know she's not here because she feels she has to be. She's here because she loves you." Chester rolled his eyes at her.

I should've known he would be on her side, Paisley thought. *Everyone always sides with her*. She watched him place two large travel bags beside her bed.

"I don't know why she's tripping," Seymone sighed.

"She's tripping because you left her high and dry when it was time to make a move and open the studio, and then you acted like it was no big deal. She's still hurt and feels that you chose your man over your friendship," Chester said nonchalantly as he reached into one of the bags and pulled out a beautiful peach lounge set. "I knew you would love this the moment I saw it."

"It's gorgeous!" Paisley smiled. "A heck of a lot better than this ugly hospital gown I'm wearing."

"Too bad there's not a tub in here. I know you would kill for a hot bath," he told her. "I got this new sea salt soak from After Effex that's to die for! Don't worry. I'ma hook you up when we get you outta here."

"I know you are." Paisley nodded.

"Hold up, hold up, wait, wait, wait." Seymone's eyes darted back and forth between Paisley and Chester. "What do you mean I chose my man over our friendship? When did all this come about?"

"Let it go, Seymone," Paisley replied. "I'm over it, seriously."

"No, you're not," Chester sighed. "That's why she's surprised you're here. She thought you didn't care about her anymore. I've been telling her for months that you two need to hash this out. But she didn't wanna bring it up."

"I can't believe you." Paisley shook her head. "No, I'm lying. I can believe you. You always pick the most inopportune times to tell my business."

"You really think I chose Bobby over you, Paisley?"

Paisley looked at her friend. She wanted to be honest, but she didn't want Seymone to get it twisted and think it was jealousy, which it definitely wasn't. Although she thought Bobby was a disgusting, arrogant prick and Seymone could do way better, she knew her friend was in love and she was happy for her. She took a deep breath and said, "I think you chose Bobby over our business and the plans we made for the future. But, it's all good."

"That's ridiculous. Bobby proposed and then he got signed to the Falcons! How was I supposed to know any of that was going to happen?" Seymone dabbed at the tears that were forming in her eyes.

"Seymone, don't cry. I understand. I said it's all good," Paisley told her. "See, Chester, this is all your damn fault."

"Look, I just opened the door, you both chose to walk in." Chester shrugged. "Besides, this is a conversation y'all shoulda had a long time ago."

The phone rang next to her bed. Paisley reached over and answered, "Hello."

After a few moments with no response, she repeated herself. Still nothing. She placed the phone back on the receiver.

"So, that's why you been so busy you ain't had time to talk to me, Paisley?" Seymone asked.

"No, you know everything I got going on. The studio has been slammed, not to mention I'm helping Diesel and the guys with remodeling and revamping the club. If I didn't want to talk to you, Seymone, I would just tell you. If nothing else, you know I'ma grown-ass woman."

"I ain't say you weren't. I guess I just thought that we were better than that and if you had a problem with me, you could just tell me. Maybe you're right, I don't need to be here." Seymone grabbed her purse and put on her sunglasses.

For some reason, Paisley started laughing uncontrollably. Chester and Seymone looked at her like she was crazy, and then they began laughing with her.

"Okay, what the hell are we laughing at?" Seymone finally asked.

"Why the hell are you putting on your sunglasses and it's nine o'clock at night and raining outside?" Paisley answered when she was able to talk.

"The same reason you wore a white fur coat over your bikini to DeeJay Terror's All White Affair last Fourth of July, wench!" Seymone smiled.

"Because you're both the true divas I raised you to be, that's why," Chester announced. They stared at him and then the room filled with laughter again. It felt good to laugh.

"I'm glad you're here, Seymone. You know that." Paisley reached out her hand.

"I wouldn't be anywhere else." Seymone grabbed Paisley's hand and squeezed it.

"Thank God that's over." Chester collapsed into the chair as if exhausted. "Whew, first I had to deal with Emma Jean's drama and now this."

"Yeah, your mom had me kinda stressed, for real," Seymone said, taking off the sunglasses and removing her jacket. Paisley's eyes widened as she looked at her friend. To the average person, Seymone looked like the beautiful model she was. At five foot eight, she was slightly taller than Paisley, who was five seven-and-a-half. Her chestnut skin, hazel eyes, and curvaceous bottom hinted at both her Puerto Rican and black heritages. Dressed in a red Baby Phat sweat suit and all red Nikes, her naturally curly hair was pulled into a long ponytail that fell to the center of her back. Even though she was curvy, Seymone had always been petite, a size eight at the most. As she stared, Paisley noticed that her friend was now easily a ten, maybe bigger. She couldn't resist asking.

"Seymone Taylor, are you pregnant?"

"What? Are you crazy?" Seymone's voice squealed. "Why the hell would you ask me that?"

Paisley shrugged. "Because you've gained weight. Wow, girl."

Chester laughed. "Paisley, you need to stop. You're acting like the girl is plus-sized or something. She's just put on a few pounds, and I think it looks good on her."

"Bobby kept telling me I was anorexic and he wanted me to put on five pounds." Seymone admired herself. "I guess I got a little carried away, but he is loving it. He can't keep his hands off me and keeps saying how good I look."

"I didn't say you looked bad," Paisley told her. "I'm just not used to you being that thick."

I shoulda known Bobby's controlling ass had something to do with Seymone's weight gain. I guess I should be grateful, because he coulda asked her to lose weight and she would be walking around here looking like Nicole Richie's twin.

"Yeah, you were always the thick one, and I was the one with the eyes." Seymone laughed. "Now I guess I can finally raid your closet, especially since you're all laid up."

"You better stay your ass outta my closet," Paisley warned her.

"We can raid it together." Chester nudged Seymone's arm and they laughed together like they were two school girls.

"I don't see anything funny," Paisley said.

Her doctor, whom she met earlier, Evan Singleton, walked in and examined her. Had she not been in excruciating pain, she probably would have been more inclined to comment on his tall, dark, athletic body and his handsome face.

"How are you this evening, Ms. Lawrence?" He smiled.

"I'm still in some pain, but I'm better, Dr. Singleton." she told him.

"Call me Evan, please," he said. "Let's try this again. How are you this evening, Ms. Lawrence?"

"I'm better, Evan," she replied dryly. She knew he was trying to be light-hearted and put her at ease, but she wasn't in the mood to laugh at all.

"That's good to hear," he replied as he shined a penlight into her eyes, causing her to squint. He pulled back the sheet and checked her legs, which were still swollen and covered with black-and-blue bruises. They had been crushed from the front-end impact and it was a miracle that they weren't broken. Paisley could barely move because of the pain.

"Can I please get rid of this catheter?" she whispered.

"I think we should give it a few more days, until you gain more strength in your legs," he said.

"I can make it to the restroom. It's not that far. And my family is here to help me if I need it," she pleaded.

Seymone nodded. "We'll be right here."

Dr. Singleton hesitated, then finally said, "I'll remove it and see how you do."

Paisley was relieved. Having the catheter removed was one small step to getting out of there and heading home. This entire situation was becoming overwhelming. She had a studio to run, and the club that she had invested in was scheduled to open in less than six weeks. Being laid up was not part of her plan. Chester and Seymone excused themselves while Dr. Singleton called the nurse to remove the uncomfortable device.

"How much longer do you think I'll be here?" she asked.

"Three days or so, another week at the longest," he answered. "I know you're anxious to get out of here. You're quite the popular patient."

"I bet," she sighed. From what Seymone and Chester told her, the press had been adamant in their search for information regarding her and Warren. Cameramen and reporters had been lurking in the hospital and security had been heightened. For Paisley, just hearing about it made her bad situation worse.

"This is gonna be a little uncomfortable," the nurse told her.

She flinched and closed her eyes. Once it was over, she thanked both of them.

"I'll be back to check on you in the morning." He smiled. "Get some rest."

"Easier said than done," Paisley sighed. "Dr. Singleton, how is Mr. Cobb?"

"As far as I know, he's still unconscious," he told her. "If I hear any news, I'll be sure to let you know."

"Thank you," she told him. She prayed that Warren was okay. She wanted to see him, talk to him, and let him know that she was fine. The nurse gave her another dose of pain meds and she drifted to sleep with thoughts of Warren on her mind.

I gotta pee, Paisley thought as she struggled to open her eyes and see. The room was completely dark. She had convinced Chester and Seymone to go home around midnight. She reached for the remote and clicked on the television; the glow from the screen provided enough light for her to check her watch and see that it was after three in the morning. It had been hard to get to sleep, even with the narcotics they were giving her for pain, because someone continually called the room, but didn't say anything. Finally, having the phone taken from the room had given her some rest. The urge to use the restroom became stronger, and knowing that it would probably take the nurse a while to get to her room, Paisley decided to struggle to the bathroom alone. She eased her body up, clenching her throbbing thighs, while maneuvering her legs over the side of the bed. As she prepared to stand up, she braced herself for the pain she knew she was about to experience. Her legs wobbled as the combination of pain and pressure shot down her body when she stood. Paisley grabbed the bed for support. She didn't know whether to call the nurse to help her struggle back into bed, but the pressure on her bladder encouraged her to grab a nearby chair, use it as a makeshift walker, and will herself into the small restroom. *I made it.* She smiled to herself. She sat on the toilet for a while after she finished, fighting off overwhelming dizziness. It was as if she were in a thick fog. Finally, after what felt like hours, she gathered the strength to stand up and stumble back toward her bed.

"Just a little farther to go," she whispered, pushing the chair closer to the bed. The sound of the legs scraping against the floor amplified and caused her teeth to clench. She had just made it to the side of the bed when she caught a glimpse of a man's shadowy figure standing near the doorway. She squinted and tried to make him out. "Who are you?"

"Uh . . . I . . . I just wanted to make sure you were okay." His voice was barely above a whisper. He was dressed in green hospital scrubs and hat, and his face was covered with a surgical mask. There was something recognizable about him, but she couldn't put her finger on what it was.

Paisley's heart began pounding and she grabbed the sheet, pulling it close to her body. "Get out!"

"I needed to see for myself. They wouldn't tell me." He took a step closer to her.

Paisley scrambled to find the call button for the nurse. "Get the hell out! I swear, I'm about to scream!"

He took another step, and before she could react, he dropped something on her bed and ran out. Paisley screamed as her fingers found the red help button and pressed it nonstop.

"Ms. Lawrence, what's wrong?" The nurse came running in.

"That man! He was just in my room. He ran out, you had to see him!" Paisley panted, struggling to catch her breath.

"What man?" The nurse seemed to be confused. "I didn't see anyone."

"You had to see him. He ran right out right before you came in. Please call security so they can get him. He put something on my bed!"

The nurse glanced at the foot of the bed to where Paisley was pointing. She pulled the blanket back, checking for whatever it was the man had dropped.

"There's nothing here, Ms. Lawrence." She shrugged.

"He was just here." Paisley frowned, her breathing becoming even more shallow.

"Ms. Lawrence, you're hyperventilating. I need for you to breathe deeply," she said, helping Paisley adjust herself in the bed. "You're pretty heavily medicated, and sometimes that can cause you to see or hear things that aren't really there."

Paisley was confused. She knew what she had seen.

There *had been* a man in her room, and he *did* drop something on the bed. *I'm not crazy*, she thought, still confused by what had just happened. *Heavily medicated my ass.*

A few moments later, Paisley was breathing normally. "Are you going to report this to security? I need someone to take a report or something."

The nurse seemed to be frustrated with Paisley's request. "Ms. Lawrence, I didn't see anyone and I was right across the hall when you screamed. If there had been a man running out of here, like you said there was, I would've at least seen him in the hallway."

Paisley felt her anger rising, and stared at the woman. "Listen, I don't give a damn if you saw him or not. Get security in here!"

"I'll be right back," the nurse said, glaring icily at Paisley. She headed out of the room, leaving the door open. "Who does she think she is? *Pulpit whore.*"

Chapter 4

"What's going on? They said you could leave?" Paisley was dressed and sitting on the side of the bed when her agent, Fallon, walked in with Seymone. "Can you grab my other bag? I don't know why Chester brought all this stuff anyway."

"I know they didn't tell her she could leave. She can barely walk. Heck, they took her catheter out yesterday." Seymone looked at her like she was crazy.

"I can't stay here. I gotta go." She groaned in pain as she tried to stand up.

"Paisley." Fallon ran over to help her. "Girl, what is wrong with you? You're in no condition to leave this hospital."

"What's going on?" Seymone asked.

"Last night, this guy . . . he was dressed in a hospital mask . . . He . . . he was in here," Paisley told them.

"What?"

"Girl, no!"

The two women spoke at the same time.

"I went to the bathroom and when I came out, he was in my room," she continued.

"Are you all right?" Fallon asked.

"What did he want?" Seymone frowned.

"What kinda question is that?" Fallon turned and shook her head in disbelief at Seymone.

"I mean . . ." Seymone started.

"Believe it or not, he said he wanted to make sure I was okay," Paisley told them.

"He said that? Wow, did you call the police? Did they catch him?" Seymone's eyes were wide with excitement. Paisley had to wonder if she was enjoying hearing about the distressful situation. "What did you do?"

"I screamed. And the fat, ugly nurse came waltzing in like I was interrupting her snack break. I told her about the guy and she told me I was hallucinating. She didn't even want to call security."

"You've gotta be kidding," Fallon said, reaching into her purse and pulling out her cell phone. "This is ridiculous. Don't worry, Paisley, I'll take care of it and get you the hell out of here."

Paisley watched as Fallon fell into management mode, demanding to speak to the hospital director and the head of security. She loved Fallon. She was the flyest white girl she had ever met, and hiring her as her manager had been the smartest move she had ever made. Fallon Baxter only had four clients, including Paisley and Seymone, all recommended by Chester, and she made sure that they were all so successful she didn't need any more. Fallon's father was one of the most successful entertainment lawyers in the nation, and she had connections all over: directors, producers, photographers, restaurateurs, bankers, doctors, lawyers, pilots. You needed it, Fallon could get it. Five foot five, dark hair, and curvy, she was a perfect combination of homegirl, high class, and hip. She was born and raised in Philadelphia and gave her family hell growing up. She had been thrown out of more private schools than her parents could count, until her mother finally said the hell with it and, when Fallon was in the eleventh grade, enrolled her in the roughest public school in the city. She had hoped Fallon would freak out and appreciate the quality, expensive education they were trying to provide. Instead, Fallon thrived. It was as if she had found her home. They had to wonder if maybe she had been a black girl in a former life because she fell right into place. By senior year, Fallon was an honor roll student, senior class treasurer, voted Most Outgoing and Best Dressed, and graduated with honors. Although it seemed odd to the rest of the family that all of Fallon's friends were black and she only dated black guys, her parents were just happy that they finally stopped getting calls in the middle of the night asking them to come pick their daughter up from a local police station.

"Seymone, help her back into bed," Fallon directed. "I'm going to meet with the administrators and their whack-ass security. I'll be back in a little while. Don't leave her alone."

"I won't," Seymone assured her. She helped Paisley back into bed, and as she reached to spread the blanket across her legs, she leaned over and stuck her hand between the mattress and the foot of the bed. She pulled something out. "What is this?"

"Let me see that." Paisley took what looked like a folded note card with something shiny attached. "This is it! This is what he dropped last night. I knew I wasn't crazy!"

She gently unfolded the card and the scent of strange cologne filled her nostrils. The written message inside read:

My heart and thoughts are with you and I am always nearby. You are and will always be mine.

Attached to the card was a gold Mickey Mouse pin. Fallon reached over and took the card from her.

"I'm taking this with me. And don't worry, I'ma have that heifer from last night's job." Fallon leaned over and kissed Paisley's forehead.

"Thanks, Fallon," Paisley told her. "I still wanna get the hell out of here."

"You will, as soon as you're well enough. But you gotta get some rest and heal first," Seymone told her.

"She's right." Fallon nodded. "Let me go handle this. By the time I get finished with them, your medical bills are gonna be on the house and they'll be naming a damn wing after you."

Paisley laughed and felt a bit more at ease. She knew that Fallon may have sounded like she was joking, but she wasn't. When Fallon meant business, she meant business, and she didn't care who got offended, whose feelings got hurt, or who didn't like it. And for that reason alone, those who knew her had no other choice but to respect her. She was a good person.

"You want me to cut the television on?" Seymone asked.

"No, I'm tired of hearing them talking about me like I'm the whore of Babylon. Are the reporters still lurking?" she asked.

"Not as many as before," Seymone told her. "You know how that goes, they've moved on to the next big story."

"Any word on Warren?"

"I haven't heard anything."

"I wanna know if he's really okay. The only thing they are telling me is that he's in critical condition. That's not good enough." Paisley sighed. She looked over at Seymone and told her, "Seymone, go tell the nurse you need a wheelchair."

"I don't need a wheelchair." Seymone frowned.

"Not for you, retarded girl, for me. I want you to take me to see Warren." Paisley sat up once again.

"Uh, I don't know if that's a good idea, Pais. Just get one of the nurses here to go check on him for you," Seymone suggested.

"You know these heifers around here ain't trying to do that. You think I haven't heard them talking about me?"

"For the right amount of money, girl, you know they'll get his chart for you."

"Seymone, come on," Paisley pleaded. "Just get the wheelchair and take me to see for myself. I need to see if he's all right."

"What's the deal with you and him?" Seymone asked. After the words escaped her lips, she took a step back. She had finally gathered the nerve to ask the question everyone had been wondering but no one had asked.

"What do you mean? Ain't nothing up with us. We're friends," Paisley snapped. "What? You thinking what everybody else is thinking? That I seduced him and caused this huge tragedy to happen upon him?" Paisley could feel tears forming, and she tried to wipe them before they fell. She lifted her left arm and nearly knocked herself out with the pink cast. "Dammit."

"Paisley, come on, you know I don't think nothing like that. I'm your best friend and if no one else knows you, I do. You don't seduce anyone unless they want to be seduced and this accident was just that, an accident. And it's just as much a tragedy for you as it is anyone," Seymone told her. Paisley looked at her best friend and saw that she was being sincere. "I was just curious because you've never mentioned that you even knew Warren Cobb."

"I guess it never came up," Paisley told her. In reality, her friendship with Warren was something so precious that she kept near and dear to her heart, and she felt like sharing it with anyone would somehow cheapen it or make it seem wrong. It was the one part of her that was hers and hers alone. Like a secret place she could go that only she knew about. "I mean, it's not like his name ever came up in general conversation or something."

"True," was Seymone's only response.

"But, I just wanna see for myself that he's all right. Please just get the wheelchair and take me."

Seymone hesitated and finally said, "You know this is a bad idea right? And what happens when Fallon comes back and finds us gone?"

"We'll be back by the time she gets back."

"Fine." Seymone stood up. Paisley ran her fingers through her nine-hundred-dollar weave and prayed that her face was decent, even though she had no makeup on. *If ever I needed Qianna Westbrooke,* it's right now, she thought about her makeup artist.

A few minutes later, Seymone came through the door pushing a wheelchair. After giving Paisley a baseball cap and some big shades, she helped her ease into the chair and they were off. Seymone double-checked the hallway for the press hounds, and, being as inconspicuous as possible, they whizzed past the nurses' station and into the elevator. The doors closed just as a few reporters in the waiting room realized that it was her and jumped up.

"That's what happens when you sleep on Paisley Lawrence." They laughed and gave each other five.

"What floor are we going to?" Seymone asked.

"The nurse I had earlier told me he's in ICU on the ninth floor," Paisley answered, her voice barely above a whisper. Her heart was beating so fast that she thought it would jump out of her chest. Seymone pushed the button; the elevator jerked and Paisley's stomach dropped. She didn't know if it was from them suddenly going up, or from her nerves. They stopped and the doors opened. Without thinking, Seymone pushed her out.

She didn't check for the press, Paisley thought. She looked around and instantly saw the mass of people grouped in the hallway and waiting room of the surgical ICU area. Dressed in suits and dresses, she knew they had to be church members. A few people stared as they passed by.

"Well, this is the right floor," Seymone whispered.

"You think?" Paisley hissed.

"You know they're not gonna let you see him in ICU. Only family is allowed."

"I just want to try. That's the least I can do."

"I'm telling you, this is crazy. What room?"

"Nine thirty-six, I think that's what the nurse said."

"What do you mean, you think? What the hell?" Seymone started pushing faster.

As they got closer, the crowd thinned and Paisley thought they were home free. Just as they were approaching the nurses' area, Paisley reached down and grabbed the wheel, stopping the chair.

"What's wrong?"

Before Paisley could answer, one of the women spoke.

"What the hell are you doing here?"

Everyone turned and stared at Paisley and Seymone. Paisley's eyes met Kollette's and they stared at one another.

"Sister Cobb, what's the matter?" one of the ladies asked.

"That's her," was Kollette's answer.

"It can't be," the lady said. "No one in their right mind would be disrespectful enough to come here to his room, knowin' how sick Brother Cobb is."

"Well, I told y'all she was crazy, because here she is right now. Look," Kollette told them. Paisley looked at the overweight, unattractive woman and started to say something. Instead, she just smiled.

"She's not crazy. This woman got out of her own hospital bed to come and pay her regards to Mr. Cobb," Seymone responded.

"Her regards aren't welcome here." The lady took a step toward them and Paisley tensed. She could feel the crowd closing in on them, and she knew the scene was about to get worse. Her eyes shifted toward the direction of Warren's room.

"I need you to leave right now! Security!"

In a flash, two stout guys looking like bounty hunters were by Kollette's side. They were dressed in all black, and neither looked too friendly. Paisley rolled her eyes at them, determined not to let them think she was intimidated by their presence.

"Ladies, I think you two need to leave," the first guy told them.

"Look, we don't want no trouble," Seymone said.

"No one said you did." The second guy's voice was so deep that a chill went down Paisley's spine, and goose bumps formed on her arm. Even through her dark shades she could see the handsomeness of his expressionless face.

"Come on, Ms. Lawrence, don't cause a scene. You know things look bad enough as it is," the first guy spoke softly.

Paisley continued to stare as she said, "It seems funny how security flocks to her side when she calls, but when I needed you last night there was no one to be found."

"I don't know what you're talking about," the second security guard said. Again, the richness of his voice caught her off guard. "We're personal security for Brother and Sister Cobb."

"I want her removed now!" Kollette snapped.

Seymone grabbed the handles of the wheelchair and started backing out. The first security guard took a step toward them and offered to help.

"I got it," Seymone told him. He continued toward them and she jerked the chair as she pulled it. Just as she turned it around, a flash nearly blinded Paisley. She covered her face, using her bulky cast as a shield against the camera. They seemed to be coming from everywhere and swarmed upon them like buzzards. The two security men sprung into action, pushing back the paparazzi and demanding that they leave. Seymone tried to maneuver the wheelchair through the frenzy, but it was as if they were stuck. Paisley tried not to panic. There didn't seem to be any way out.

"See what you've caused!" Kollette yelled. She began crying hysterically. "All this is your fault; this madness, not to mention that my husband is laid up in a coma, is all because of you!"

Uniformed security guards pushed their way through what was now a crowd, and tried to gain control of the situation. Seymone shook her head in disbelief. Kollette was escorted farther down the hallway by the two security men.

"There's no way outta here," Seymone groaned.

This is not good. God, please help us get up outta here, Paisley prayed, and tried to think. She glanced up and saw the door to Warren's room open. The deep-voiced security guard stepped out and beckoned for them. *Oh, hell no*, she thought, and shook her head.

"He wants us to come that way," Seymone said, leaning over.

"The elevator's the other way. We'll be trapped if we go that way," Paisley told her.

Seeing that they weren't following his instructions, the guard came toward them. He grabbed the chair from Seymone and told her, "Come on."

"What do you think you're doing?" Paisley growled.

"Helping you find a way out of here," he said, then turned to Seymone. "Follow me."

His strides were so long that Seymone could barely keep up with him down the hallway. He made a left turn down another corridor and kept moving. Paisley was quiet, hoping that he wasn't some crazed man planning to kill them.

"There's a patient elevator this way," he finally said, slowing down. Paisley spotted it and relaxed a bit. After checking that the coast was clear, he made sure they got on safely.

"Thank you," Seymone said.

"Don't mention it," he said.

Paisley removed her sunglasses and asked, "Can you tell me how Warren is? That's all I was trying to do, get an update on him."

He stared at the floor and shrugged. "He's stable."

"What does that mean? I need someone to give me more info than that. Hell, you're in there with him when the doctors come in. What are they saying?"

For the first time, he made eye contact with Paisley. "They're saying pray."

The elevator doors closed, and again, Paisley's stomach dropped. This time it was because, from the security guy's tone, she knew there was a strong possibility that Warren might not make it.

Fallon

See, this is exactly why I don't deal with a whole lot of people. The four clients I do have keep me running around enough. How hard is it to lay your ass in a hospital bed and stay there until I come back? Is that too much to ask? This situation that Paisley has gotten in is crazy enough without adding more issues for me to deal with. Here I am, handling business with the damn hospital suits, and security comes in telling me that Paisley's ass is upstairs in ICU trying to see Warren Cobb and all hell is breaking loose. What the hell is she thinking?

Fallon adjusted the blazer of her Donna Karan pantsuit and set off to find her most prized client and friend. For the past five years, she had been Paisley's agent, and they had made more money than she could ever wish for. Paisley's unforgettable looks, perfect statuesque body, sensuality, and natural ability to move in front of the camera combined with the business-savvy, industry-connected, no-nonsense Fallon resulted in a successful business partnership and win-win situation for them both. Together they had worked and built Paisley's career and persona, known in the music industry as the *"Sensual Seductress."* She had become a phenomenon in the music video industry and they both became very wealthy. They had never had a problem until now. It was as if the moment Chester had called and told her about the accident and who was involved, the floodgates opened and poured a PR nightmare into their lives.

The nature of Paisley's relationship with Warren Cobb seemed like something the world wanted to know; and something Fallon didn't even know herself. She had held off giving a statement, waiting until she and Paisley had discussed the situation. The phone calls, e-mails, text messages, and voice mails were endless. For the most part, they were harmless. There were a couple that seemed a little over the top, but it wasn't uncommon for her to get a message or two from an overzealous Paisley fan. It came with the territory. But there was something disturbing about one message in particular, especially after hearing about the man is Paisley's room. She clicked on her BlackBerry and scrolled through the messages from Paisley's fan site until she found the one she was looking for. The words seemed to leap from the small screen and she blinked as she read them:

Paisley, your sleeping beauty will soon awaken in my arms and I will be by your side. I am right nearby and just a whisper of my name from your lips would make my day complete. In time.

Chapter 5

"Okay, diva, Seymone is waiting downstairs in the car. You ready to roll?" Paisley looked at Chester. "Do you really need to ask?"

"Let me check you out." He took a step back and gave Paisley the once over. Even after almost losing her life four days ago, she still looked fierce. He made sure she was picture perfect just in case a snapshot of her was taken during her exit. Paisley didn't know what she would do without him. Qianna, her regular makeup artist, was booked, but he had beckoned for Camille, her protégée and one of the hottest new makeup artists at After Effex Salon, to come over and not only do her face, but give her a fresh manicure and pedicure as well.

"Chester, I really think you're going too far. I'm going straight home and I don't think anyone is gonna notice my feet, especially since I'll be wearing sneakers." She looked down as Camille helped ease her feet into the fresh pair of white Nikes.

"We're not taking any chances," Chester told her. "Besides, you know your nails and toes should always match, don't trip."

"That is true." Camille nodded.

"Don't encourage him, Camille. I didn't think there was much you could do with all these bruises and scratches on my face, but you worked it out, girl." Paisley smiled at the pretty, young girl. The phone began ringing and Paisley stared at it.

"I got it." Camille reached over to answer it but Paisley emphatically stopped her.

"No!"

"Sorry, I forgot," Camille apologized, and quickly snatched back her hand.

"Let's hurry up and get the hell outta here." Paisley sighed. She was finally going home.

Considering the lurking press, the crank phone calls, the stranger appearing in her hospital room in the middle of the night, and the chaos caused when she tried to visit Warren, the doctor agreed that Paisley would probably recover better away from the hospital. She remained in the hospital for two more days. Her friends made sure she was never alone, making her a bit more at ease. The nurse had just come and given Paisley her discharge paperwork when Fallon walked in, looking very much like Posh Spice in her cute dress, large sunglasses, and fly haircut, and made an unexpected announcement.

"Warren Cobb regained consciousness."

Paisley was speechless. Her first instinct was to rush to see him, but that desire was instantly suppressed by the memory of Kollette calling security and having her escorted off the floor.

"That's great," Chester remarked.

"Wow," Camille said. "That's good news."

"I just got the call," Fallon said, "and I wanted you to hear it from me rather than hearing it on the radio on the way home."

"I appreciate that." Paisley nodded. Warren was awake. Knowing that he was no longer in a coma made her feel a little better. "I'm glad."

"I knew you would be," Fallon told her. "Paisley, I gotta get a press release together. I know you said you weren't up to dealing with it, but we have to say something."

Paisley knew Fallon was right. There was so much speculating going on and everyone was waiting for the full story. Paisley still hadn't said anything to anyone, not even her friends. She was grateful that they were giving her space and respecting her privacy, but she knew they wanted to know just like everyone else did.

"I know," Paisley agreed. A knock on the door grabbed their attention.

"Ms. Lawrence?" A petite, well-dressed, brown-skinned woman stood in the doorway.

"Can I help you?" Fallon asked, removing her shades.

"Yes, I'm Ebonie Monroe, Warren Cobb's agent." The woman's voice was sharp. "May I come in?"

Fallon looked over for Paisley's approval before saying, "Come in."

"I'm glad I caught you before you left so we could talk. They told me you were being discharged today." Ebonie looked around the room. Even though Paisley had donated most of the bouquets, balloons, and stuffed animals she had received to the pediatric ward and the nursing home down the street, there were still flowers everywhere. "I'm glad you're well enough to go home."

"How is Warren?" Paisley asked. "I was told he's conscious."

"Yes, he woke up this morning, thank God. It's truly a blessing. Well, his surviving that terrible accident was a miracle in itself. God is good," Ebonie said.

"All the time," Chester chimed in, like he was the backup choir. Paisley frowned at him and he shrugged.

"I'm just glad he's awake," Paisley sighed. "What did you need to talk to me about?"

"I am preparing to make a statement and a press release and I wanted to just go over what needs to be said," Ebonie said to Paisley.

"Yes, exactly what will you be saying in this statement?" Fallon walked over and stood in front of Ebonie.

"This is Fallon Baxter, my agent, Ms. Monroe." Paisley turned to Fallon.

"Nice to meet you." Ebonie extended her hand and Fallon shook it. "I'm sure you've already prepared a statement of your own, then."

"We're in the process of doing so," Fallon said knowingly.

"I don't want to say anything until I talk to Warren," Paisley told both of them. They turned and stared at her. "I just want to get his take on things and find out how he wants to handle it. I know things are looking really crazy right now, and I promise you, it's not as bad as it looks. And I'm not trying to be funny or disrespectful, but before we give any type of statement to anyone, Warren and I need to talk first."

"Um, Mr. Cobb isn't really up to talking to anyone at this time. And this needs to be handled sooner rather than later. Look, I'm sure you want this to be over and done with, and right now, the media is having a field day . . ."

"You think I don't know that?" Paisley frowned.

"Why don't you just agree to a generic statement thanking everyone for their prayers and support during this time, and that both Paisley and Warren ask that their privacy be respected during their recovery period?" Chester offered.

"Sounds good to me," Paisley agreed.

Both Ebonie and Fallon remained quiet. They both knew that the future of their clients' careers were riding on them. One wrong move, and both of their careers were down the toilet.

"Ms. Lawrence, I understand your wanting this to remain a private matter. But you of all people should know that both you and Mr. Cobb are very public people. Although for different reasons," Ebonie started.

"What the hell is that supposed to mean?" Paisley snapped.

"Oh, hold up." Chester glared at Ebonie.

"Calm down." Fallon addressed Chester and Ebonie, "I think what Ms. Monroe is trying to say is that you both have strong fan bases who support you, and you know people are going to want more than that."

"I don't give a damn what people want. And besides, I'm sure if you ask Warren what he wants said, he'll tell you to talk to me first," Paisley said.

A strange look came across Ebonie's face, and Paisley asked, "What? Did Warren say something about me or the accident?"

There was a brief silence, then Ebonie told her, "Warren doesn't remember the accident. And when I asked him about being with you, he said he doesn't even know who you are."

Paisley was stunned.

"I'm sure that's because he just regained consciousness," Fallon suggested to Paisley.

"Yeah, Pais. You didn't remember the accident yourself until we told you about it," Chester agreed, rubbing Paisley's shoulders.

She knew they were trying to make her feel better, but it wasn't working. How the hell could he say he didn't know her? Ebonie had to be lying.

"That is possible," Ebonie remarked. "Listen, I don't have a problem releasing the generic statement and release another statement later."

"We'd appreciate that." Fallon nodded.

"There's something else I need to make you aware of," Ebonie continued. "We have received some messages that are cause for concern."

"What kinds of messages?" Paisley mumbled.

"As I stated, Mr. Cobb has a large, dedicated fan base and some of the messages have made reference to Ms. Lawrence's safety." Ebonie shrugged. "Hospital security told me about the trespasser in your room and I think you should consider getting some personal security."

"I agree." Fallon nodded.

"What? I don't think so," Paisley snapped, her mind still distracted by the fact that Warren said he didn't know her. "I'm fine, and the sooner I get the hell outta here, the better I'll be!"

"Home, sweet home," Chester said as he helped Paisley ease onto the sofa in her living room. "You sure you don't want me to carry you upstairs?"

"No, I'm good," Paisley told him, settling into the thick plushness. As she leaned back, she was glad that she had chosen the comfortable, oversized living room set, rather than the black leather she had almost gotten.

The brown decor of the room was accented with red and gave the room a welcoming feeling from the moment you walked in. Paisley loved her house. The four-bedroom, three-and-a-half-bath, four-thousand-square-foot home was nestled in the heart of Wellington Heights, one of the most prominent neighborhoods in the city. The moment she saw it, she fell in love. It didn't matter to her that it was too big for just one person to live in. It didn't matter to her that the upkeep of the yard and the pool would be a pain in the ass. It didn't matter that for the price she paid for it, she could've very well bought three smaller homes, and a car for that matter. What did matter was that it was her dream home. The home that she always wanted, but never in a million years thought she could have. It was hers.

"You want something to drink?" Seymone asked, taking the dark red cashmere blanket from where it hung on the back of the sofa, and spreading it across Paisley's legs.

"No, I'm fine. Can you get my Mac?" Paisley asked. She had been asking for her laptop for days, but was told that she couldn't use it in the hospital.

"Why don't you get some rest first?" Chester suggested.

"I am resting," Paisley told him. She looked over at the empty television stand. She had planned on picking up a new plasma, but had been putting it off as she spent most of her time upstairs in her bedroom when she was home. "It's bad enough I don't have a TV to watch. At least I can surf the Web."

"Fine," Chester sighed. "Where is it? Upstairs?"

"Yeah, in the sitting area," she answered, watching him gather her bags and take them up the steps. "Wait, I need my cell phone out of my purse."

Seymone reached into the large, black Coach bag and passed Paisley the BlackBerry she had been demanding for the past three days. Paisley turned the phone on and stared as it began lighting up. She had more text messages than she felt like reading and her voice mail was full. She started listening to the messages, mostly from her clients at The Playground, and smiled.

"Okay, who is making you smile like that and what did he say?" Seymone asked.

"It's not a he," Paisley told her, "it's one of my Strip Hop students, Mrs. McNeil. She told me her husband asked when she was going back to class because he needs her to keep learning."

Seymone laughed. "He probably wants her to become an honor roll student."

"Probably so, they've been married sixteen years and she decided to take the class to add some spice to their love life."

"Wow, that's what's up. I'm glad The Playground is doing so well, Pais. I went over there with Chester yesterday to make sure everything was all right and I saw the waiting list. And you had about thirty messages on the answering machine from people wanting to make appointments."

"Yeah, business is booming. We have a blast," Paisley replied, then looked down at the cast on her wrist. "I don't know what I'm gonna do now."

"I told you a long time ago you needed to hire some help. But no, you swore you had everything under control," Chester said, coming down the steps carrying her leather laptop case.

"I did have everything under control. This is just an unexpected setback." Paisley rolled her eyes at him. She took her laptop out of the bag and clicked it on. She checked her business Web site and was happy to see numerous get well wishes from her students and friends posted. Her eyes widened when she read the messages in her e-mail and MySpace accounts. She was just finishing up when the doorbell rang. Seymone rushed to answer it.

"I'm here to visit the sick and shut in," Diesel said as he walked in carrying his silver motorcycle helmet. He quickly looked around the room and asked, "Your mama ain't here, is she?"

"If she was, do you think I'd be here?" Chester answered.

"What's up, Diesel." Paisley smiled.

"I'm good, baby doll," he said, leaning down and kissing her cheek. The scent of his Kenneth Cole cologne filled her nostrils. "You look good."

"Liar," she told him, closing the laptop.

"No need for me to lie. You know if you ain't look good, I would be the first to tell you."

"That's true," Seymone laughed.

"Now he's lying." Chester said. "You know my ass would be the first to tell you."

"He's right about that." Diesel sat next to her.

"So, is everything still a go at the club?" she asked him. Diesel, along with his boys Scooter and Leo, had made a major power move and bought one of the biggest nightclubs in the city, State Streets. Paisley was their silent partner. Diesel had been one of her biggest supporters when she opened the studio nearly two years ago. He had helped her with everything from painting the walls to passing out flyers. When he told her about his desire to purchase State Streets, she offered to help him without his even asking. She decided to reinvest the money she was making at the studio, into his club.

"So far, so good. We signed the final paperwork and we're planning the grand opening in six weeks. You gonna be up for it?" he asked.

"You think I'm not?" She laughed.

"I don't know, I mean, I ain't know since you've been sneaking out with the church folk in the middle of night." Diesel laughed heartily. "Good ol' Warren Cobb. Who woulda thought? No wonder Scooter can't get no play, he ain't your type."

Seymone and Chester cracked up.

"That shit ain't funny." The look Paisley wore on her face was as stern as the tone of her voice. They stopped laughing and stared at her, realizing she was serious.

"Come on, Paisley," Seymone said. "You know Diesel was just playing."

"That's nothing to play about." Paisley glared. The room got quiet and tension filled the air. "Warren almost died. He's still not out of the woods. And I wasn't sneaking around with nobody."

Tears began stinging her eyes and she tried to blink them back. Her head began throbbing, her legs ached, and she had the overwhelming urge to lie down.

"Paisley, are you all right?" Chester asked.

"Yeah, I'm just tired." She closed her eyes.

"Diesel, can you help her upstairs?" Seymone suggested.

"Not a problem, baby doll." He stood up, gently scooped her into his arms, and took her to her bedroom.

"Thanks," she said as he laid her onto the bed.

"Look, I'm sorry about what I said. I didn't mean to offend you, seriously." Diesel looked as if he was about to cry, making her feel worse than she already did.

"You know you didn't offend me. It's just that all of this is too much for me to even deal with. I got mad hate mail on my MySpace, e-mails calling me all kinds of whores and tramps. It's just not a good day I guess." She sniffed and told him,

"And did you hear that Warren says he doesn't even know who I am?"

"He got amnesia?" Diesel frowned.

"I don't think so. From what his manager says, his ass is remembering everything else," she snapped.

"Well, you didn't remember the accident yourself, Paisley."

"He's faking. I think him and his manager came up with this amnesia to cover up something that don't even need to be covered."

"Maybe so."

"While he's having *selective memory*, I gotta deal with people saying all kinds of stuff about me. What kinda shit is that?"

"Shit that you've always had to deal with. From the moment you became known as the Sensual Seductress and you started blowing up, you had haters. This ain't nothing you ain't had to deal with before, Paisley. Remember when that rapper Python started bragging that he slept with you after the video shoot, we all knew he was lying.

And when they called you to be in the next video what did you tell him?"

Paisley looked over at the best friend who was more like a brother to her and smiled, wiping the tears from her eyes. "I told him that it would be double because he shortchanged me on the last one since he came and I didn't."

"And that nigga paid you, didn't he? Because he liked that. That was your M.O. and you decided if they were gonna lie about sleeping with you, your ass was gonna get something out the deal. Remember you said you had to take the good with the bad and keep it moving and you would just brush them haters off."

What Diesel didn't know was that Paisley had caught Python in the trailer with another male dancer on the video shoot. She was stunned when she walked in and found the two fine brothers engaged in a passionate kiss. He had panicked and was about to have an anxiety attack, when Paisley assured him that she wouldn't say anything. Somehow though, when they got back to the set, word got out that Python was sleeping with one of the dancers. When asked if it was her, Paisley neither confirmed nor denied the rumor, so she became the dancer he was sleeping with. Python was one of many entertainers she was rumored to have bedded, but in reality never did.

The talk became rampant, and at first she was bothered by it, until Fallon actually began marketing her as the "seductress" of the music industry; the reputation opened more doors and gave her more opportunities than she could ever imagine. Soon after, she was invited to the hottest parties and premiers, booked club appearances and magazine spreads, and had a yearly calendar.

All because she allowed all of the down low rappers and singers, erectile-dysfunctional producers, and anyone else who could afford to be seen with her to brag about being "seduced."

"Okay, that was because people were gonna talk regardless, Diesel," she responded, recalling how she allowed the males in the industry to lie on her because it made her a hot commodity. At the time, it seemed like a brilliant idea. It was easier brushing off the haters and their talk because she gave them permission to lie; this was different.

"And they're still gonna talk, Paisley." He smiled. "What? Now because you got hate mail coming from the church folk it makes it worse?"

"No, I just thought Warren was going to help explain things," she admitted.

"Be real, Paisley," he laughed. "Warren Cobb has more to lose than you do. I don't blame him for playing it off. He's being the typical man: 'It wasn't me.' "

"You're not making this any better. Warren and I are just friends, Diesel, I swear."

"I believe you. You don't owe me or anyone else an explanation," Diesel told her. "Look, I gotta get outta here. I will call and check on you later. Get some rest. We got a lot of work to do."

"Thanks, Diesel," she said as he leaned over and gave her a quick hug.

"What are you gonna do about The Playground?" He turned just as he was walking out her bedroom door.

She took a deep breath. "That's a whole 'nother issue I gotta deal with. I either gotta hire someone to help out while I'm out of commission or close up shop for a while."

"How long is Seymone gonna be here?" He gave her a knowing look.

"Hell no, that will definitely not work. We tried that before and the moment her man calls, she'll be out," Paisley replied. "'I'll figure something out.'"

Exactly what that something was, she didn't know.

Diesel

Man, I'm glad Paisley is home. That makes me feel a little bit better. I was kinda worried that the accident was gonna cause a setback with all that we're trying to do, but if Paisley says she'll be ready in six weeks, then I know she will. I love that woman. Not in a romantic, sexual way, although she is fine as a mutha. At five six, a hundred and fifty pounds, with cocoa brown skin and them gray-ass eyes, damn. She is definitely what my granddaddy would call a bad mamma jamma: full D-cup breasts, her waist is small, and those hips and ass are perfect. But her body is nothing compared to her gorgeous face. Those thick, long lashes and her full lips, and when she smiles, she has the deepest dimples I have ever seen. I've witnessed her instantly become every man's fantasy woman when she smiles at them. All my boys have tried to hit that, thinking Paisley was easy, and none of them have succeeded. I can't blame them for trying though. Paisley is fine. They've even tried to call me out a time or two for not trying. But Paisley is my girl, and I love her like a sister. Which is why when Seymone flaked out on her when they were supposed to open The Playground together, I stepped up. Who would've thought that converting a warehouse into a dance studio with some mirrors and stripper poles would be a financial gold mine? But, it worked and I'm happy for her. And now she's paying it forward by helping me open the club.

Hopefully, her business luck will continue and the club will be just as successful as The Playground.

Diesel had been developing plans for his nightclub for a couple of years now. His promotions company had grown and he had been waiting for the right time to make his move. A few months ago, the owner of State Streets approached him about possibly buying the club, and he knew it was just the opportunity he had been waiting for. He talked with his best friends, Scooter, who was a regional director for the YMCA, and Leo, who was a pharmacist, and they all decided to put up the money. As a silent partner, Paisley's funds provided cushion money in case they needed backup funding.

"How's my baby doing?" Scooter asked. He was sitting at the bar of TGIF's where they were meeting Leo for lunch.

"She's good. She says she'll be good to go for the opening." Diesel sat on the barstool next to him.

"So, is it true? Is she really sleeping with Warren Cobb?"

Diesel looked over at Scooter and replied, "In my opinion, hell no. But you know Paisley. If she was, she'll never tell and we'll never know."

"She is the seductress, with her fine ass," Scooter told him. "I just don't understand."

"Understand what?" Diesel said after getting the bartender's attention and ordering a beer.

"Why she would never give a brother like me a second look. Hell, I look better than Warren Cobb."

"Maybe, but unlike you, Paisley doesn't think Warren Cobb is an asshole." Diesel laughed so hard he nearly choked on his beer. He was so busy trying to breathe that he didn't notice the strange look on Scooter's face.

"He who laughs last, laughs best," Scooter told him. "We'll see who the last man smiling is."

Warren Cobb will probably be smiling long after you will, friend, Diesel thought.

Chapter 6

"Come on, Paisley, I'm ready to go." Warren held out his hand and Paisley tried to reach for it, but her legs ached and buckled under her. She tried to stand as he helped her up, but the pain was unbearable. She couldn't get up.

"Warren, I can't move," she cried out.

"I can't wait, I have to go," Warren told her.

Paisley reached out to him, pleading for him to take her with him, but he walked away, leaving her sprawled in the middle of her bedroom floor. She was crumbled, devastated that he was gone. Suddenly, she felt another presence in the room. She could hear someone breathing and she smelled the strong scent of cologne. It was the same scent she smelled that night at the hospital.

"Warren, Warren, Warren!"

Paisley's eyes opened and she glanced around the dark room. She had been dreaming, but she knew someone had been there in her room.

"Paisley, are you all right?" Seymone came rushing in.

"Seymone, someone was in here. They were here, in my room!" Paisley told her, sitting up and reaching for the lamp on her nightstand.

"What?" Seymone asked, rubbing her eyes.

"Here, in my room," Paisley repeated. "I could feel them. I could hear them breathing in the dark. And I could smell them. Don't you smell that?"

Seymone inhaled and nodded, "Smells like cheap cologne. Maybe . . ."

"Maybe nothing. You know the only men who have been in here today are Chester and Diesel. And they don't wear cheap cologne." Paisley's heart began pounding. "It was him, I know it was."

Seymone spotted something in the corner and frowned. She walked over, reached down, and picked up a rubber band–wrapped stack of fan mail that Paisley was sorting earlier.

"See," Paisley said, "that mail was on my desk and you know it. Someone was in here and they were going through my shit!"

"I'm calling the police."

Paisley began shaking from a combination of pain and fear. Her body ached and mental exhaustion sank in. It was too much for her to bear. "How the hell did someone get in my house?"

"I don't know," Seymone answered, hurrying over to the nightstand and grabbing the phone. "But we'll find out."

"This is crazy." Paisley shook her head in disbelief. She twisted her body in an effort to get out of bed, but was stopped by the pain. "Dammit!"

Seymone gave the address of the house and then said, "I'm going to make sure the doors are locked!"

"It's a little too damned late for that!"

"I don't want him to come back in."

"He was already in! He may still be in! Don't leave me in here by myself!"

The two women went back and forth, both of them in a panic, trying to figure out the best thing to do.

"I'm calling Chester." Paisley took the phone from her. "I'ma tell him to come over here. We need a man in the house."

"Chester? Paisley, for real." Seymone looked at her like she was crazy. "You know Chester can't protect us from nothing but . . . bad fashion ideas!"

Paisley couldn't help laughing. She knew Seymone was right. Chester would've been just as scared as they were. She hung the phone up before he answered.

"Shh. You hear that?" Paisley listened more closely.

"I think it's the doorbell," Seymone replied.

Bam, bam, bam!

The knocking coming from downstairs caused both of them to jump.

"That's probably the police." Seymone turned to head out the door.

"Wait!" Paisley hissed. "What if it's not? He may have come back. Don't leave me!"

"It's not him!"

"How do you know?"

"Because his ass wasn't polite enough to knock the last time he came in. Why would he knock now?" Seymone said matter-of-factly.

Bam, Bam, Bam!

The knocking got louder.

"Let me go let them in," Seymone said.

"At least help me down the steps. I don't wanna stay up here alone."

Seymone gave an exasperated sigh and walked over to the bed. "Fine."

Paisley moaned as she rolled her legs over the side of the bed and wobbled to stand up. She leaned onto her friend, and they made their way out of the room. They barely made it into the hallway when the phone began ringing.

"This isn't gonna work," Seymone said. They made their way back and Paisley got back into bed.

"I gotta get downstairs before they break the door down," Seymone said, and rushed out.

Paisley snatched the ringing cordless phone and answered it.

"Hello."

"Who the hell called me and hung up?" Chester demanded. "I am entertaining and I don't have time to be playing on the phone."

"It was me. Someone broke in," Paisley told him.

"What? I'm on my way," he said, and hung up.

Paisley looked around her room. It was what she considered her sanctuary, large and open with a connected sitting room, complete with a fireplace. Her king-sized, brass bed sat in the center of the room, held up by four tall bedposts. The walls held a plasma television, surround sound speakers, and large framed black-and-white, poster-sized photos of Paisley on the covers of various magazines, and still shots. She had decorated the room in blues and greens, which were calming and soothing. The last thing she felt at the moment was calm. She felt violated. She strained as she rose out of bed and peaked out of her window into the street below. An unfamiliar black Jaguar was easing past her house. She tried to see the license plate number, but it was too dark.

After what seemed like hours, Seymone finally called up the steps, "Paisley, the officers wanna talk to you. Can I bring them up?"

"Yeah," Paisley told her. She adjusted the shirt of the gray lounging outfit she wore, making sure she was decent.

Seymone walked in, followed by two uniformed officers; a man and a woman.

"How ya doing, Ms. Lawrence," the brown-
skinned man asked. "I'm officer Mike Jenson.
This is my partner, Dorian Bell."

The pretty, light-skinned woman smiled and
extended her hand. "Nice to meet you. We understand that the intruder actually came into
your bedroom?"

"Yeah, he was in here." Paisley nodded.

"You said it was a he, can you describe him?"
Officer Jenson asked, taking a small notepad
from his pocket and writing in it.

"Not really, it was dark. I didn't see him this
time," Paisley replied.

"This time? He's been here before?" Officer
Bell frowned.

Paisley explained the incident in the hospital
room and the hang-up calls she had received. "I
don't even understand how he got in here."

"From what we can tell, it looks as if someone
came through the utility room door. We'll process downstairs for prints and we'll do the same
thing in here," Officer Jenson told her.

"There was a black Jaguar driving past right
after we called you. That may have been him,"
Paisley told them.

"Did you get a good look at the driver or a tag
number?"

"No, I tried, but I couldn't."

"Black Jaguars aren't that unusual in this neighborhood, but we'll check it out."

Paisley nodded. Chester had arrived and was in her room on the phone with Fallon when the officers finished up.

"I'm here, she's fine. I don't know," he said into the phone, sitting on her bed. "Fallon says she and Gotti are on their way."

"Tell her she doesn't have to come all the way over here." Paisley sighed. It was after two in the morning and she was exhausted. She didn't see the need for Fallon to drag herself out of bed along with her fiancé, Gotti, just to stand watch over her.

"Uh, we'll call you back," Chester said, glancing up at the officers as they walked into the bedroom.

"Ms. Lawrence, do you have anywhere you can stay tonight?" Officer Bell asked as she came into the room.

"I'm not leaving my home," Paisley stated.

"Look, under the circumstances, I suggest you not stay here until either we find this person, or you get some type of security system," Officer Jenson told her.

"I've been telling her to get an alarm system for months now." Chester shook his head.

"Paisley rolled her eyes at him, then told the police, "Thanks. I'll call the security company tomorrow and have them come out. But I'm not having this man drive me out of my home."

"I understand how you feel." Officer Bell gave her an empathetic look. "But right now, it's not safe."

"My cousin is here with me now. I think we'll be all right with a male in the house," Paisley told her. All eyes turned to Chester, sitting on the bed in his yellow plaid pajama bottoms, leather slippers, and "My boyfriend loves me and so does yours" T-shirt. His massive afro was tied in a black satin doo rag, tied at the back of his head.

"Are you trying to be funny?" he asked Paisley.

"No," Paisley told him. "Can't you spend the night?"

"I guess so." He shrugged.

"Oh God, we're dead." Seymone shook her head.

"We'll make sure there are extra patrolmen in the area and keep an eye out," Office Jenson assured her.

"Here's my card." Officer Bell passed her the small card. "Call me if you need me."

Paisley thanked them and Seymone walked them out.

"Guess we'll be having a slumber party." Chester smiled. "Good thing this bed is big enough for all three of us."

A couple of days later, Paisley was hooked up with the latest and greatest alarm system, and moving around more easily. Fallon had just arrived with lunch for everyone from Paisley's favorite deli, and they were about to eat when Seymone's cell phone rang.

"I'll take this in the other room." Seymone looked at it and hopped up from the table.

"She's really been there for you, huh?" Fallon smiled. "I knew Seymone wasn't gonna desert you in your time of need."

"It's only been a week." Paisley opened the top on her chicken Caesar salad and covered it with dressing. "You act like she's been here for months."

"Damn, Paisley, give the girl some credit. She left her fiancé in ATL, in the middle of planning their wedding and building their house, and has been here."

"I didn't know she was doing all that. Seymone hasn't mentioned anything about her wedding or a house since she's been here." Paisley stopped mid-bite and frowned.

"She probably hasn't had the time to think about it with everything that's going on." Fallon shrugged. "She hasn't really said anything to me about it either. She just mentioned it the other day when I was telling her about the bachelorette parties people have at The Playground. Speaking of which, have you started looking for a substitute until you get back on your feet?"

Paisley shook her head. She knew she had been neglecting her business and she needed to get it together. But between dealing with the intruder in her home and worrying about Warren, The Playground wasn't at the top of her priority list. "I can't even think about that right now. I tried calling the hospital and speaking to Warren, but they wouldn't put me through to his room. I know he's not in ICU anymore. He's in a regular room."

"Yeah, they moved him yesterday. He's much better."

"How do you know? Where the hell are you getting your information from?" Paisley asked.

"Ebonie told me. She called to see how you were doing and compare some press information that she had." Fallon reached toward the middle of the table and grabbed a napkin.

"Did she say if Warren admitted to knowing me?"

"No, he still says he doesn't know who you are or why you were together. He doesn't remember anything about the accident, going to a bar, nothing. As a matter of fact, Ebonie says Warren doesn't even drink," Fallon told her.

"He's lying." Paisley sat back and stared at her in amazement.

"I get the feeling that Ebonie knows he's lying too," Fallon said, sounding more like a black girl from the hood than the white girl she was.

"Really?" Paisley's eyes widened. "How so?"

"Something about the way she talks about him and you. It's like she knows that there's something up with his story. Then again, Paisley, this convenient bout of amnesia may be her idea. It's her job to protect his career at all costs. Saying he doesn't know you is the perfect explanation."

"For him, not for me. Nothing happened between us, Fallon. You know if it did, after all this, I woulda told you. If nothing else, we always agreed to be honest with each other."

"I know, Paisley. And I hear what you're saying."

"Why does it sound like there's a 'but' somewhere? What?"

"I went by Charley's and the waitress told me that you two clearly were together. She also told me that unlike Warren, you didn't have anything to drink. Why didn't you tell me that Warren had been drinking?"

"He wasn't drunk." Paisley began fumbling with her salad.

"Even still, it was something you should've let me know. We need all the pertinent information we can get regarding this, Paisley. We don't know how Ebonie and Warren's record label are going to try to carry this." Fallon gave her a smug look. "And you know me, I have no problem leaking info that Ebonie damn sure don't want to let get out."

"No," Paisley said emphatically. "I don't want you to leak anything."

"We don't know how they're gonna try and play this out. We gotta be ready to fight fire with fire," Fallon replied.

"There's not going to be a fight. Warren won't let it get that far," Paisley said assuringly.

"You don't know that. And I'm just gonna let you know that not only am I your friend, but I'm your manager. I've always made the best decisions where your career is concerned and I'm not gonna stop now because you're more worried about what Warren Cobb is going to say."

Paisley looked Fallon in the eye and the two stared, neither one saying a word for a moment. Only time would tell which one would be the victor in this argument.

"Don't make me *fire you*." Paisley knew she had to say something to make Fallon see how serious she was.

She was stunned when Fallon responded by saying, "Don't make me *quit*."

Chapter 7

"Paisley, telephone," Seymone said as she walked into the room. Paisley was so into *The Young and the Restless* that she didn't feel like talking on the phone.

"Take a message," Paisley said.

"I think you wanna take this one," Seymone said, walking in and passing her the phone. "It's important."

"Hello."

"Ms. Lawrence, this is Becca. I'm calling from Dr. Singleton's office. You missed your appointment this morning, so I was calling to reschedule." The woman was so perky that it was irritating. "Can you come in tomorrow?"

"I'm sorry, I'm really not up to it," Paisley told her. "I have some personal issues I'm dealing with and I have to call you later next week sometime."

"Okay, that's fine. I understand. I hope things get better for you and I'll talk to you next week," Becca told her.

"Why don't you wanna go to the doctor?" Seymone asked.

"I don't feel like it," she told her. "I just wanna stay in bed."

Paisley was moving around a little better, but she rarely got out of bed. It was as if she had no energy. Seymone was really becoming concerned.

"I think you need to go and get checked out," Seymone suggested.

"I'm fine. I'll go when it's time to get this cast off. It's the only thing bothering me at this point." Paisley reached for the remote and turned on the TV. It was almost time for *The Young and the Restless*. Soap operas had become her new vice. She hoped Seymone would get the hint and leave her alone.

"Warren was released from the hospital this morning." Seymone passed Paisley a stack of mail.

Paisley quickly turned off the television and focused her attention on her friend. "What? How do you know?"

"It was just announced on the radio. I heard it while I was on my way back from picking up the mail at The Playground. Some ladies stopped by while I was there, too. Mrs. Nancy and Mrs. Blake. They both send their love. Really nice ladies."

"Yeah, they are. What did the radio say about Warren?"

"Nothing. He was released from the hospital this morning, that's all." Seymone hesitated, then said, "I told the ladies that classes would resume next week."

Paisley looked at her like she was crazy. "Why would you tell them that? In case you didn't notice, I still can hardly walk and not to mention I have a big-ass cast on my arm!"

"I know." Seymone nodded and turned to walk out of the room.

"Wait, where the hell are you going? You come in here making two announcements like that and you think you're just gonna walk out like it's no big deal?" Paisley was confused.

"What? OK, Warren got out the hospital. I thought that would be good news for you. You've been moping around for days because you were worried about him. He's well enough to leave and go home." Seymone folded her arms and then said, "You've got clients beating down your door and the studio is booked for weeks. I know you were in an accident, but you've also been acting like your head is so far up your ass that you can't even think about the success of your business."

"What the hell do you mean?"

"Everyone has been asking you about the studio and you brush them off like it's no big deal. It's been damn near two weeks since the accident. I go to that studio two or three times a week: picking up mail, making sure it's locked up, checking the messages, and not once did you ask me to resume the classes for you."

"And I'm *not* going to ask, either. Why would I do that? Hell, let's be real. I figured the success of my studio wasn't your concern. The same way your wedding and your new house isn't mine," Paisley snapped. *There, I said it. I didn't want to, but I did. Who the hell does Seymone think she is? It was one thing to sit with her at home while I healed, but now this wench is coming in and trying to take over. Hell no.*

"So, are we back on that again? Me and Bobby?"

"I don't give a damn about Bobby! That nigga don't mean shit to me! This is about you not telling me you had even started planning the wedding or you were building a house," Paisley huffed.

"First of all, I'm not building a house. Bobby and I were looking at houses the day before you got into the accident, and had talked about hiring a builder. Second, you know I'm engaged. I am thinking about what I want in my wedding, but we haven't even set a date yet."

Paisley stared at Seymone and processed what she had just said. She felt bad because she had had an attitude with Seymone since the day she and Fallon squared off over Warren.

"I know you're going through a lot, Paisley, but I'm here for you whether you like it or not and if that means I work at the studio until you hire someone, then that's what I gotta do." Seymone turned and left the room before Paisley had the opportunity to respond.

When she was alone, Paisley lay back on her pillow and cried. It was as if she were on some fast moving carnival ride that was taking her up and down, through flips and turns, and she couldn't get off. Her life was turned upside down and she couldn't get right-side up. She picked up her phone and dialed Warren's cell phone number. Her heart began pounding when, instead of going straight to voice mail as it had the last few times she called, it rang. She prayed that he would answer. Instead, after five or six rings, the voice mail did pick up. She thought about hanging up, then, in a moment of boldness, she decided to leave a message.

"Warren, it's me. I heard you were released from the hospital and I . . . I'm relieved . . . I'm

glad you're okay. I was hoping I could talk to you
. . . Just call me when you get this message." Her
voice was shaking. She ended the call and threw
her phone onto the nightstand. She snuggled
deep under her covers and decided to lose herself in a heavy slumber.

"Paisley." There was a knock at the door, and
Seymone stuck her head in. "You have a visitor."

"Who is it?" Paisley said without opening her
eyes.

"Dr. Singleton."

Paisley's eyes popped open. She wondered if
she had heard Seymone wrong, and sat up. "On
the phone?"

"No, here . . . Downstairs."

"What do you mean downstairs?"

"Damn, Paisley, wake up. He's downstairs."

"What is he doing here? How did he even
know where I lived?"

"You keep asking me questions that you need
to be asking him." Seymone frowned.

"Tell him to give me a few minutes to get
dressed," Paisley told her.

"Okay," Seymone sighed, and went back down
the stairs where the handsome doctor was waiting.

Paisley went into the bathroom and washed
her face. She glanced at her reflection in the mir-

ror and realized how horrible she looked. Her hair was pulled back into a messy ponytail and badly needed washing. She still had scrapes on her forehead and bruises under her eye and on her cheek. Her neck was peeling from the chemical burns. In addition, having missed her weekly facial resulted in blemishes and pimples, which were especially worse since it was almost time for her period.

I gotta get it together, she thought. *I'm breaking down and it's damn sure not a good look.*

"Paisley, Dr. Singleton says you don't have to come down. He can come up," Seymone announced through the bathroom door. "He came over to check on you. Fallon told him it was okay."

"I'm gonna kill Fallon," Paisley hissed. "Fine, bring him up."

Paisley hurried and got herself together as best as she could. Instead of getting back into bed, she went into the sitting area and settled on the sofa.

"And how are you?" Dr. Singleton asked, entering the room. Seymone sat on Paisley's bed, staying nearby in case the doctor tried anything funny. She didn't care how fine he was, she wasn't taking any chances.

"I'm good." She was surprised to see that he was dressed in jeans, a crisp, white shirt, and a sports jacket. He was carrying a small, black medical bag.

"What's that look for?" he asked.

"I guess I thought you'd have on a lab jacket." She smiled.

"I only wear that in the hospital," he told her. "If you would've come into the office like you were supposed to, I would've had it on."

"I really wasn't up to coming out," she told him.

"Yes, that's what Ms. Baxter said when I called her."

"You called Ms. Baxter?" Paisley blinked.

"Yes, my receptionist was concerned about what you told her, and I had some concerns of my own," he confessed. "So, I called her this afternoon. She had given me her card when you were released from the hospital."

"That doesn't surprise me," Paisley responded.

"How have you been feeling?" he asked.

"I'm getting better," she told him.

"If you don't mind, I just wanted to come by and check you out. I know you have some reservations about coming into the office, and that's understandable," he said, reaching into the bag and taking out a stethoscope.

He gave her a brief checkup and made sure she was healing properly. "Everything looks good. It looks like minimal scarring from the chemical burns on your neck. The bruising on your legs and face is improving, so that's a good thing. We just need to get that cast off in about five weeks. And I would like to schedule some physical therapy for you, just to make sure your leg muscles are getting exercise and you can regain your full strength."

He reached into his bag and passed her a piece of paper. "Here's a referral to a great therapy center near the hospital."

"That's not necessary," Paisley told him.

"Ms. Lawrence, I'm really trying here, but you're being a difficult patient. I'm only trying to help you." He frowned, still holding the paper out. "I know you're going through a lot—"

"I beg your pardon, Dr. Singleton," Paisley interrupted him. Pointing to the degree hanging on the wall near her desk, she informed him, "I'm a licensed physical therapist myself. The best in the business."

"Oh, really? I'm sorry I didn't know that. I just thought you were . . . a . . . model." Dr. Singleton gave her a weak smile.

"It's all good," Paisley told him, glancing at Seymone. "It's not something a lot of people know about me."

"Well, do you work at a facility or at a center in the area?" Dr. Singleton put the paper back in his bag.

"She works in the area." Seymone smiled.

Paisley gave her an ugly look. "I choose not to work in a clinical setting."

"But you say you're the best in the business," he reminded her.

"I am," she replied. "I tried the clinical setting for a while. I worked at two different facilities, but the staff at both of them always had something to say about who I was and my 'other' career that I was known for. I found that I was becoming more of a distraction than anything."

"That's a shame," he told her.

"She has her own private practice now," Seymone volunteered.

"Really? Where?" Dr. Singleton's attention was now drawn to Seymone.

"She runs The Playground," Seymone answered.

"The Playground?" Dr. Singleton looked deep in thought. "I've never heard of that. Is that a pediatric facility?"

Seymone could no longer hold her laughter. Paisley closed her eyes and shook her head in embarrassment. "No, it's not. It's a fitness facility for women."

"Paisley teaches Strip-Hop and Eroticize classes. It enhances their sexuality while promoting physical fitness."

Seymone walked into the sitting area and sat on the arm of the sofa. "It also gives women a boost of self-esteem."

"Wow, sounds interesting," Dr. Singleton told them.

"Dr. Singleton, you said you had some reservations about me coming into the office. Why was that?" Paisley decidedly changed the subject.

"Well, we received some strange calls at the office questioning the time of your appointment this morning. And when we refused to give out the information, the person became a bit threatening." Dr. Singleton looked uncomfortable.

"Oh, hell no." Paisley shook her head. "What do you mean, threatening?"

"How did they even know Paisley had an appointment?" Seymone frowned.

"I don't know, but they did," Dr. Singleton said. "That's when I called Ms. Baxter and she gave me the go ahead to come by."

Paisley wondered why Fallon didn't call and tell her all of this herself. She began to get the feeling that even having a security system wouldn't keep her safe.

"I appreciate your concern and coming," Paisley said, distracted by what he just told her. "I'll call when it's time to get the cast off."

"No, I'll come by to check on you. I want to make sure you're regaining the strength in those leg muscles."

"I'll call and schedule an appointment." Paisley fought the urge to stare into his handsome face.

"No need. I'll be here same time next week. I'll save you the trouble of trying to come up with an excuse to cancel in case you try to." He passed her his card. "Call me if you need anything before then. And get some rest, Ms. Lawrence, doctor's orders."

"Yes, sir." Paisley took the card from his hand.

"I'll walk you out," Seymone offered. She walked him downstairs and thanked him again. "I really appreciate your making a house call."

"It wasn't a problem. After the strange phone calls, and after talking to Ms. Baxter, I knew it was the right thing to do. She needed to be checked out, but I can understand her hesitance. And, considering the circumstances, it's probably a good thing she didn't come in. It wasn't safe." Dr. Singleton's eyes were filled with as much concern as his voice. They stood in the foyer of Paisley's house, talking.

"It's pretty rough for her."

"You're a good friend for being there for her through all of this," he said.

"Thanks, sometimes I wonder." Seymone laughed.

The doorbell rang, catching both of them off guard.

"Who could that be?" Seymone's eyes widened and her heart began beating with fear.

"You're not expecting anyone?" Dr. Singleton asked as Seymone stepped in front of him and looked through the peephole.

"No," she told him. She made a small gasp and opened the door. "Bobby!"

Bobby

See, this is the bullshit I'm talking about. I fly all the way the hell down here to make sure things are cool, and what's the first thing I see when I get to Paisley's house? Seymone talking to another nigga. I swear, I try to give that girl the benefit of the doubt, but she can't be trusted. Maybe I went against my better judgment when I proposed to her. I mean, at twenty-seven, I am still young and I have my whole life ahead of me. But, Seymone Davis is a helluva catch. She's fine as hell and all my boys want her. Sometimes, I can't believe I got her ass. But then again, why should I be surprised?

I'm Bobby Taylor, all-star running back for the Atlanta Falcons. I'm the catch. I just gotta refine her ass a little bit. Even if she is gorgeous and successful, she still got some major changes to make before I make her my wife. I wanted her ass to thicken up a little bit, because I was never one for skinny chicks, and she's put on about ten pounds. That's cool, but she betta be careful because I can't be with no fat chick either.

Now, I gotta get rid of that damn Paisley. I can't stand that trick. She thinks she's all that and she ain't. Granted, she's the one I was trying to go after until I found out what a bitch she was. I can't believe she laughed at me when I told her I thought she would be the perfect woman for me. It's cool though, because Seymone ain't find nothing funny about my ass, and before Paisley could even blink, I had her on my arm and wearing my ring.

Hahaha, my timing was perfect. Paisley had come up with this whack-ass idea about some stripper school and actually thought Seymone would be dumb enough to go into business with her. I stopped that shit real quick. There's no way any woman of mine was gonna be shak-

ing her ass for all the world to see. Not if she's gonna be Mrs. Bobby Taylor. Hmph. Seymone is a quick study though, I gotta give it to her. She hasn't been in a video in a couple of months, and I know the offers have been pouring in. That white girl Fallon ain't been too happy about that. But I bet her ass don't say nothing to me about it. Things were moving in the right direction until Paisley got into this accident. Now I see I gotta come give Seymone's ass a quick intervention.

"What's up, baby?" Bobby stepped into the house and gave Seymone a kiss. He looked Dr. Singleton up and down, then turned back to Seymone and asked, "Who is this?"

"Baby, this is Paisley's doctor, Evan Singleton. Evan, this is my fiancé, Bobby Taylor."

"Nice to meet you." Evan nodded.

"I ain't know doctors made house calls." Bobby continued to stare, his arm remaining around Seymone's waist and holding her close to him, marking his territory.

"The dedicated ones still do." Dr. Singleton shrugged. "Seymone, I'll see you next week when I come back to check on Paisley. Until then, you both have my number."

"Okay, Dr. Singleton." Seymone opened the door for him.

"Evan," he told her.

"Evan," she repeated.

Bobby didn't like the way Dr. Singleton was looking at Seymone. *It's a good thing I got here when I did*, he thought. *I gotta nip this shit in the bud*.

Chapter 8

"Lord, you've gotta help me. I am trying to do the best I can, but it's not working. It's bad enough I feel like I'm a prisoner in my own home because of some sick bastard out there trying to get me. But now, of all people, Bobby Taylor is in my house. I can't stand his arrogant, pragmatic, wanna-be-bad, thinks-he's-God's-gift ass and I know he can't stand mine. I know I asked you to help me out with my mother, and you did. But can you please help me out one more time, please? Oh, and God, thanks for healing Warren and making him better . . .

Bzzzzzz. . . . Bzzzzzzz. . . . Bzzzzzzz.

Paisley's cell phone began vibrating. She picked it up and saw that she had a text message. She went to the inbox, and rubbed her eyes to make sure that she wasn't mistaken. There was a message from Warren. She hurriedly opened it and read:

I'm OK, baby, and I'm gonna make sure you're
OK too. Love you.

She dialed his number, but again, only got his
voice mail. Although she was relieved to hear
from him, she was frustrated that she still wasn't
able to talk to him. She sent him a text back telling him to call her ASAP and waited, hoping her
phone would ring and his voice would be on the
other end. She had to find out why he was saying
he didn't know her; what the method to his madness was.

"So, how long do you plan on being here?"
Bobby's voice drifted into her room. Paisley crept
over to her bedroom door, opened it a crack and
strained to hear them. She still couldn't believe
he was even at her house. When Seymone had
walked into her bedroom and told her he was
there, she almost made a smart comment until
she saw him standing in the doorway.

"What's up, Paisley?" He nodded.

"Chilling," Paisley said, her voice flat. His
quick glance to her breasts didn't go unnoticed
by her and she folded her arms in disgust.

"I see you're changing genres, huh? Going for
the gospel cats now?" He smiled, and Paisley had
to restrain herself from jumping out of bed and
slapping him.

"Bobby, that's not funny!" Seymone gasped.

"Well, Seymone tried slumming it and look what she ended up with." Paisley faked a smile.

"Funny," Bobby remarked, then turned to Seymone. "I got us a suite at the Radisson."

Seymone frowned at him. "I can't leave Paisley here alone. You can just stay here."

Both Paisley and Bobby looked at her like she was crazy.

"Whoa." Paisley did a double-take.

"Aw, hell naw," Bobby commented.

"Y'all both are tripping." Seymone grabbed Bobby's hand and pulled him out of the room. Paisley didn't know what Seymone was trying to pull, but there was no way Bobby Taylor would be staying overnight at her house. She knew an argument was going to take place and she wanted to hear exactly how Seymone was gonna handle it.

"I don't know," she heard Seymone tell him.

"Damn, Seymone, it's been two weeks. Her ass don't look all that hurt to me. She still got a smart-ass mouth," Bobby commented.

"And so do you."

"What? You better chill the hell out. Look, you know we got a lotta shit to take care of. You said you wanted to find a house, how the hell are we supposed to do that if you're here?"

"I know."

"And what about the wedding? You putting that on hold, too?"

"We haven't even set a date."

"I was gonna do that after we got the house situation settled."

Yeah, right, Paisley thought. *He is such a liar and I don't see why Seymone even deals with him. Everyone and their mama knows that he's been partying it up for the past two weeks while Seymone was here. Hell, he was partying while Seymone was there with him.*

"She's my best friend, Bobby. What do you want me to do? I'm not just gonna leave her."

"You said yourself that someone tried to break in the other night. You don't think I'm worried about you? What if you get hurt?" Bobby's voice became seductive. "Seymone, I love you. I don't want anything to happen to you."

"I love you too, Bobby," Seymone said. It got quiet, and then Paisley heard a soft moan.

Gross. Well, I guess Seymone will be packing up and leaving tonight. I'd better call Chester and tell him to come over. This is stupid. Maybe I should've just let my mother stay.

"You want me to wait downstairs while you get your stuff?" she heard Bobby say a few seconds later.

"Baby, I'm not leaving her. I can't."

"What?" Bobby's voice got louder.

What? Paisley was just as surprised as he was.

"Paisley needs me," Seymone said.

"I need you," Bobby snapped.

"She needs me more. Don't trip, baby. I don't know why you can't just stay here. I thought you were working on compromising. I cut back on work; I go to all your games during the season, I help out with your charity events. When are you gonna give a little, Bobby? What are you compromising on?"

"I flew my ass all the way here to see you. That was a compromise. I'm gone to the hotel. Call me later after you're done playing nursemaid for Paisley. My flight leaves tomorrow night."

"Bobby!" Seymone yelled.

Paisley listened to the chirping of the alarm system as the front door opened, then closed. Suddenly, it was eerily quiet.

Did she leave? Paisley eased the door open a little wider. *She went after him.* She stepped farther out into the hallway and peeked down the steps. She turned to go back, and screamed, seeing someone standing in front of her.

"What the hell is wrong with you?" Seymone squealed, dropping the basket of clothes she was carrying.

"I thought you left . . . I mean . . . I heard the door close," Paisley said.

"Where the hell am I gonna go? And why would I leave without telling you?" Seymone bent over and picked up the scattered items. "No, your ass was eavesdropping probably."

"I was not," Paisley lied. "I heard the alarm when the door opened and I thought maybe you went with Bobby."

"No, I didn't," Seymone sighed. "He threw his little temper tantrum and went back to the hotel."

"Why?" Paisley pretended like she didn't already know.

"Because he wanted me to go with him. He can be so selfish," Seymone said, "just like someone else I know. But I refuse to call names."

"I know what you mean. I keep telling Chester he needs to be more considerate of others." Paisley smiled.

"Yeah, that's definitely not who I was talking about. But, Bobby'll get over it. He's probably mad because he thought he was gonna get some." Seymone laughed.

Paisley looked at her best friend and thought about the sacrifice Seymone had just made. "Why don't you go over and be with him tonight. I'll get Fallon or Chester to come and stay a couple of days."

"Are you serious?" Seymone grinned.

"Yeah, it's cool. You've been cooped up with me in this house long enough. Besides, go so at least one of us will be getting their back blown out," Paisley remarked. It had been so long since she had even been out on a date, let alone had sex. It wasn't that she didn't want to be in a relationship, but she didn't have the time, energy, or patience to deal with meeting someone, getting past all the bullshit, and trying to figure out if he was even worth it. The guys she had dealt with in the past had all proven to simply be disappointing in one way or the other. Most of them had put up a pretty good front as if they were the real deal, but when it came down to it, they were intimidated by her success, more interested in dating the Sensual Seductress rather than Paisley Lawrence, or were just straight up liars about who they were or what they were about. Dating had become sickening, and at this point in her life, she wondered if there was even anyone out there for her. And to this day, she had only fallen in love once, with Warren, and look at how that had turned out.

"Girl, you are the best." Seymone gave her a quick hug and she moaned in pain. "Oh, my bad."

"Whatever. You better enjoy yourself, because when you reopen The Playground next week, you ain't gonna get no rest. I'ma work you to death."

"Deal." Seymone nodded.

Chapter 9

"Marcus, you are *not* the father!" "I knew she was lying!" Paisley said, watching the man dance on the TV screen while Maury Povich tried to comfort a screaming girl who had just been publicly humiliated in front of millions on national television. "That baby don't look nothing like him. Run girl, that's what you get. Your lying tail."

"I can't believe you're actually watching this crap, Paisley." Seymone sat on the opposite end of the sofa in Paisley's den and shook her head. "There has to be something better on TV."

"What can be better than trying to figure out which one of these seventeen guys is this chick's baby daddy? I haven't slept with that many men in my life." Paisley laughed.

"That ain't what I heard, Sensual Seductress." Seymone ducked as Paisley tossed a throw pillow at her.

"Don't go there," Paisley warned her. "It ain't about what I *heard* about you, it's what I *know* that you need to be worried about."

"I'm not worried, because I know just as many of your secrets as you know mine, Paisley Pooh!"

Paisley cringed at the nickname her mom used to call her. It had been a long time since she had heard that name, and it brought back a ton of childhood memories. It was hard to believe that they had grown as far apart as they had, and barely spoke to one another. When she ran away from home when she was seventeen, she decided she would never look back. Now, ten years later, it seemed harder than ever not to.

"Stop, please," Paisley begged, covering her ears.

"Have you talked to your mom since you've been home?" Seymone's voice became serious.

"No, I've talked to my father. You know I wasn't one of my mother's favorite people before the accident; now, after all this, I don't think we'll be arguing anytime soon," Paisley told her.

"Don't be like that, Paisley. You know your mom loves you. If she didn't, she wouldn't have been right there by your side at the hospital," Seymone said.

"Believe me, she was there out of maternal obligation, that's it." Paisley rolled her eyes.

"Yeah, maternal obligation, what's that other word it's called? Oh yeah, *love!*"

"No, she probably didn't want my father to make that nine-hour drive all the way out here by himself. She was afraid he would get here and I would corrupt him, maybe introduce him to some pretty, young thing that would make him laugh and he would leave her evil, controlling ass," Paisley teased.

"Paisley, that's just plain wrong, and you know it." Seymone shook her head. "Your parents love each other a lot and they both love you. You need to stop and be grateful. Hell, sometimes I wish I could take my mother on Maury and find out who my father is."

Paisley looked over at her best friend and saw the longing in her eyes. Seymone rarely talked about her family, especially her absentee father. They had grown up in two different environments: Paisley in a comfortable, two-parent home, and Seymone in the hardcore Ninth Ward of New Orleans, by her here-today, gone-tomorrow mother. Paisley ran away from home and began stripping because she wanted to live life in the fast lane. Seymone had no choice; she did it to survive.

"I'm sorry, Seymone," Paisley said, feeling guilty.

Seymone shook her head and smiled. "No, you're not. You're Paisley."

"You wanna watch something else?" Paisley asked. "Divorce Court is on I think."

"No. Can't we go somewhere? Let's get out of this house." Seymone stood up and stretched. "I'm starting to get cabin fever."

"I can't go anywhere. Don't you know I was in a car accident, Seymone? I almost died," Paisley reminded her, "unlike the driver of the other car who walked away with a freaking bump on his head!"

"You didn't die, Paisley. You've been cooped up in here long enough. You can't stay in here forever. Get up and get dressed." Seymone pulled her by the arm.

Paisley hesitated. "I can't. You know people are still talking."

"Great. We want to keep them talking. As a matter of fact, let's give them something to talk about. Or did you lose some of your fabulousness in the accident? Hell, I'm fat now, and I don't care. Let's go to the mall and then let's hit a party. I'm calling Chester, he'll know where the hot spot is tonight! Come on, Paisley, let's get to it!"

Paisley reluctantly agreed, and they were getting into the car when a black Lexus pulled into the driveway. Evan stepped out, dressed in a pair of khakis and a pale orange soft-collar shirt, and walked over to them.

"Good afternoon, ladies," he greeted them.

"Hey, Evan, I guess we forgot you were scheduled to come by this afternoon," Seymone said.

"Yeah, we did." Paisley couldn't help again noticing how handsome he was. *I wonder if he's a good kisser?* This time, she was drawn to the fullness of his lips. They seemed soft and inviting, *definitely kissable*. She loved kissing, and actually had a personal theory that a man's kissing ability was indicative of his sexual prowess. The better he kissed, the better he was in bed. If his kiss was soft, gentle, and sensual, that was the type of lover he was. If he couldn't kiss at all, then nine times out of ten he was whack in bed. Many men didn't get another date with Paisley after that initial kiss; to her, there was no point. *I wonder if he's a good kisser, she thought again.*

"Isn't that right, Pais?" Seymone asked.

"Huh?" Paisley realized that not only had she been staring at the doctor, but she had missed everything they were saying. She immediately began blushing. *What the hell is wrong with you,* she scolded herself. *He's your doctor and you're his patient. He's too goody-goody for you anyway, definitely not your type.*

"I was telling Evan that we were headed out for a little therapy at the mall." Seymone looked at her strangely, and then added, "I left my phone in the house. I'll be right back."

"Therapy at the mall?" Evan asked.

"The best kind," Paisley said.

"Well, I guess retail therapy counts as physical therapy." Evan smiled. "I'm sure there will be plenty of walking involved."

"Definitely." Paisley nodded.

"Well, would you like for me to reschedule your appointment for tomorrow or another day this week?" he asked.

"Look, Dr. Singleton . . ."

"Evan," he corrected her.

"Evan," she repeated. "I'm fine, really. With the exception of this itchy cast and a little soreness in my legs, there's nothing wrong with me."

"And that's a good thing," he said, "but I still want to check you out."

Paisley couldn't help smiling at the way he said it. "Really?"

"I meant make sure you're healing properly." It was his turn to blush, realizing how his comment sounded.

"I know what you meant," she laughed. "But I feel like I'm putting you out of your way."

"Not at all," he assured her, staring at her so hard that she had to fight the urge not to become lost in his eyes. "I tell you what, I'll let you off the hook today since you already have a physical therapy appointment. But I'll be back same time next week, unless of course you need me before then. Agreed?"

"Agreed," Paisley said, wondering why the thought of his returning next week was actually making her giddy inside. *Don't do it, girl*, her inner voice warned, *don't even bother. You'll only be setting yourself up for the big letdown again.*

A little while later, she and Seymone were strolling out of the mall. Walking was becoming easier for Paisley, although she still hurt a bit. The heat of the sun felt good on her face, and the fresh air was a welcome change from the lingering scent of the candles she kept lit throughout her house.

"So, what's up with you and the doc?" Seymone asked.

"What are you talking about?" Paisley looked at her as if she was crazy.

"I saw you checking him out, Paisley. Giving him the 'hmm, I wonder if he can kiss' look."

"I was not," Paisley lied, amazed at how well her best friend knew her.

"Well, if you weren't checking him out, then maybe you need to. That man is fine and he's got it going on, not to mention he grins every time he looks at you."

"What man doesn't grin when he looks at me? They're all perverts." Paisley shook her head. "I have no interest in him at all. I don't have any interest in any man, as a matter of fact."

"Whoa, hold up there, friend. I hope you're not saying what I think you're saying. You're not interested in women, are you? Please don't tell me that, Pais, because I'm not ready to deal with that right now."

"Don't play with me, Seymone, you of all people should know that I'm strictly dickly!" Paisley began laughing so hard that her body began to ache. Of all the things she had been accused of being in her life, no one had ever insinuated that she was a lesbian. "Ouch!"

"You wanna sit for a minute?" Seymone asked her, pointing to a nearby bench in front of a PetSmart.

"Sure," Paisley said. As soon as she took a seat, a small dog came running up to her.

"Biggie! Biggie, come back." A little blonde girl came running behind it. The dog jumped into Paisley's lap and she squealed.

"Oh my goodness," Seymone laughed, reaching for the small dog and passing it to the girl.

"I'm sorry, ma'am," the little girl said.

"Meagan!" a woman called. "You'd better get that dog back on the leash right now!"

"I am, Mom." The little girl took the dog and slipped the leash on it.

"I'm sorry," the woman said as she walked up. "Paisley, is that you?"

Paisley saw that it was one of her clients from The Playground. "Hey there, Christie! How are you?"

"I'm doing great now that I see you're OK. Lord knows we've been missing you. When is The Playground opening back up?"

"Soon," Paisley assured her. "This is my friend, Seymone. She's gonna take over the classes for a while."

"Nice to meet you, Seymone. I'm glad to hear that because you know my husband has been in Iraq for seven months and he'll be home soon. I gotta have some moves for him, ladies!"

"We got you covered," Seymone laughed.

The dog started barking and Paisley reached down and patted its head. "Aww. It's so cute. I want one!"

"Stop lying," Seymone laughed. "You don't even like dogs."

"What kind is it?"

"A Yorkie and a pain," Christie said. "We've gotta go. I will be seeing you next week then, right?"

Paisley nodded. "Classes start next week." They hugged and waved good-bye.

"She's nice," Seymone commented. "She doesn't look like the type that would be taking classes at The Playground."

"Honey, please. I have all the undercover freaks from Wisteria Lane," Paisley laughed, referring to the clients that she called "Desperate House-wives."

Suddenly, she felt as if someone was staring at them. She turned around, hoping to catch whoever it was, but didn't see anyone. Her eyes scanned the parking lot, and she saw the black Jaguar with dark tint that she swore she had seen driving by her house the night someone was in her room.

"Well, well, well. I thought I was dreaming when I passed by and saw that ugly-ass truck parked outside."

Paisley looked up from the chair she was sitting in and stuck her middle finger up at Scooter, who had walked into the main dance room where she was guiding Seymone through one of the aerobic floor routines to the tune of "Don't Cha" by the Pussycat Dolls. Seymone walked over to the stereo and turned down the music. After their little field trip to the mall, instead of hitting a party, they had gone to the studio to start preparing to reopen.

"I saw that," Diesel said, walking behind him. Both men looked like they had just stepped off the cover of *GQ* magazine dressed in custom-fitted suits: Scooter in smoke gray and Diesel in navy blue. She didn't know which one was sexier: Diesel with his smooth coffee skin, muscular body, and bald head, or the dark chocolate–complexioned Scooter, with his thick, curly afro and medium build.

They walked over and hugged both girls.

"You look good, Pais," Diesel said.

"She damn sure do." Scooter winked at her.

"Thanks, fellas, even if I know you're both lying," Paisley said. Hanging out with her friends made her feel as if things were returning to normal. "And I told you about hating on my truck, too."

The guys often teased Paisley about the Toyota Tundra pickup truck she loved. It was her pimp ride, painted hot pink, dropped with a set of twenty-two-inch rims on it.

"You know they're just hating." Seymone nodded toward them.

"We definitely ain't hating on you," Diesel said to Seymone. "I ain't seen you move like that in a minute. I didn't know you still had it in you, girl."

"Whatever." Seymone sucked her teeth at him.

"What are y'all doing here on a Friday night?" Scooter asked, sitting in the chair and pulling Paisley into his lap. She started to protest, but he smelled so good and the warmth of his body was so inviting that she remained there.

"Getting ready for this week," Seymone answered.

"What's this week?" Scooter ran his fingers along Paisley's hand and commented, "Your pink cast matches that ugly truck."

"Shut up. The studio is reopening this week. Seymone is going to run the classes for me," Paisley told him.

"Cool. Now whose ingenious idea was that, I wonder?" Diesel raised his eyebrows at Paisley.

"So, that means you can work with our girls?" Scooter asked Seymone.

"What girls?" Seymone reached for a towel and wiped her face and neck.

"We're hiring a couple of go-go dancers for the club," Diesel said. "Paisley was supposed to train them."

"Damn, I forgot about that," Paisley mumbled. She had agreed to teach a couple of routines to the girls who had been hired.

"I can do it." Seymone shrugged. "Paisley can give me the songs and walk me through the choreography."

"Bet, that's what's up." Scooter nuzzled Paisley's shoulder.

"Ouch," she whined and pulled back. "I know you see these scars on my neck."

"I only see beauty." He stared at her.

She shook her head and stood up. "You play too much. Where are you two headed, anyway?"

"We're going to hang at Jasper's for a minute," Diesel replied.

"Aw man, Jasper's. I wish I could go," Paisley commented. Jasper's was one of her favorite restaurants, known for its live jazz and awesome food. The owner, Uncle Jay, was a character and she loved hanging out just to talk with him.

"Come go with us," Scooter suggested. "Then I won't be a third wheel."

"Why are you a third wheel?" Seymone asked.

"Because he's going to hook up with Qianna. He thinks I don't know it." Scooter cut his eyes at his boy.

"Man, you tripping," Diesel said. "I'm going to eat."

"You still got a crush on Qianna after all these years?" Seymone laughed.

"Hell yeah, and he still ain't made a move," Scooter said, nodding.

"Oh, ye of little game," Paisley sighed. "Didn't you almost lose her to another man a little while ago?"

"All of y'all are tripping. Yaya and I are just good friends, and I don't wanna jeopardize that by making a wrong move," Diesel explained, then aimed at Scooter. "Some friendships are too precious to ruin by trying to throw unwarranted romance in the mix."

"But everyone knows that she's feeling you too," Paisley said. All Paisley had to do was say Diesel's name and Qianna's face would light up. There was no doubt in Paisley's mind that the two of them had feelings for each other. Paisley's cell phone rang. Her thoughts shifted to Warren, and she hoped he was finally calling. She struggled to get up from Scooter's lap. He gently used his arms to steady her.

"I ain't taking no chances." Diesel shook his head. "Man, you ready? We gotta get outta here and these ladies gotta get back to work."

Paisley answered her phone. "Hello."

"Ms. Lawrence, this is Kevin with ADT. Is everything okay?"

"What do you mean?" She was confused by his question.

"Your alarm is going off."

Paisley began to panic. "I'm not at home."

"Okay, ma'am, we'll dispatch the officers to your home," he told her.

"I'm on my way now," Paisley said, frantically looking for her keys.

"Don't go into your home until the police arrive," she heard him say before she ended the call.

"Paisley, what's the matter?" Seymone ran to her side.

"Someone just broke into my house." She broke down crying. It only took a matter of seconds for them to lock up the studio. Scooter drove her home in her truck while Diesel followed with Seymone in his silver Chrysler 300. They could see the flashing lights of police cars as they turned into her cul-de-sac. Paisley rushed out and headed for the front door as soon as Scooter pulled into the driveway.

"Paisley, wait!" he called after her. Paisley ignored him, spotting Officers Jenson and Bell standing in front of her door.

"We've secured the area and it's all clear. You can relax," Officer Jenson told her.

"It was a false alarm," Officer Bell told her.

"Thank God." Paisley sighed. "I was so scared."

Scooter walked up, shaking his head. "For someone whose legs were just crushed in a car accident, you sure can move."

"They said it was a false alarm," she told him just as Seymone and Diesel got to her.

"That's good," he said.

"Yeah. It happens all the time." Officer Jenson nodded.

"Your front door was unlocked, and we checked everything out. The sensor was probably alerted by your dog. He is so cute." Officer Bell smiled. "He was yipping at us as soon as we walked through the door."

They all stared, looking at her like she had just fallen from the sky.

"What's wrong?" Officer Jenson asked.

"I don't have a dog," Paisley said.

Scooter

I wish there was something I could do. I feel so helpless. The woman I'm in love with is being stalked by some psychopath and I feel like there's nothing I can do. I must admit, when the cops said the alarm was set off by the dog, I was kinda freaked out my damn self. Especially because I know Paisley doesn't have a dog. And then, we walk in the house and who comes bouncing down the steps, barking like crazy, but a six-pound, gray Yorkie. A Yorkie, for God's sake. Then, Seymone leans over and picks him up and around his neck is a Juicy Couture bracelet with a Mickey Mouse charm attached.

I swear, whoever this dude is, he's not only slick, but he's stupid, too. Ain't no way I'm spending five hundred dollars on a bracelet and have the chick I bought it for not know who I am. After seeing the bracelet, Paisley had a meltdown. She just shook her head and withered down to the floor, then started rocking back and forth.

"Why is he doing this to me?" she kept repeating over and over.

I took her into my arms and carried her upstairs to her bedroom. Seymone and Diesel dealt with the cops and called Fallon to let her know what was happening. After I put her on the bed, I took a quick look around the room. Paisley has the biggest bedroom I've ever seen, and I have a few fantasies about what I could do to her in that bed. If only she knew . . . how much I do . . . I mean, besides the fact that she's beautiful and you can't help but see how fine she is Paisley is the epitome of the woman I want to marry. She's a no-nonsense woman who knows what she wants out of life and is not afraid to speak her mind. For years now, I've been dealing with these gold-digging chickenheads who don't mean anything to me, and I realize now how much I care about Paisley. Her accident has made me see that. I know Diesel thinks that my making a play for her is stupid, but

there's something there between us. I can feel
it. I refuse to be like him and Qianna, acting
like they're still in middle school, scared to take
their friendship to the next level. I ain't wasting
no more time and missing out on what I know
is meant to be.

"Come on, Pais, it's all right." Scooter sat
beside Paisley and pulled her close to him. She
buried her head in his chest and cried for several
minutes. He stroked her hair and rubbed her
back, whispering, "You're gonna be fine."

"Come back here, you little runt!" Diesel yelled
from downstairs.

Suddenly, the little dog came running into
the room and began barking at Scooter. Paisley
raised her head and stared at it. Scooter stood up
and tried to grab it. The dog leaped onto the bed
and curled up beside Paisley, and the barking
stopped. Again, Scooter reached for the dog and
it growled and snapped at him. Scooter took a
step back and the dog quieted down.

"Pais, the cops are calling Animal Control to
come pick up the dog," Diesel said as he walked
into the room. "Why the hell is the dog on your
bed?"

"It jumped up here." Paisley wiped her eyes.
Diesel reached for it and the dog growled.

Diesel laughed. "This dog really thinks he can
protect somebody."

Paisley's phone rang and she grabbed it. Her eyes widened and she wore a strange look on her face. "I gotta take this in private."

Scooter helped her off the bed and she went into the bathroom, the dog following right behind her. He could've sworn he heard her say the name "Warren," but he knew better than that.

Scooter shook his head and smiled at Diesel. "Man, this is wild."

"You got that right. I guess she's cool with the dog." Diesel sighed. "I'll go tell the cops they can leave."

"All right, I don't feel right just leaving them here alone tonight. I'm probably gonna hang out here," Scooter told him.

"Isn't that noble of you?" Diesel gave him a knowing look. "Man, I respect your wanting to be here for her safety and all. I just hope that's all you're trying to do."

"All I can say is, it's a start." Scooter smiled. *If only she knew how much I do. . . .*

Chapter 10

"Warren?" Paisley said into the phone.

"Hey, sweetheart. It's so good to hear your voice." He sounded winded. "How are you doing?"

"I'm two seconds away from losing my mind, that's how I'm doing." She couldn't believe she was talking to him. It had been a month since the accident and she had so much to tell him.

"What's wrong? They said you were released from the hospital a week before I was and you're doing fine."

"Who is they? And how do they know how I'm doing?" Paisley snapped.

"My people," was his response.

"Well, that's interesting, Warren. Because according to your people I've talked to, you don't have a clue who I am." She caught a glimpse of her reflection in the mirror and shook her head, wondering if the bruises would ever go away.

"What? That's crazy," he told her.

"I'm just going by what Ebonie, your publicist, says." Paisley stepped back onto the tiny ball of fur that she hadn't noticed follow her into the bathroom. The dog yelped, and she looked down at it. "What the heck are you doing in here?"

"Was that a dog?" Warren asked.

"Yeah," she answered, leaning down and picking it up.

"When did you get a dog? You don't even like dogs."

"Some crazy man who's stalking me broke into my house and left it." She explained to him all the drama she had been dealing with since the accident, then added, "And to top it off, they said you didn't even know who I was."

"Baby, I'm so sorry," he replied. "I swear, you know I didn't mean for any of this to happen. I didn't have any recollection about the accident, but I don't even think they asked me about you. I'm really worried about this guy, though. What are the police saying?"

"He's like a damn ghost, Warren. No one sees him except for the two times I woke up and he was in my room. And even then, it was dark. I don't know what I'm gonna do." She felt the tears begin to form, and sniffed.

"Paisley, don't cry. I'm gonna take care of it for you. I promise. I'ma make sure you're safe," Warren told her.

"How?"

There was a pause. Finally, he said, "Look, I gotta go. But I love you and I'm gonna take care of you. I'll call you in a couple of days."

"Warren, wait!" she said into the phone, but he was gone. She tried calling him back but it kept going straight to voice mail. Paisley was so confused by what Warren had said, she didn't know whether she was coming or going. She wanted to talk to someone, but felt she had no one to share her feelings with. She looked down at the dog she was holding and it licked her face. Something about that moment touched her inside.

"Gross," she said, wiping her cheek with the back of her hand and putting the dog on the floor. "If you plan on staying here, you'd better chill with the licking."

"I don't think we should stay here tonight," Seymone said.

"Where are we gonna go?" Paisley frowned.

"We can go to a hotel," Seymone suggested. "I mean, Paisley, even with the security system, this fool got inside."

"I don't wanna leave my house," Paisley replied. Even though she was just as freaked out by the incident, there was no way she was going to be forced to leave her own home.

"I don't wanna stay here, Pais. What if he comes back?"

"I don't think it's safe either," Diesel told them, "at least not until we get all these locks changed and the security system checked out."

Scooter cut his eyes at Diesel and then said, "I can stay here with you guys."

"You don't have to do that." Paisley smiled at him.

"That's not a bad idea." Seymone nodded. "At least he'll be more help than Chester would be."

"You can't stay here by yourself, Paisley," Scooter told her.

"But I know you had plans," Paisley said.

"I'm staying, that's final," Scooter said. "Cool?"

"Cool." Diesel nodded. "I'll be back in the morning to check on you guys."

He went to give Paisley a hug and the dog began yapping again. Seymone laughed and picked it up.

"See, we're good. We got Scooter and a watchdog." Paisley rubbed the dog's head.

"I can't believe you're actually gonna keep this loud-ass dog." Scooter shook his head.

"She shoulda let the cops haul it right off when they left," Diesel added.

Seymone nodded. "And kept the bracelet."

Even though Scooter was at the house, Paisley was still afraid that maybe her intruder would return. She couldn't sleep because she feared that she would wake up to find him standing over her again. For the umpteenth time that night, she got out of bed, hobbled downstairs, and checked all the doors, making sure they were locked.

"What are you doing?"

She jumped and nearly peed on herself, turning to find Scooter standing in the doorway. "Dammit, Scooter! You scared the hell outta me. I was checking the doors."

"Didn't we already check them before you went to bed?"

"Yeah, but I was just making sure. I locked them before I went to the studio yesterday too, but he still got in." Noticing his striped boxers and white tank undershirt, she couldn't help smiling.

"What's funny?"

"Cute pajamas." She winked.

"It's not like I knew I would be staying here tonight. It's not like a brother came prepared. And for your information, these are Yves Saint Laurent, baby."

"Gosh, can't you take a compliment? I told you they were cute."

Paisley gave Scooter's body the once over. He wasn't as built as Diesel, but Scooter was fine in his own right. She had always found him attractive and she knew that he had a slight crush on her. But even though he had the looks, job, and security she desired in a man, Scooter had an air of arrogance about him that turned her off.

"Where is your new rat?"

"He's not a rat, he's my watchdog. I put him in my bathroom with some newspaper. I ain't wanna take a chance of him going to the bathroom all over my house."

"I still can't believe you kept that damn dog. You don't know where it came from. You don't have no papers on it." He sighed. "That means you can't even breed it."

"I'm going back to bed," she said.

"I'll carry you," he said, scooping her into his arms in one motion. "You don't need to be going up and down these steps anyway."

"You are crazy." He was such a good person, but although she tried to imagine being more than friends with him, she just couldn't see it happening. She put her arms around his neck and held on.

"Look, if it'll make you feel better, I'll just bunk in here," Scooter said when they got to her room.

"Yeah, right," she giggled. "I don't think so. You know it ain't even that type of party between us."

"See there, I was talking about sleeping over there." He gestured toward the sofa in her sitting area. "You were the one talking about the bed. You must want me there."

"Oh, please." She rolled her eyes. "Don't even try it."

He began massaging her shoulders.

"That feels good." She groaned.

"I tend to have that effect sometimes," he whispered. "You should think about going on a vacation. I know a great little spot in Hilton Head."

"Vacation? What's that? You know I can't go on a vacation, and neither can you."

"Why not?"

"I have a studio that I can barely run and you have a nightclub that's about to open in less than a month, or have you forgotten?"

"Those are minor details that can easily be worked out." Scooter's hands travelled from her shoulders to her neck. "Let me ask you a question, Pais."

"Ask away." She rolled her head forward, enjoying the feel of his hands a little more than she probably should have.

"Have you ever thought about going out with me?"

Paisley's eyes opened and she shook her head. "No, Scooter. To be honest, I haven't. I don't think that's something I would ever want to consider. I value our friendship too much, you know that."

"Come on, Pais. You know I've been digging you for a while now. And I think you and I would be good together." For a moment, she thought he was teasing her, and then she saw the sincerity in his eyes and heard it in his voice. "When you were in that accident and we didn't know if you were gonna make it, I was scared. Not because I thought you were gonna die, but because I thought you would never know how I felt about you. The fact that there's some psycho stalking you and I can't do anything about him frightens me. I wanna protect you, be there for you, and take care of you."

Paisley was speechless. It was as if Scooter had left his body and someone else had jumped in it and taken over.

"I know it's a lot to take in, but I had to tell you. Just meditate on it and we'll talk about it later. In the meantime, I'ma grab one of these blankets and catch me some 'z's. Get some sleep, Paisley. The doors are locked and I'm right here. I'm not gon' let anything happen to you." He kissed her softly on her neck, then made himself comfortable on the sofa.

"Good night." She was shocked by his confession.

"Night," he replied.

The next morning, Paisley woke to the sound of her cell phone ringing.

"Hello," she answered without seeing who it was.

"Who is this?" a female hissed into the phone.

Paisley sat up, and replied, "You called me. Who is this?"

"Someone keeps calling and paging my husband from this number. Now who the hell is this?"

Paisley glanced down at the face of her phone and grimaced as she saw Warren's name. "Kollette, it's me, Paisley."

"What? You've got to be kidding me. Why the hell are you still trying to contact my husband?" Kollette screamed.

"First of all, you need to lower your tone with me, and if you're concerned about who's calling Warren, you need to ask him yourself." Paisley looked over and saw Scooter stirring on the sofa.

"I don't have to ask my husband anything. You're the one who's been blowing his phone up, so I'm asking you!"

"Look, I don't owe you an explanation about anything. I'm hanging up." Paisley's voice remained calm. It took all she had not to say that Warren had called her first, but if Kollette had gone through Warren's phone, she had to see that he had made the call.

"I'm warning you, stay away from my husband."

"Are you threatening me?"

"You call it whatever you want." Kollette was breathing so hard, Paisley wondered if the woman was about to have a heart attack while she was on the phone. "But I can make your life a living hell and I will. Stay away."

"You're crazy," Paisley told her.

"You ain't seen crazy yet," Kollette said, and hung up.

Paisley looked at the time on her phone and saw that it was five o'clock in the morning. She couldn't believe Kollette had the nerve to call her with that madness. *I got enough in my life I'm dealing with than to worry about Kollette's fat, insecure ass. What I should've done was let her know that The Playground was about to reopen and suggest she come and try to take some classes.*

Chapter 11

"I can't understand why you kept that damn dog," Seymone snapped, walking into Paisley's office after her first class had ended. "I think he peed on my gym bag."

"That's because you didn't let him out like I asked you to," Paisley replied. She had to admit, she hadn't realized how much work having a dog would be. She was constantly cleaning after it chewed something up, went to the bathroom on the floor, or knocked something over. Then there was letting him outside and making sure he had food and water. *If this is anything like having a kid, I'm glad I decided to wait on motherhood. Although, at almost thirty, my ticking biological clock is starting to concern me.*

"Scooter had just let him back in before he left," Seymone answered, "and that was because he crapped on the floor. I swear, if he doesn't kill that dog, I will."

"Neither one of you are gonna do anything. Dammit, I think I left my laptop at home." Paisley swiveled in her chair away from the computer, where she was working.

Today was the day that classes were resuming at The Playground; she had a lot of work to catch up on, and typing with a cast on her wrist wasn't as easy as she thought it would be. Diesel and Scooter made sure that not only her security system was intact at her house, but at the studio as well, complete with surveillance cameras. It had taken some persuading, but she had even convinced Scooter that he could leave her side and go to work, something he hadn't done in two days. Paisley was determined to regain some sense of normalcy in her life. Returning to the studio and seeing her students walk through the doors, greeting her with hugs and smiles, renewed her spirits instantly. She had expected funny looks or questions regarding her and Warren and the accident, but there were none. She had mentally prepared herself for the snide comments and accusatory glares, but no one gave her any. They didn't even seem to notice her still very bruised and scarred face and neck.

"So, how did it go?"

"It was so much fun! The ladies are nice and we had a ball. I'm looking forward to the next one, but I'm tired right now." Seymone laughed and plopped into one of the chairs in front of Paisley's desk.

"Now you see why I space them out like I do." Paisley gave her a knowing look.

"By the time you're healed and back in full swing, I'ma be back to a size four." Seymone rubbed her hands along her now size-ten hips.

"Girl, you know you weren't a four! You were a solid six, sometimes an eight!" Paisley said, thinking that even with her slight weight gain, Seymone still looked damn good in her white baby T-shirt blazoned with The Playground's logo, and white leggings. She pulled a pair of white stiletto heels out of her gym bag, which were a requirement for the pole class she was about to teach in the next hour, and slipped off the white Reeboks that were on her feet.

"I don't think so. I'm an eight now." Seymone squinted at the monitor sitting on top of the file cabinet. "Is that Fallon?"

Paisley looked over and watched Fallon standing at the front door, which now automatically remained locked until someone buzzed it open. Paisley pushed the button and Fallon pulled it open.

"When the hell did this turn into Fort Knox?" They heard Fallon say from down the hallway.

"Don't be mad because we're all about safety."
Paisley laughed.

"I understand that, but damn." Fallon glanced
up at the security monitors. "Wow, you can see
all over the building."

There were cameras located in each area of the
studio: the Big Room, where the Strip-Hop classes were taught; the Pole Room, which held ten
stripper poles where pole dancing was taught; the
Workout Room, which was set up like a typical
gym, and held cardio equipment and free weights;
and the Hot Spot, which was the boutique where
students could buy workout attire, or bedroom attire. The cameras were also placed in the parking
lot, and by the front and back doors. They knew
what was going on in the studio at all times.

"Looks like The Playground is back in action
and you got a full house." Fallon pointed at the
women on various equipment in the Workout
Room. Paisley smiled, feeling grateful as she
watched her faithful clients getting their workout on.

"Yeah, word must've spread fast. The phone
has been ringing off the hook all morning," Paisley said.

"Speaking of the phone, that's why I'm here."
Fallon tucked her hair behind her ear and took
a seat beside Seymone, leaning her black Prada
briefcase beside her. "We need to talk."

"You're not here for class?" Seymone feigned shock.

"Honey, I don't need Strip-Hop. I wear my man out enough as it is, don't act like you don't know." Fallon grinned.

"Whatever." Seymone stood up. "I got a class to get ready for and a pissy gym bag to clean."

"Why is her gym bag pissy?" Fallon asked when Seymone was gone.

"She claims the dog did it." Paisley shrugged.

"You're really keeping a dog that a stalker gave you?"

"Yeah." Paisley nodded.

"I don't mean any harm, Paisley," Fallon told her, "but that's some real white-people shit to do."

Paisley began laughing so hard that her body began aching. "Fallon, you are truly crazy."

"I'm serious. It is." Fallon shook her head. "Believe me, I'm white and I know."

After a few moments, Paisley regained her composure. "All right, so what's going on?"

"I got a call from Ebonie Monroe." Fallon sighed, pursing her lips. "It seems that Warren's wife, Kollette . . ."

"Is crazy as hell," Paisley finished the sentence.

"Huh?"

"She called me from Warren's phone the other morning and threatened me." Paisley smirked.

"Well, according to Kollette, you've been calling and texting Warren all times of the night and she's kind of pissed. She's threatened to go public and say that you're stalking her husband," Fallon informed her.

Paisley couldn't believe it. "You're joking, right? How the hell am I stalking someone when someone is stalking me?"

"That's what I told Ebonie. And she admitted that not only is Kollette a drama queen in the worst way, but she's a lot to handle. I've assured Ebonie that you have your own personal issues you're dealing with. Now, I totally understand if on occasion in the past few days, you called or texted Warren to make sure he's getting better, am I right?"

Paisley wondered where Fallon was going with this, so she simply said, "Yes."

"And Ebonie even pointed out that after looking at Warren's cell records, he has called and texted you."

"Yes."

"After all, as you've told me, you're friends, and not only that, but you two were involved in an accident together. But we all know the sensitivity of the situation and I assured Ebonie that

Kollette won't have any other reason to even think that you 'want' her husband."

"This is crazy." Paisley sat back and shook her head in amazement. "Did Ebonie point out to Kollette that Warren called me?"

"I didn't ask and, to be honest, Paisley, I don't care. Like I told you, Warren Cobb is not my concern, you are. We know this chick is crazy, but we don't want to give her any other reason to be crazier than she already is and drag your name into anything. You understand?"

"I guess." Paisley sighed. What she didn't understand was why Warren didn't handle his wife and was allowing this to continue. Then again, maybe he didn't even know Kollette was doing any of this. One thing was for certain; she was gonna make damn sure he found out.

"Who is that guy?" Fallon asked, staring at the monitor.

Paisley glanced up and saw a strange man lurking outside in the parking lot. "I don't know."

The man seemed to be checking things out, as if he wanted to make sure no one was watching. He walked from the parking lot and disappeared from their view.

"I guess he was lost." Paisley shrugged.

"Now," Fallon opened her bag and took out a day planner, "your Web site numbers are incredible. We're running another print of the calendar. You've gotten mad calls for jobs. I know you're not up for working just yet, but I just wanna give you the heads-up that Paisley Lawrence is back in demand. I know this is gonna sound crazy, but in a way, this accident has jump-started your modeling career again. If you want the work, that is."

"I don't know, Fallon," Paisley said. "I'm really getting too old to be a video vixen. I'm damn near thirty. I'm supposed to be transitioning, remember. That's why I opened The Playground."

"And that's cool. But Paisley, I'm telling you, there are some big time offers on the table. Enyce is launching a new lingerie line and they want you to be the spokes model."

"What? Are you serious?" Paisley was shocked. She had been featured in ads, but she had never been the actual spokesmodel for anything.

Fallon nodded. "I'm serious. They're talking print and video; the whole nine yards. The entire line will be created around you and The Playground."

"How much are they paying?"

Fallon reached into her briefcase and passed Paisley a sheet of paper with numbers written on it. "I almost said yes without consulting you first."

"All these zeros? You should have said hell yeah!" Paisley laughed. The wheels in her head started turning. "We should let Chester design the line."

"That's brilliant. Look at all the items he's already done for The Playground." Fallon nodded.

"Yeah, you know designing is his pleasure, girl." Paisley laughed. "Oh, snap! That's what the line can be called. Pleasure!"

"I love it," Fallon squealed. Within minutes, she was on the phone with the execs from the fashion label and Paisley was calling her cousin with the news. She was explaining the concept and title to Chester when Fallon called her name.

"Paisley, look, dude's back."

Paisley saw that the guy they had spotted earlier was now hanging in the back of the studio. She stepped forward to get a closer look.

"I don't know what's going on, but I'm about to call the police." Paisley picked up the phone, dialed 911, and told the dispatcher that there was a suspicious black man dressed in blue jeans and a black and red jacket lurking around the premises.

"Maybe we should gather everyone into the Big Room," Fallon suggested.

"No, I don't want them to panic. The police will be here in a few minutes and they'll get him.

Come on, let's go and wait in the lobby." Paisley grabbed her cell phone and saw that she had missed a call from Scooter. She called him and told him what was going on.

"Hold tight. I'm on my way," he said, and hung up.

"Scooter's on his way," Paisley said, peeking out the door, waiting for the police to arrive.

"He's sure becoming a regular knight in shining armor." Fallon gave her a knowing look. Paisley told her about Scooter's confession the other night. "I always knew he had a thing for you. But then again, most guys do."

"You know I don't like him like that. He's really not my type," Paisley told her.

"Scooter is fine. And he can dress his ass off. Not to mention he's well-educated, has a corporate job, a house, several cars . . . let's not even mention that he just bought a nightclub. What more are you looking for, Paisley?"

"I don't know . . . I just never considered dating Scooter . . . He's Scooter."

"Exactly my point. He's Scooter, and you know him, I know him, we all know him and know that he's a good guy."

Paisley looked down the street and saw the police approaching. "Cops are here."

Fallon said, "Uh, Paisley, the guy is walking toward the door."

Sure enough, he was walking straight toward them. Paisley took a step back and wondered what she should do. The bell rang and the guy looked inside. There was something familiar about him, and Paisley took a step closer as she tried to figure out where she knew him from.

"Don't let him in," Fallon cried out.

"I'm not," Paisley snapped.

They watched as a policeman got out of his car and called out to the guy. Another police car pulled up into the parking lot. The guy turned around and Paisley braced herself, praying that he wouldn't do anything like pull out a gun and go on a shooting rampage.

"I hope he doesn't try to run from the cops and they end up shooting him in the parking lot. I definitely don't wanna see The Playground on the news because of a shootout. We've been in the press enough," Fallon commented.

The guy said something back to the officers, and began walking toward the squad cars. Suddenly, Paisley watched as, instead of guns being pulled, the three men began laughing and talking to one another as if they were old friends. One police officer gave the guy a hug.

"Wow, that's not what I was expecting to happen," Fallon commented.

Confused by the sudden camaraderie among the men, Paisley opened the door and walked outside. Fallon was right behind her.

"Excuse me, can someone explain to me what's going on? Who are you and why the hell are you loitering around my studio?" she asked.

"Yes, please do. We called you all out here to protect and serve and somehow it's turned into a frat meeting!" Fallon exclaimed.

The three men walked over to the women.

"Uh, sorry, ma'am," one of the officers said. "This man fits the description of the man we were looking for, and it turns out that we know him, that's all."

"She knows me too," the guy said, the richness of his voice catching her attention. "You called the cops on me?"

Paisley frowned and again stared at the familiar man. She tried to recall where she knew him from, but she still couldn't place him.

"You know this guy, Paisley?" Fallon asked.

The door opened and Seymone rushed outside. "What's going on? Why are the police here?"

"She called them on me," the guy said. Again, his voice rang in her head.

Seymone looked over at the guy. "Oh, hey! How are you?"

Paisley was even more confused. "You know him?"

"Yeah, he's the guy who helped us that day at the hospital when we went to see Warren. He got us out of the craziness that Kollette started," Paisley replied. "You're one of Warren's security guys."

Paisley instantly recalled who the guy was and felt embarrassed. "That's right. I'm sorry."

"It's all good," the guy said, unsmiling.

"Well, we'll double check the outside premises, just to make sure. Landon, nice seeing you again." The officer extended his hand and the guy shook it.

"I'll catch you guys sometime next week, hopefully," he told them.

"Will do," the cop said.

"Uh, people are kinda staring. I think we should take this inside." Fallon pointed out the ladies who were now gathered in the lobby.

They all went inside and assured everyone that everything was fine. Paisley, Fallon, and the guy, whose name Paisley assumed was Mr. Landon, went into her office.

"Have a seat, Mr. Landon," Paisley offered.

"Landon," he corrected her.

"That's what I said," she reacted. She sensed that he had an attitude, and gave him a once over.

"Landon is my first name. My last name is Malone," he informed her.

Fallon sat down and he sat beside her. "Well, Mr. Malone . . ."

"Landon," he repeated.

"Landon," Fallon said, "how can we help you? Why are you here? And why were you creeping around outside?"

"I was checking things out, basically," he replied.

"Checking them out for what?" Paisley leaned on the edge of her desk and waited for his answer.

"To familiarize myself with the outside of this location, the parking lot, the doors, et cetera." He stared at Paisley. His eyes were piercing, as if he was trying to intimidate her, but she was never one to back down easily.

"What? You were casing my place? Because that's what it sounds like you were doing." She paused. "Are you working for the tabloids? I know that's how you security cats are."

"Is that really what you think I was doing?" She could hear the anger in his voice, but she didn't care.

"No, Landon, I think she's just trying to figure out why you're here, that's all. You of all people should know that with everything that's happened, it does seem a little weird for you to show up out of nowhere," Fallon explained.

"Okay, no one called and told you I was coming?" he asked Fallon.

"No, why would they?" Fallon was now confused.

"I was hired as Ms. Lawrence's personal security. I'm to be with her twenty-four, seven. She's my new assignment," he announced as he sat back in the chair and folded his arms.

"You're kidding, right?" Paisley asked. "This is some kind of joke."

"No, it's not," he told her.

"Who the hell hired you?" Paisley demanded.

"I don't ask any questions, OK? The agency I work for called and told me my assignment changed. They pay me and I just go where I'm assigned," he said.

"And how long did they pay you for?" Fallon asked. Paisley frowned at her and she commented, "I'm just wondering."

"Right now, six months," Landon answered.

"What?"

"That's deep."

Paisley and Fallon both spoke at the same time.

The bell rang, startling them all. Paisley looked up at the monitor and saw Scooter standing at the door.

"I forgot he was coming," she said as she buzzed him in.

"Where the hell are the police? Did they catch that fool and take him away?" Scooter walked in, dressed in a shirt and tie, his suit jacket casually tossed over his shoulder.

"No, we have the suspect in custody." Fallon giggled.

"That's not funny," Paisley replied.

"Nice shades," Fallon commented to Scooter. "Let me see them real quick."

"Hell no, these are Dior, special order. You ain't touching 'em," he quickly told her. Looking over and seeing Landon, he asked, "Who are you?"

"Landon Malone," Landon answered.

"He's Paisley's new personal security," Fallon informed him.

"Personal security?" Scooter looked at Paisley. "You hired him?"

"I didn't hire *anybody*," Paisley said.

"Someone hired him for her," Fallon said. "Landon, I can give you a tour of the premises, as you said. I can also fill you in on the other stuff that's been going on."

Scooter stepped aside as Fallon and Landon exited the office. When they were gone, he said, "Who hired this guy? Do we even know he's legitimate?"

"He's legitimate. He's worked for Warren. I saw him when I was in the hospital," she told him.

"So, I guess *Warren* hired him for you." Scooter stared at Paisley, waiting for her answer.

Something about the way he asked made her uncomfortable. "I don't know . . . I doubt it. I really don't know who hired him."

"Then fire him," Scooter said. "This guy coulda been hired by the tabloids or working in cahoots with the crazy dude who's stalking you. Tell him his services aren't needed and he needs to leave."

The thoughts in Paisley's head were going a mile a minute. She had wondered herself if Warren had hired Landon. *Landon has been working for Warren, and Warren did tell me he was going to take care of it and make sure I was safe. He would have only had to make one phone call to have Landon's assignment changed. That would make sense. It has to be Warren. Then again, what if Landon is working for a tabloid or, even worse, with this crazy-ass stalker? I don't know.*

"Wow, Paisley, someone hired your ass a bodyguard." Seymone's head popped into the office. "What's up, Scooter?"

"Hey, Seymone, what's good?" Scooter looked her up and down. "Nice outfit."

"Shut up," she told him.

"Look, you want me to fire him for you?" Scooter turned and asked Paisley.

"Fire who?" Seymone asked.

"That *Landon* cat," Scooter replied.

"Why? I think having him around is a good thing. Makes sense to me," Seymone said.

"We don't know anything about him. We don't even know who hired him. Do we even know he's really hired? Did you see a contract confirming that?" Scooter demanded.

"He just got here moments before you did, Scooter. I'm still trying to figure all this out." Paisley's wrist began itching in her cast, making her even more irritated.

"Okay, we have a pretty good idea who hired him, especially since he was working for Warren. And it'll only take a phone call to check him out. Let's be real, if someone meant to harm Paisley, would they go outta their way and *hire* someone to protect her? That's crazy. Paisley's not the only person dealing with this stalker issue. I live with her, and the thought of having a *trained* security guy around makes me feel a little better about this entire situation."

"That's true," Paisley commented.

"Oh, I guess I was just there for decoration, huh?" Scooter glared at Seymone.

"I didn't mean it like that, Scooter. Don't start tripping." Seymone gave him an apologetic look.

"I ain't tripping. It's all good, baby girl." He shrugged.

"I gota class to teach." Seymone walked out.

"You know she didn't mean anything by that, Scooter," Paisley said softly. "I'm gonna check Landon out and make sure this whole thing is legit. If it is, having him nearby makes sense. You know I appreciate your being here for me, but you got your own stuff you gotta take care of. The club opens in three weeks and I don't feel like hearing Diesel and Leo popping off at the mouth because you've been hanging around me instead of handling your business."

She stepped closer to him and put her arms around him. He stared down at her and smiled. "So you admit, you like having me around, huh?"

"I knew you were gonna take it there."

"No, this is where I wanna take it." He leaned in and kissed her gently, taking her by surprise. It had been so long since she had felt a man's lips on hers, and it felt so good, that she forgot about who it was kissing her. Before she realized it, she was kissing Scooter back.

"Paisley, what . . . Oh, sorry." Fallon's voice interrupted them.

Paisley quickly stepped back, feeling like a kid caught with her hand in the candy jar. "What's up?"

"I . . . uh . . . oh, I just wanted to know what the rest of your schedule looked like," Fallon said quickly.

"Right now, I don't even know," Paisley said. "I got some calls I gotta make. After that, it's hard to say."

Scooter looked down at his watch and said, "I got a meeting to get to. I'll call you later and check on you, okay?"

"Yeah." Paisley nodded.

He leaned over to kiss her again, but this time Paisley moved her head and instead of getting her mouth, his lips landed on her cheek. She glanced over at Landon, who was staring, and she quickly looked away.

Ebonie

All right, I'll be the first to admit that I took the job working for Warren Cobb because I thought he was the sexiest thing to ever grace the gospel stage, and I wanted to get with him. Yeah, it paid very well, and it was the opportunity of a lifetime, especially for someone who had literally just graduated from Tuskegee with a business degree. But I had an agenda, and an ulterior motive: I wanted Warren Cobb. That voice, those songs, that man, I wanted him. Then, I found out, Warren was married. Not only was he married, but he was married to, for lack of a better term, a bitch. A fat, ugly bitch at that (forgive me, Lord). How the hell Kollette managed to rope him in and get him to put a ring on her finger, I will never know. But, unfortunately, she was Mrs. Warren Cobb and he was my boss. I learned two things early on: one, she made sure everyone knew that she was his wife, and two, Warren really didn't like her. I mean, anyone close to him couldn't help but notice that he couldn't stand her. But it was as if she had a root on him and there was nothing he could do about it. He tolerated her for whatever reason.

Warren was resilient when it came to work. He toured nonstop and when he wasn't, he was locked away in a studio somewhere working on a project. It got to the point where he told me instead of "asking" if he wanted to do a gig, "tell" him the gigs he was working. He didn't care whether it was big or small, I was to book it. His dedication to his ministry was remarkable. I had never seen anything like it before in my life, and it made him even more appealing not only to his fans, but to me as well. The man was relentless. After a while, I realized the reason he worked so hard and so much was so that he wouldn't have to be at home. I didn't blame him though. I had more than my fair share of being laid out by Kollette for working Warren so hard. She blamed his constant travelling on me.

I knew that in addition to handling damage control after the accident with Warren and Paisley, I was gonna have to deal with Kollette in some capacity. After all, as she pointed out to me for the umpteenth time, she was Mrs. Warren Cobb. But she was getting on my last damn nerve and I was tempted to curse her out and quit.

"Ebonie!" Kollette screamed as she and Neil, who was the bishop's son, walked into Ebonie's office. The sound of her voice made Ebonie's blood boil.

"Yes, Kollette," Ebonie said as calmly as she could.

"Did you set up the interview with the *700 Club* for me and Warren?"

"I scheduled the interview for next Thursday, Kollette. But it's only for Warren. They didn't mention anything about having you there," Ebonie replied.

"What do you mean? Warren is recovering from a horrific accident. Not only did he almost die, but he had a video ho in the car with him. I think I need to be there to show the solidarity of my marriage," Kollette snapped.

"That's smart," Neil said as he gave Ebonie a snide look. It took everything within her not to turn her nose up. She didn't like him any more than she liked Kollette. Neil was the adopted son of Bishop Arnold, Kollette's uncle. Besides the fact that he and Kollette were always together, there was something about them that made Ebonie think that they were more than the "cousins" they claimed to be. They were a little too touchy-feely for her taste.

"Warren wants to do it alone. He feels that would be best," Ebonie informed her.

"Well, I'm telling you that I'm gonna be there with him. Set it up. And set up one with BET. People need to recognize that Warren Cobb does have a wife and whether they like it or not, he's happily married. Maybe if I had been with him at more of these appearances you've been scheduling over the years, that skank Paisley wouldn't have felt so comfortable jumping in the car with him."

"That may be true," Neil said, touching Kollette's back.

Ebonie's only response was to stare at them.

"Speaking of that skank, did you tell her agent she'd better stay away from Warren or I'ma blow up her spot?"

"I have that situation taken care of," Ebonie responded.

"Good, now take care of the interview. Call and let them know Mr. and Mrs. Cobb are looking forward to it." Kollette walked out the door. Neil looked back and gave Ebonie a wink before following right behind her.

Ebonie reached for the phone and called Warren, telling him about his wife's request.

"Don't change anything," he advised her.

"Don't worry, I won't," she assured him. "I know better."

"I know you do, and I appreciate it. Did you take care of the other thing?"

Warren had assured her that he and Paisley were merely passing acquaintances, but Ebonie knew better. Kollette had called her first thing Monday morning, going off about Paisley calling Warren's phone. Ebonie immediately called Warren to let him know Kollette was snooping, and he said fine. He then told her to call the security company Landon Malone worked for and have him sent to Paisley, and prepay them for six months. Ebonie didn't ask any questions, and he didn't offer any answers. She did what she was told. That's how it was between them. *I got an agenda, and an ulterior motive.*

Chapter 12

"So, how do we do this?" Paisley asked Landon. The last class had ended and they were ready to leave. Fallon called and let her know that she had checked with Full Armor Security, the company Landon worked for, and they verified that his services had been retained for her for the next six months. The only other thing they would tell her was that it was paid for.

"Where are we headed now?" Landon asked.

"Home," Paisley answered, tugging at the cast that was again itching.

"Well, you can go ahead and I'll follow you in my car."

"Oh, I thought I had to ride with you." She shrugged.

"I'm your security, not your chauffer."

I really don't like him, she thought. "I didn't say that you were. Seymone, are you ready?"

"Yeah." Seymone's voice drifted down the hallway.

"Is this what time you leave every day?" Landon asked.

"Most days. We do have night classes two nights a week. But the studio is just reopening and we haven't really gotten back into our regular schedule yet," she answered, passing him one of the monthly calendars with the normal schedule on it.

"Strip-Hop, Floor Play, Pump & Grind, Pole Seduction," Landon read the class titles aloud, "*Ho* Down, Hell on Heels?"

"Yep, we offer a broad variety of classes," she said, nodding. He continued to stare at her and she asked, "What? This is a playground for women."

"I didn't say nothing." Shaking his head, he folded the paper and put it into his back pocket. From the way he said it, Paisley could sense his disapproval. It was the same disapproving look her mother had when she saw Paisley on a magazine cover. The same look of disgust that the women at the physical therapy clinic gave her when she praised a male patient. The look that made her feel like even though she knew that she was doing what she wanted to do in life, and living out all of her dreams, she should feel unworthy.

"Seymone, hurry up," Paisley yelled, twisting her arm back and forth, trying once again to ease the constant itching.

A few moments later, Seymone met them at the front door, her gym bag in one hand and Paisley's keys in the other. "I'm ready."

"It's about time." Paisley snatched the door open, glaring at Seymone. "What are you waiting for? You have the keys and I have to set the alarm and lock the door."

Seymone aimed the keys at Paisley's truck and hit the button. The truck chirped and the lights flashed. "Truck's unlocked. Go ahead and I can lock up."

"Hold up a sec," Landon told her. "Let me go out first."

Paisley followed him, watching as he looked around. He opened the door for her and helped her get in. She mumbled a brief, "Thanks."

"Uh, nice truck. But, considering everything that's going on right now, you may wanna think about getting a vehicle that's a little less conspicuous," he said, his voice dripping with sarcasm, and closed the door. She watched him get into his black Intrepid. Just as they were about to back out, a large, silver Hummer pulled behind them.

"Who the hell is that?" Seymone asked.

Paisley's heart began pounding and she became nervous as she looked in the rearview mirror. The door to the huge truck opened and a tall figure jumped out. She relaxed as she recognized the guy and opened her own door. "Girl, it's Python!"

Python headed toward her, his own security guard, Mack, right beside him. Before they made it to her truck, Landon was rushing after them, yelling. Mack turned around, his hand resting under his shirt. Paisley knew Mack carried a gun and had no problem using it when it came to protecting Python. She didn't hesitate as she jumped out of the car and toward the three men.

"Mack, it's cool!" she yelled out.

"Girl, you know Mack is crazy!" Seymone said.

"Chill, Mack," Python ordered him. Mack slowly put his hands to his side and everyone relaxed a bit. Python grinned at Paisley. "What's up, gorgeous? How you doing?"

Paisley gave him a big hug, wondering to herself how a man this fine, with so many women at his disposal, could be on the down low. "Hey, sweetie. I'm better."

"I just got back off tour a couple of hours ago. I heard what happened. That's fucked up. You sure you're a'ight?" Python gave her a concerned look. "Did you get my flowers? I texted you a million times and tried calling you."

"Yes, Python, I'm fine." She nodded. "I got your flowers, but my phone got damaged in the accident, so it was out of commission for a while. I got a new one and it's up and running. How you been, Mack? Has he been working you to death?"

Mack grinned shyly at Paisley and shrugged. "You know how he is."

"Indeed, we partied hard and rocked the stage harder." Python turned his attention to Seymone, walking over and sweeping her into his strong arms. "Girl, you know I been missing your fine ass!"

Seymone squealed, "Python, put me down!"

"You fall in love and get ghost on us! You know that ain't right!" he teased her.

Not wanting to seem rude, Paisley introduced Landon, who had been watching them. "Python, this is Landon, my security guard."

"What's up." Python extended his fist to Landon, who gave him a pound. "This is Mack, my right-hand man. I'm glad you're with my girl. I been telling her a long time that she needed to get some firepower watching her back. She always acted like it was no big deal. I'm glad you finally decided to get some sense."

"It's not my choice, believe me." Paisley rolled her eyes at Landon.

"Well, thank whoever chose to hire him," Python said, then he looked at Landon. "Good luck, bro. She's more than a handful. I hope you can handle her."

"I think I got her covered," Landon replied.

"Well, I gotta get outta here. I just wanted to come by and see you. Call me, ma," Python said. Paisley and Seymone gave both him and Mack hugs.

"You think you can get in the car and we can leave now?" Landon asked when Python was gone. Paisley rolled her eyes at him and returned to her truck.

"All set?" Seymone asked.

"Yeah, let's go." Paisley climbed into the passenger side of her truck.

"What's your problem?" Seymone asked, pulling on her seatbelt and turning on the ignition.

"I don't like him," Paisley said. "He's a jerk."

"You don't know him well enough not to like him," Seymone said, pulling off.

"I know that he doesn't like me, either. And I know that there's something about him that puts me on edge. How can I be around him twenty-four, seven when I don't even feel comfortable? This isn't gonna work."

"Paisley, he's not here to be your friend. He's here to protect you and make sure you're safe.

You're his job. You don't have to like each other."
Seymone laughed.

"I'm glad this is so amusing to you," Paisley
said. "How the hell is he gonna guard me when
he doesn't like me? That's more reason for him
to let something happen to me."

"You are so conceited, you know that?" Seymone glanced over at her and shook her head.

"Where the hell did that come from?"

"I'm just saying, you're so used to guys falling
all over you, and Landon didn't, so you naturally assume he doesn't like you. To me, that just
shows that you're conceited. Everything has to
be about you." Seymone sighed.

"You don't understand." Paisley reached over
and turned the radio on. She glanced in the side
mirror and spotted Landon's car behind them.
They rode the rest of the way home in silence.

A sleek, black Mercedes Kompressor was sitting in Paisley's driveway when they pulled up.
Seymone parked right beside the car and Landon pulled behind her. The door of the Mercedes
opened and Chester stepped out.

"Oh my God! I've been sitting here forever,"
he yelled when they were out of the truck. "I told
you I was gonna be here at six o'clock. You're
late."

Paisley shook her head. "It's only six-twenty. Calm down."

"We forgot you were coming, Chester. My bad." Seymone walked over and gave him a hug, and he kissed both her cheeks in his dramatic fashion.

"What is her problem? I am not in the mood to be dealing with an attitude." Chester rolled his eyes at Paisley. "What's wrong with you?"

"Paisley, hold up," Landon yelled.

"Oh my, who is that?" Chester asked, looking at Landon.

"That is who is causing that attitude," Seymone told him. "That's Paisley's new security guard, Landon."

"He is fine," Chester hissed. "Reminds me of a clean-cut Method Man. Sexy."

"That's who he looks like. I was trying to figure out who it was." Seymone snapped her fingers. "Method Man!"

"How you doing?" Chester grinned as Landon walked up.

"Sup." Landon nodded. He seemed to be caught a little off guard by Chester.

"Landon, this is my cousin, Chester," Paisley introduced him.

"Nice to meet you," Landon said, trying not to stare at Chester's bright orange hair.

"Believe me, the pleasure's all mine," Chester replied.

"Can we go in now?" Paisley asked.

"You said you have a security system?" Landon asked as they walked toward the front door.

"Yeah," Paisley answered.

"You have your house key?"

"Seymone has it."

Seymone held out Paisley's house key on the ring and he took it. "I'll unlock the door and make sure it's all clear. What's the code to the alarm?"

"What? You want me to just give you my security code?" Paisley looked at him like he was crazy.

"Yeah, I do," he answered. "I need to cut the alarm off when I get in, right?"

"Yes, but . . ."

"Pais, he is your *security*," Seymone told her.

"Yes, he is." Chester winked at her.

"Fine." Paisley rolled her eyes. "Five-two-seven-eight."

"Hey, that's our birthday," Chester commented.

"I know." Paisley faked a smile.

They waited while Landon unlocked the door and went inside. A few moments later, he returned and told them it was okay for them to come in.

"I gotta go let my dog out," Paisley said as she headed toward the laundry room. "Killa! Where are you? Killllaaaa!"

"Hold on," Landon told her. "Whoa! Killa?"

In a flash, he was headed toward the door.

"Landon, wait!" Seymone called after him.

Paisley opened the laundry room door and the five-pound dog came running out. He ran straight to Landon and began barking. Paisley began laughing so hard that she almost peed on herself. Seymone and Chester were nearly in tears.

"Okay, you got me." Landon smiled, bending down and rubbing the dog's head. "Killa?"

"That's right," Paisley told him.

"She needed to name him Pissa or better yet, Shi—" Seymone commented.

"Leave my dog alone," Paisley said before she could finish. "Come on, Killa. You wanna go outside?"

Later that night, Scooter called. "What's going on?"

"Nothing, just getting out of the tub." Paisley wrapped a large bath towel around her body. She walked into her bedroom and made sure the door was locked.

"My meeting ran late, but I still wanted to come by and check on you," he sighed.

"You don't have to. It's been a long day and I'm going to bed after I check my e-mail." She grabbed a bottle of Johnson's baby lotion from the dresser and clumsily put some in the palm of her right hand. She rubbed it on her body the best she could, trying to maneuver with one hand. *I gotta get a pedicure tomorrow*, she thought, looking at her feet.

"Are you sure?"

"Yeah. Chester hung out over here for a while. He just left."

"That's cool. Where's your bodyguard?"

"He's in his room, I guess." She grabbed the tank top and shorts she slept in from her bed and slipped them on. Landon now occupied the large bedroom over the garage, right down the hallway from hers. It was close enough that he could get to her if needed, but far enough away that they had their own privacy.

His room; that sounds so weird. Not only do I have a bodyguard, but he has his own room in my house. If he thinks he's really living here for six months, he's crazy. This is only until they catch that fool who's stalking me.

"You know I had no problem staying there and guarding your body,"

"I bet you didn't." She was too preoccupied to even think and hoped he wasn't about to talk about their being together. Reaching for the remote, she clicked the TV on and went to get her laptop bag from where she usually set it on the side of the bed, but it wasn't there. *Where is my computer?* she asked herself, trying to remember where she had it last.

"Where's the rat?" Scooter asked.

Paisley looked around and realized that she hadn't seen or heard Killa since she had gotten out of the tub; which was unusual because he rarely left the room unless she did.

"I don't know. Look, let me call you back," she told him.

"Is everything okay?" Scooter asked. "You sure you don't want me to come through?"

"I'm all right," she said, now looking around the room for the dog and her computer bag. "I just gotta figure out where I put my laptop."

"A'ight." Scooter seemed disappointed.

Paisley walked down the hall and heard Seymone's voice singing in the bathroom across the hall from her room. She knocked on the door and called out, "Seymone, is Killa in there with you?"

"*But each time I try, I just break down and cry,*" Seymone sang, "*cuz I'd rather be home feeling blluuuuueeeeeee.*"

Paisley knocked on the door again, "Seymone!"

"What? Hold up a sec." A few seconds later, Seymone cracked the door open, naked with the exception of the shower cap on her head. Steam poured from the bathroom. "What?"

"I can't find Killa. Is he in there with you?" Paisley asked.

Seymone looked at Paisley like she was crazy. "No you didn't call me out of the shower to ask me that. Hell no."

"I can't find him." Paisley frowned.

"Good, and he better stay where he is because he pissed in my room again!" Seymone started to close the door.

"Wait!" Paisley stopped her.

"What, Pais? It's cold." Seymone bounced up and down, shivering from the water dripping on her body.

"Have you seen my laptop? It's not in my room either."

"Naw, I haven't seen it," Seymone told her. "I don't think you took it to the studio this morning, either."

"A'ight." Paisley sighed.

Seymone closed the door and Paisley cringed as she resumed singing, "*We'll be making love the whole night through, cuz I'm saving all my love for yooooooouuuuu.*"

Paisley stood at the top of the stairs, and called out, "Killaaaaa, here Killa, Killa!"

She waited for him to come running, but he didn't. She went downstairs and searched in the kitchen, living room, and utility room, but he wasn't there. She walked into the den, and gasped when she saw that the sliding door leading to the backyard was slightly open. Her heart began pounding. Her first thoughts were that her stalker had gotten inside, killed her dog, and was waiting in a closet, wearing a hockey mask, with a butcher knife in one hand and a hacksaw in the other. *Oh God, he's in here somewhere, probably watching me right now. There's no way I'm gonna die with my feet needing a pedicure and my weave needing to be redone. I ain't going down without a fight.* Paisley went into the kitchen and quietly opened a drawer, pulling out the biggest knife she could find. She grabbed the cordless phone from the wall and was about to dial 911 when she heard a dog barking. Knife in hand, she walked into the den. She wielded the knife as the sliding glass door opened wider, and she prepared to slice up the intruder. Within seconds, Killa came running past her. Oh God, he's really out there. Her grip on the knife tightened.

"Ahh!" she screamed when a shadow figure stepped inside.

"What the . . ." Landon jumped when he saw her standing in the middle of the floor.

"Jesus," was her only response as she realized it was him and dropped her arms to her sides. She was breathing so hard that she could see her chest rising and falling.

"What are you doing and why do you have a knife?" He stared at the sharp blade she was holding.

"I thought someone had broken in," she told him. "The door was open . . . and I kept calling Killa . . . and I didn't know where he was . . ."

"I took him out to go pee. He was about to take a squat in my room," Landon told her.

My room. The words echoed in her head as he said it. *He's really living here, that's crazy.*

"Oh, sorry." She shrugged. She watched as his eyes fell to her feet, and she put one foot on top of the other in an effort to hide the chipped polish on her toes. "Uh, have you seen my laptop?"

"Huh?" He frowned.

"I can't find my laptop. I was wondering if you may have seen it lying around," she said, twisting her arm, which was now itching in the cast. She looked down at the knife, and before she thought about it she was sliding it into the irritating cast, trying to scratch.

"Stop it!" Landon eased the knife out and took it from her. "Are you crazy! What if you woulda nicked your vein?"

"It itches, okay? And the Doctor says I have to wear it for three more weeks. You betta be glad I ain't using the electric knife to take it off!" she told him.

Landon shook his head at her. "You really are crazy. No, I haven't seen your laptop. Do you mind if I hang out down here for a while and watch TV?"

"No, that's cool. Come on, Killa!" Paisley called the dog. He came running beside her. She looked at Landon. "Thanks for taking him out. I know that's not part of your job description."

"Yeah." He shook his head again. The two stood staring at the dog, neither one saying a word until he finally asked, "You need some help going up the stairs?"

"No, I got it," she told him.

"Your legs look pretty banged up." He pointed to her thighs, which were still covered with bruises in various shades of purple and blue.

Paisley looked down, now feeling uncomfortable. She had been so self-conscious about her feet, that she forgot that her legs were visible in the shorts she wore. "I forgot you could see it. My bad."

"You sure?" he asked her.

"Yeah, I got it," she said, and walked out. *Hmm, maybe he's not so bad after all. Maybe I judged him too soon.* Just as she made it up the steps, she heard his cell phone ringing.

"What's up," she heard him answer. "Yeah, I'm here. The house is amazing. I've never seen anything like it in my life."

Stop being nosy, she tried to tell herself, *that's that man's personal phone call and you don't need to hear it. Why? He's talking about my house, so that makes it my business.* Her curiosity got the best of her and she continued eavesdropping.

"No, it's her and her best friend, Seymone Davis. Yeah, I'm serious. Both of them live here. Man, stop, you know ain't nothing like that even jumping off. Naw, no orgies. Naw, none of that, either. Man, come on, I only been here a day, but no, she ain't seduced nobody since I been here and I haven't met anyone famous. This wild cat named Chester came over tonight. He was a little over the top, but he was cool. I guess she's a'ight, but Seymone is really nice. No, she owns this dance studio where she teaches other chicks how to striptease and pole dance. I swear. It's totally disrespectful."

Paisley could feel her anger building as she continued listening.

"What do you mean? How am I tripping? I don't agree with it at all. I think this would've been more a job for you, not me. You know the changes I've made in my life and I don't feel comfortable being around this. It's immoral. I know, I know. You're right. Naw, I'ma do my job and I'ma make sure nothing happens to her. Regardless of what she does and how I feel about it, her life is my responsibility and I'm gonna make sure she's safe. Yeah, I agree."

Paisley was so angry that she could feel tears building up. How dare he talk about her like she was a common whore on the street? *What I do is not disrespectful; it's a support haven for women. I hate him.*

"No, I haven't talked to her. I thought about calling her and then I figured what's the point. I don't even know how I'm even feeling about that right now. Yeah, I got you. Cool, I'll talk to you tomorrow. Naw, I ain't taking no pictures with my cell and sending 'em to you. You're a fool, boy! Peace."

Paisley returned to her room and closed the door. She climbed into bed and released the tears she had been holding in. Hearing Landon say those things about her reminded her of her mother, and the way she made Paisley feel. She was used to people talking about her; it was a major part of her life. But there were times like this, when the reality of what was said, true or not, hit home and made her realize that even with all she had accomplished in her life, the fame and fortune she had gained, she would always be judged on what she did rather than who she was as a person.

Landon

A'ight God, I know this is a test, right? It's gotta be. I was living foul, doing my dirt, headed straight to hell with gasoline drawers on and then I changed my life. You wanted me on the straight and narrow; I got on the straight and narrow. You wanted me to stop drinking and smoking, I did. You wanted me to stop gambling, I did. All the bad things in life that I enjoyed the most, that made me the man I was at the time, that I knew were wrong, but I did them anyway because they brought me so much pleasure. I gave all of that up because you told me, you assured me, you promised me that none of those things would bring me the pleasure I would find if I turned my life over to you. And

I did, God, I did. You told me to stop strong-arming for the dope dealers, loan sharks, and kingpins and be a warrior for you.

You told me to join the right side of the law and protect the streets on your behalf. It was you who lead me to become a state trooper. It was hard, especially at first, because I knew my street fam was gonna be pissed and think I was a sellout, but I did it anyway. And you worked it out, too, I gotta tell you. Strong-arming from the time I graduated high school until you told me to stop.

All the lives I threatened, the bones I broke, the teeth I knocked out, the drug deals I protect-ed, the tears I brought grown men to, and not one record of arrest. Amazing. You opened the doors and got me the job, and it was all because of your grace. You stood true to your promise, and even after I became a trooper, I still had the respect and admiration of the street fam I thought I would lose forever, because they knew I was doing what you told me to do.

Even when I almost lost my life while on the job, you spared me. And although my injuries cost me my job last year, you spared my life. You even gave me a better job with Full Armor, a Christian-based security firm that provides services to those Gospel celebrities and churches that are all about doing your work, Lord, like I am. You even gave me a new love in my life, Kenya. I thank you for her, even though she plucks my nerves and we really aren't speaking right now. If she's the woman you would have me marry, then I'll take her. Believe me, I trust you, God. But, for the life of me, I don't know why you have me in this house guarding this . . . this . . . sinful seductress of a woman. With her beautiful face and perfect body. This woman, who has no virtues, and has the nerve to encourage her immorality to other women, Paisley Lawrence. Even her name is gorgeous. And those eyes . . .

"Hello," Landon answered his phone for the second time that night. The first time, he had been speaking with his twin brother, Benjamin, who was beyond excited when he found out Landon was not only Paisley's security guard, but living with her.

"Hey, baby, what are you doing?" Kenya asked.

In a way, he was glad to hear from her. It had been a few days since they had talked, but their last conversation had gotten heated and he wondered if this one was going to be the same way. "Nothing. Watching television. What are you doing?"

"Leaving work," Kenya sighed. "It's been a long day. We had college night at school."

Landon prepared himself for the ten-minute venting he was about to hear. Kenya was a high school guidance counselor and constantly complained about her job. With her it was always something, whether it was the students, the parents, or the administration. Landon had to wonder why she even stayed because she seemed so miserable.

"So, other than that, what's going on?" He tried changing the subject.

"Nothing. How's your new assignment? Is she all that they make her out to be?" Kenya said, her voice dripping with sarcasm.

"She's nice," Landon answered. One of the reasons he and Kenya hadn't really been speaking was because of his new assignment to Paisley. She had been livid when he told her he was going to be staying there. Kenya told him to tell his boss no and when he didn't, she called him selfish and disrespectful.

"I bet she is. She's probably prancing around in front of you half-naked all day," Kenya told him. "I can't believe you're even there with her, Landon. You're supposed to be saved, for Christ's sake. Your staying there with her is wrong on so many levels."

"It's my job, Kenya. You act like I volunteered for this."

"I'm just saying, you know what Paisley Lawrence is all about: sex, sex, and more sex. I hear she even has a sex school where she teaches sex classes. Call Full Armor and tell them you can't do it. It not only goes against your own personal beliefs, but those of the company as well. How hard is that?"

"Kenya, you know I'm not going to do that," Landon told her.

"Why? Do you wanna be there? Is that what it is? Do you want her to seduce you?"

"You're really tripping. It's not that at all." Landon wondered if the reason Kenya was so edgy lately was because she needed some reassurance about him and their relationship. "Baby, you know that I'm already seduced by you. There's no way any woman, not even Paisley Lawrence, can do for my heart the things that you do. Stop tripping."

"Whatever, Landon. I'm telling you, you better stay prayed up and mindful. After all, she seduced Warren Cobb and it nearly killed him. I gotta go. Love you."

"Love you too." He hung up the phone. He clicked on the television and tried to focus on the news, but the oil painting of Paisley hanging over the fireplace caught his attention and he became engrossed. He stared at it, and smiled as he thought about her trying to use the huge butcher knife to scratch under her cast. The perfection of her body was clearly visible in the shorts and tank top she'd had on. Trying not to stare at her breasts had been a struggle. After all, he was a man and, Lord knows, she was a woman.

I'm trying, Lord, I promise you, I am. But this is a test that I don't know if I'ma be able to pass.

Chapter 13

Paisley tossed and turned all night long, unable to fall asleep. She was so angry and hurt by Landon Malone and the things he said about her. Not only that, she was pissed at Warren for just tossing Landon into her life without even discussing it with her. She called Warren's cell phone and left several voice and text messages, not giving a damn if Kollette heard them.

"Warren, it's me. I don't know what the hell you were thinking when you hired Landon Malone, but you can unhire him. I don't like him. He's pragmatic, hateful, and demeaning. I know you called yourself looking out for me, but I don't need you and I damn sure don't need him. I want him gone, ASAP!"

Paisley got dressed quickly and headed downstairs with Killa right on her heels. The house was so quiet the chirping of her disarming the alarm seemed deafening. She opened the back door and the dog ran out of the house, barking at some ducks who were hanging out near the pool. The time on the microwave in the kitchen read six-fifteen. *Damn, it's early*, she thought as she filled the dog's bowls with food and water. A few seconds later, Killa came running in and began eating. Paisley leaned against the counter and watched as he devoured the food. She was tired. *Coffee.* She reached into the cabinets and was disappointed when she didn't find any. She spotted the keys to her truck, grabbed them from the counter, and headed out the door.

It was the first time she had been behind the wheel of a car since the accident. Paisley was extra careful, making sure her seatbelt was on and all of her mirrors were positioned just right. Her foot slowly pressed on the brake and she eased the gear shift from park to reverse. *Knock, knock, knock.* Paisley nearly jumped out of her skin and slammed on the brake.

"What the hell is your problem?" she screamed, throwing the car back into park.

"I should be asking you that same question!" Landon yelled back.

She hadn't even seen him come out of the house. Dressed in a wife beater, black sweat-pants, and a pair of Nike flip-flops, he seemed menacing and she could see his anger, but she didn't care. She was angry too.

"I'm trying to leave." She glared at him.

"I can see that. Why are you sneaking and—"

"Sneaking? Please. I'm a grown-ass woman, I don't have to sneak anywhere," she told him.

"You know I'm supposed to be with you at all times in case something happens." He frowned.

"I'm good," she told him, "nothing's gonna happen. As a matter of fact, I don't even need you to be here. You're fired."

"Yeah, right. You can't fire me," he said smugly.

"Really? Watch me," she snapped at him. His smugness made her even angrier.

"Whatever. Look, I don't know why you're tripping this morning, and I'm not even gonna argue with you. You wanna go somewhere, fine. Move over so I can drive you," Landon demanded.

"Yeah, right. You're not my damn chauffeur. Just leave, Landon, for real. I don't need you. You're fired," Paisley told him, kicking the truck into reverse and pulling off, nearly running him over.

I hope his ass is gone by the time I get back. She turned the radio up and allowed the comedy of Steve Harvey and his morning crew to help improve her mood. Before long, she was laughing and singing along with Chris Brown as she pulled into the parking lot of Java's, her favorite coffee shop.

"Well, well, well, I haven't seen you in a while." Dobie, the owner who regularly waited on her, smiled. "How are you?"

"I'll be better once you hook me up." She smiled at him.

"The usual?" he asked.

"Of course," she said, nodding. He quickly made her cappuccino exactly the way she liked it without her having to give instructions, placed a slice of coffee cake on a plate, and slid it across the counter. Paisley smiled as she took a bite, savoring the buttery goodness. "Damn, I missed this."

"We missed you too," Dobie laughed. "My brother has been asking about you. He heard about your accident and he was worried to death."

"How is he?" Paisley asked. "I wish he were still here so he could come by the house."

Dobie's brother was what Paisley called her "all around guy." Whatever she needed done, he was always there to do it. Whether it was yard work, cleaning the pool, detailing her cars, he was always ready, willing, and able.

"He's good. You know we miss him a lot." Dobie sighed.

"You know he's been bragging to all of his Army buddies that he knows you."

"I gotta send him a care package." Paisley smiled.

"Uh, Dobie, I finished mopping the back room," A young guy came in and announced. He was dressed in a Java's T-shirt and blue jeans. Paisley smiled at him, but he quickly turned away.

"Okay, Nick," Dobie told him. "Can you go ahead and start taking inventory for me?"

"Uh, sure." The young man nodded.

"New blood?" Paisley teased.

"Hey Nick, this is Paisley Lawrence, one of our regulars. Paisley, this is Nick," Dobie introduced them.

"Nice to meet you." Nick barely glanced up.

Paisley looked over at Dobie. "Shy guy?"

Dobie nodded. "Yeah. I'm trying to break him out of it. He's a really smart kid. A whiz when it comes to anything electronic. He set up the new Internet cafe for me in the back. That's why I hired him."

Nick wore an embarrassed look.

"And I'm sure you paid him every dime he's worth?" Paisley asked, finishing up her cake.

"Of course. Tell her, Nick, when everyone else around here wanted to pay you minimum wage, I stepped up and paid you eight-fifty an hour."

"Yes, sir," Nick said.

"I hate to tell you this, Nick," Paisley said, twisting her itching arm, "but you got ripped off."

"What? I can't believe you of all people said that." Dobie laughed. "Nick, before he joined the service, my brother used to be Paisley's personal gopher and she paid him peanuts."

"That's a lie." Paisley giggled. "If that's the case, then why did he work for me so long?"

"For the view, of course," Dobie laughed.

"Man, this cast is itching me to death," Paisley groaned. Her cell began ringing and seeing that it was Warren, she quickly answered, "Hello."

"What am I gonna do with you, Paisley? Why is it that you have to be so difficult?" he asked.

"How am I being difficult, Warren? I didn't ask you to hire personal security for me. You took it upon yourself to do that," Paisley hissed into the phone.

"I hired him because I was concerned for your safety and you need him."

"I don't need him and I don't want him. As a matter of fact, I fired him this morning," Paisley told him.

To her surprise, Warren laughed. "You what? You can't do that."

"Why not?" Paisley asked.

"Because you ain't hire him."

"That doesn't matter." Paisley rubbed her wrist harder. She glanced up and saw Nick staring at her. She gave him a quick smile and again, he turned away. "I don't like him and I want him gone."

"It's not about what you want, Paisley. It's about what's best. Get over it and get used to Landon being there. He's the best in the business, and like it or not, you're stuck with him."

"We'll see," Paisley told him.

"Yeah, we will." Warren sighed. "Other than that, how are things going? I miss you."

As he said it, her heart melted. "I miss you too. Things are going OK. I reopened the studio this week."

She continued filling him in on the happenings since the last time they had spoken, days before. He told her about his progress and plans for the next few days. For a moment, it was like old times; them catching up on each other's lives like everything was normal.

"Well, I gotta get going. I got physical therapy this morning," he sighed.

"Too bad I can't help out with that," she teased. "You know that's my specialty."

"I know it is," Warren said. "Look, Paisley, I need for you to know that I had ulterior motives in hiring Landon."

"I don't care why you hired him, Warren. I don't want him in my house and I don't want him in my life."

"You're being difficult," he told her.

"Call it what you will, Warren," Paisley told him, remembering the conversation she'd over-heard Landon having and becoming angry all over again. "You know I don't deal with people I don't trust."

"What are you talking about? Landon is a great guy and he's the best personal security guard in the business," Warren went on to tell her.

"I don't give a damn if he's Secret Service for the president of the United States. He's fired," Paisley snapped. "Go ahead and get ready for your appointment. Love you."

"Pais, wait . . ."

Paisley hung up before he could say anything else. She took a long swallow of her coffee and sat back, trying to clear her head. Deep in thought, she nearly jumped when she felt someone touch her shoulder. She turned around and saw that it was Nick. He didn't say anything as he held some-thing out.

"What's this?" she asked, reaching for the small wooden item. Taking it in her hand, she saw that it was several coffee stirrers taped together.

"Uh . . . I . . . You can slip it into your cast and scratch," he said, slowly sliding the small sticks into her cast and wiggling them back and forth. Her arm was immediately relieved.

"Oh my God," she moaned. "That feels wonderful!"

Nick quickly pulled his hand away and stepped back.

Dobie laughed at his employee. "I told you he was brilliant."

Noticing that it was after seven, Paisley told Dobie, "Let me get another one to go and a large caramel mocha for my friend. If I go home without a cup for her, she's gonna have a fit."

"No problem," Dobie told her. She paid him and promised to be back soon.

"Give your brother my love and tell him I promise to write him soon." Paisley hopped off the stool and Nick held the door open for her. "Thanks again for my scratcher, Nick. See you next time."

"Uh . . . sure . . ." he said shyly.

As soon as she stepped outside and into the parking lot, she heard clicking and spotted two cameramen out of the corner of her eye. She covered her face the best that she could, trying not to drop the coffee as she rushed to her truck. The men ran after her and continued taking photos.

"Paisley! Ms. Lawrence! Double S! Sensual Seductress!" they called after her.

"Get the hell away!" she yelled, and almost ran them over while backing out of the parking space. She glanced into her rearview mirror and saw the black Jaguar parked in the lot next to Java's. *Was that car there before? Her heart began pounding.* She tried to recall seeing anyone in the restaurant, but couldn't remember. She hadn't been paying that much attention. *Maybe I'm tripping. There are a million black Jaguars in this city,* she tried to convince herself as she drove home.

Seeing Landon's black Intrepid still sitting in front of her house when she turned onto her street didn't help her frustration. *I know I told this dude I wanted him gone.* She walked into the house, placed the coffee on the counter in the kitchen, and was about to go find her ex-security guard when Seymone came into the kitchen.

"Where the hell have you been?"

Paisley tilted her head to the side and replied, "I went to Java's and got us some coffee."

"You gotta be kidding me." Seymone shook her head. "What the hell is wrong with you, Paisley? You just leave without saying anything to me? Then, on top of that, you don't even take Landon with you."

"I told Landon he was fired," Paisley informed her.

"I heard," Seymone snapped. "Just what is up with you? Do you have a death wish for real? Because guess what, I don't."

"What is that supposed to mean?"

"Look, Paisley, I swear, I'm trying. But damn if you're not making it hard for me." Seymone exhaled. "I told you, I promised you that I'd be here for you and I have. With all this craziness, I've been here."

Paisley was confused and didn't have a clue what Seymone was talking about, nor why she seemed to have an attitude. She immediately became defensive. "What? You wanna leave, Seymone? It's cool. I'll be fine, I told you that."

Seymone's eyes widened and voice shot up an octave. "What? See, this is what I'm talking about. You are so damn selfish. If I wanted to leave, Paisley, I would be out. But this is about me staying here, which I am. And my need to feel safe while I'm here. I mean, I know this crazy dude is stalking you, but guess what? I do worry about him harming me also. I'm just as scared as you are. I don't give a damn about how you feel about Landon. But him being here is a safety measure that I'm grateful for. Having him nearby does make me a little less anxious and a little safer."

Paisley stared at her best friend, who was dressed and ready to go to work at the studio. *A job that Seymone doesn't have to be doing.* She didn't know what to say.

"Does any of that matter to you, Paisley? Did you ever stop to consider that maybe I appreciated that he was here? Or did that even matter to you this morning when you decided to tell him he was fired and ran off like a sixteen-year-old?" Seymone leaned against the counter.

Paisley shrugged. She wanted to tell Seymone about what Landon had said, but she knew that it wouldn't make a difference. Landon was there to do a job, and how he felt about her or what he did was none of her concern. Having the paparazzi hounding her this morning was a clear indication that maybe she did need to have him nearby.

"You guys ready to roll?" Landon asked as he walked into the kitchen.

Paisley rolled her eyes. "I thought I told you to leave."

"And I told you I wasn't leaving," he said nonchalantly. He looked over at the two steaming cups of coffee and picked one up, removing the top and taking a sip. "Mmm, this is good. Next time, you can just get me green tea. Then again, we'll be together when you go."

Paisley stared at him, hoping he could read the hatred in her eyes. His eyes met hers, and she prayed that their involvement would be short-lived.

"Paisley, why don't you leave Mickey and drive something else today," Seymone suggested after Paisley had locked the dog up and they were walking out of the house.

"Why?" Paisley frowned, knowing it probably had something to do with Landon. Especially since he had commented about her truck the day before.

"Well, if you take another vehicle, we can all ride together. Plus Mickey is a bit noticeable," Seymone replied, "and gas is kinda high. Taking more than one vehicle is pointless."

Again, Paisley glared at Landon, who had the audacity to shrug as if he was innocent.

"Fine," Paisley said, and lifted the door to her four-car garage. Inside sat her black Acura MDX SUV, her chocolate BMW 745, and her silver Infinity Coupe. She watched Landon's eyes widen and she smirked. "Fine, what do you wanna drive today?

Chapter 14

"Damn, I look good." Paisley smiled, looking into the mirror. She had spent most of her afternoon in After Effex being pampered by the staff, getting a manicure, pedicure, facial, and even a much-needed massage. The high class salon was like a sanctuary to her. The welcoming atmosphere of glamour, beauty, fashion, and serenity was definitely what she needed. Not to mention the laughs she always got when she was around Yaya, Taryn, and the other staff members. She had been at the salon since one o'clock, and her watch now read five-fifteen. Any other time, she would've been in and out of the salon in a matter of three hours, but in an effort to irritate Landon, she had taken her own sweet time; even changing her nail color three times. "Yaya, you are the best."

"Girl, please, you were beautiful before you walked in here. I just enhanced what you already had." Qianna laughed.

"No, you are a miracle worker. I swear, I feel like a new person," Paisley said, looking at her reflection. Her scars were still there, but not as visible. She actually had to look for the remaining bruises. The tension in her neck and shoulders that she had when she had arrived were gone.

"I'm glad you feel better, Paisley," Qianna remarked. "It's nice to see you out and about. I know you've been going through a lot since the accident and I'm just glad that you're still doing your thing."

"I don't have a choice," Paisley sighed, putting the mirror down. "You know I've always been the one to brush them haters off."

"I know that's right. And you know I've always had your back. Whenever they come outta their mouths crooked, I shut 'em down on your behalf," Qianna assured her.

"And I appreciate your having my back." Paisley nodded. "Things have really been crazy."

"I know, Diesel told me. He also told me that Scooter stepped to you." Qianna gave her a knowing look.

Paisley looked over at Landon, who was sitting in the waiting area, and saw that he was engrossed in a magazine and listening to his iPod. Sitting up in the chair, she told Qianna, "Yeah, he did. Yaya, he says he's in love with me and wants us to be together . . . like in a relationship . . . me and him."

Qianna nodded. "I know. I mean, you shouldn't be surprised. We all know that Scooter has always had a thing for you, Paisley."

"He's always flirted with me, yeah. But I never thought it was anything serious."

"And how do you feel about him?"

"Scooter is cool. We've always been friends and we always will be. I like being around him." Paisley shrugged. "He's an amazing man."

"But can you see yourself with him?" Qianna asked.

Paisley thought long and hard before she finally said, "Honestly, there are times when I can't see myself being with any man."

"That's crazy." Qianna frowned. "Why not? Oh my God, Paisley, are you gay?"

Landon glanced over at them and then looked down. Paisley gave him an ugly look and quickly answered, "Hell no. What's wrong with everyone these days? That's the second time someone has asked me that."

"You said you couldn't see yourself with any man. I just thought . . ."

"You better stop playing, Qianna. And since we're talking about love and relationships, what's up with you and Diesel?"

Qianna actually began to blush. "What about us?"

"We all know that he's been feeling you for a while. How do you feel about him?" Paisley questioned.

"Diesel and I are friends."

"You're more than friends. I can look at the two of you and see how much you care about each other," Paisley said. "He loves you."

"And I love him," Qianna said, "but it's not the right time. We both got too much going on right now. Hell, we all gotta get ready for the opening of the club. What time are we supposed to meet at the studio tonight?"

"Nine o'clock," Paisley answered. They were holding auditions for dancers for the club opening. Diesel, Scooter, Paisley, Seymone, Chester, Leo, and Qianna were all scheduled to be there.

"Damn, I guess I need to hurry up and get outta here," Qianna said, standing up and stretching.

"Me too," Paisley said.

"Your bodyguard is cute," Qianna teased.

"He's an asshole," Paisley told her. "He's one of those crooked mouth ones we were talking about earlier."

"For real? That's foul." Qianna shook her head.

"Yep, but like I said, I'm used to being the topic of many conversations. It's all good." Paisley reached into her large Michael Kors bag for her wallet and paid Qianna. She gave her a hug and said, " Thanks, girl. I love you—no homo."

"Shut up," Qianna laughed. "I'll see you in a little while."

Paisley walked over to Landon and told him, "I'm ready."

He looked her up and down, responding with, "Cool."

After making sure it was safe, they got into Paisley's MDX and rode in silence. Paisley used her BlackBerry to check her e-mail while he drove. She still couldn't locate her computer. She had looked everywhere at home and in the studio but it was nowhere to be found. Someone had to have taken it.

"You mind if we stop and get something to eat?" Landon asked.

Paisley looked over at him. "Fine," she said, realizing she was hungry herself.

"What do you want?"

"It doesn't matter." She shrugged. "Let me call Seymone and see what she wants because it's probably gonna be a long night anyway."

Paisley dialed Seymone's cell number and they all decided the easiest thing would be to get enough food for everyone coming tonight. They arrived at the restaurant, and Paisley was headed inside when she heard someone calling after her.

"That's her! That's her! Paisley!"

A small group of teenage boys headed toward her. Her heart began pounding, but she tried to remain calm. Landon instantly blocked her with his body before they could get any closer.

"Hold on, fellas," he told them.

"Man, we just trying to say hello, that's all," one of the guys said, trying to see past Landon.

"Now's not the time, guys. She's just here to get some food, not make a personal appearance. Respect her space, for real," Landon told the young men. The guys moaned and complained, but left them alone. She spotted the photographer she'd run into outside Java's that morning passing by in his car. Paisley eased into the restaurant, praying that she hadn't caused a scene.

The owner of Jasper's, Uncle Jay, had their food ready and waiting for them. He was a frisky, flirtatious, older man who always made Paisley laugh. In a matter of minutes, they had paid and were heading out again. Paisley was relieved to see that her mini-fan club had dispersed, and they had no interruptions as they left.

By the time they made it to the studio, everyone had arrived. Paisley moved to open her door and get out, but Landon stopped her.

"Don't get out yet," he ordered.

She looked at him like he was crazy. "Why not?"

He looked into the rearview mirror. "I think the guys from the restaurant followed us. Don't move."

Paisley turned around and watched as Landon got out and headed for the small blue car that had pulled into the parking lot behind them. A couple of the guys got out and she could see Landon talking to them. Paisley's phone began ringing.

"Why are you just sitting out there?" Seymone asked. "You need help with the food?"

"Some guys followed us from Jasper's and Landon is trying to make them leave," Paisley said, still watching to see what was happening.

"Do I need to call the police?"

"The police? For what?" Chester's voice asked in the background.

"What happened now?" Diesel yelled.

"Some guys are outside. They followed them from Jasper's," Seymone announced.

Within moments, the door opened and Scooter was headed for her car.

"Are you all right?" he asked, opening Paisley's door.

"I'm fine, Scooter," she told him. She glanced in the side mirror and saw that Landon was still talking to the guys, who were now getting back into their car.

"I love you, Paisley!" one of them yelled as he got into the backseat.

"Come on, I'll walk you in," Scooter said, holding out his hand and helping her out of the SUV. Paisley was about to get out when she spotted movement in another car.

"There's someone in that car," she told Scooter.

"Where?" Scooter looked around to see who she was talking about.

"There's a camera guy in that car over there. He got shots of me this morning when I was going into Java's." Paisley pointed him out. "He tried to catch me when I went into After Effex, but I went in through the side and he missed me."

"Let me go deal with this fool," Scooter told her. "Don't move."

"Scooter, wait!" she called after him, but he kept walking, removing his tie and unbuttoning his shirt with each step he took. Paisley got out of the SUV to follow him.

Seeing Paisley, the teenagers hopped back out of their car and began calling her name. Landon turned to see Paisley chasing Scooter, who was rushing toward the cameraman getting out of his car, capturing everything on film.

This isn't gonna be good, Paisley thought as her gaze met Landon's. He shook his head and ran toward them.

"Yo, what the hell is your problem?" Scooter yelled at the cameraman.

"I'm just doing my job, man," he said, still snapping pictures. "It's public property."

"Get the hell away from here!" Scooter demanded, within reaching distance of him.

"Scooter, let's just get inside," Paisley pleaded. She knew Scooter had a temper and didn't have any problem throwing the first punch.

"Paisley, Paisley!" the teenage boys called.

She turned and saw the four boys running toward her, camera phones in hand. She didn't know what to do. She was dead center in a tornado of chaos, and she didn't see a way out of it. Paisley felt herself panicking. She was too far from the studio door or her car, and her legs still weren't well enough for her to run. The small group of guys was headed straight for her and the paparazzo was getting it all on film. She glanced up to see Scooter's arm grabbing the camera from the guy's hands.

"Scooter!" she called, but it was too late. The guy yelled as Scooter collared him and tossed him on the hood of the car. The studio door opened and Diesel came running out, followed by a well-dressed Chester.

"Scooter! Man, stop!" Diesel ran and tried to come between the two.

"Paisley!" Landon called her name and before she could turn around, she felt herself being lifted off the ground. Landon scooped her up into his arms and rushed her to the door, which was now being held open by Seymone. Once she was safely inside, Landon rushed back out the door.

"What the hell is going on?" Seymone asked.

The small group of girls who had come to the audition was now gathered in the front and watching the action unfold. Embarrassed, Paisley pushed her way through the crowd and made her way into her office. She couldn't believe the turn her life had taken.

"Are you okay, Paisley?" Qianna and Seymone rushed in and asked.

Paisley turned to the window and watched as Diesel and Scooter pushed the photographer back into his car and he drove off, followed by the car full of teenage boys.

Seymone walked over and rubbed her back as Paisley began crying. It was all too much to handle and she was sick of dealing with it all.

"Your ass shoulda been doing your job and none of this woulda even jumped off!"

Paisley's eyes widened as she heard Scooter yelling from down the hall. They rushed to see what was going on.

"That wasn't the problem. If *you* wouldn't have been trying to do *my* job, none of this would've happened." The distinctness of Landon's baritone voice was apparent, even though it was loud and an octave higher than usual.

"Man, please. Paisley said that dude had been following her since this morning when she went to Java's!" Scooter huffed.

Landon turned to look at Paisley. "You've been seeing that cat all day and you ain't say nothing?"

"If your ass woulda been with her this morning like you were supposed to be, you would know that," Scooter added.

"Scooter, that's enough. Paisley ran off this morning in one of her temper tantrums and Landon didn't know where she went," Seymone explained. "That's not his fault. Landon has been by her side all day."

"That's true." Qianna nodded. "He sat at the salon for about five hours."

"Do you have a death wish or something?" Landon asked her, his voice filled with anger. "If this man has been following you all day, why didn't you mention it? How do we know he isn't the one stalking you? Do you like being stalked?"

"What? Are you crazy?" Paisley asked.

"Do you get some type of cheap thrill by all this?" He stood right in front of her. She looked into his eyes and could see the hatred in them. He told her, "I take protecting someone's life very seriously. I don't have time to be looking after someone who thinks all this is a joke."

"I think maybe we all need to calm down," Chester suggested. "We got auditions and rehearsals. The situation has been handled and it's over. Paisley, you need to apologize to Landon."

"For what?" Paisley snapped at her cousin.

"For being difficult, for one," Chester replied. "This man is laying his life on the line to protect you and you're not making it easy for him. That's not fair and you know it."

Paisley looked down, realizing that not telling Landon about the cameraman following her all day had been a mistake, and had resulted in the chaos that erupted in the parking lot. Not only had it jeopardized Landon's life, but the life of Scooter, who had gone out of his way to be her hero.

"I'm sorry," she apologized.

"Now can we go eat and get started? We got a lot to do and a short time to get it done," Chester said, then walked into the Main Room where the applicants were waiting and announced, "Ladies, the drama is over. It's time to show us what you got!"

"You sure you're okay?" Scooter leaned over and touched Paisley's cheek.

Paisley nodded. "I'm fine. Thank you, Scooter. I appreciate your coming to my rescue. Even if it is all my fault."

"You can't help being as beautiful as you are, girl. You know fame comes with a price. People are gonna be after you, that ain't nothing new to you. You're Paisley Lawrence, it comes with the territory," he said, then looked at Landon and added, "Not everyone can deal with that."

"Look, why don't you take Paisley and go on back to the house," Diesel said. "It's been a long day for her."

"I'm all right, Diesel," Paisley said. Truth was, she was tired and her body was now aching. It was as if the massage she had gotten hours earlier had never happened. The tension in her body had returned. "I agreed to handle this part and I am."

"Go ahead, Paisley. We can handle the auditions and we know that whoever we decide on has to have your seal of approval," Seymone told her.

"You want me to take you home?" Scooter smiled at her seductively.

"No, I'm fine with Landon," she laughed. Seymone made Paisley and Landon a plate and they left.

"Um, I really am sorry," Paisley said to Landon while they were riding to the house.

"Look, I'm not one of your little conquests or one of your male fans who is so amazed by you that I can't think straight, understand?" Landon rolled his eyes at her. "I'm not one of your flunkies."

Paisley could not believe his attitude. "What the hell is that supposed to mean? I never said that you were."

"I just wanna get that straight. That little stunt you pulled with your little boyfriend coulda got someone killed. Like I told you, this isn't a game to me."

"What boyfriend?"

"Scooter. Sending him over to that photographer the way you did," Landon responded.

"I didn't send Scooter over there, he went on his own," she said, fighting the tears that were now forming. "I tried to stop him from going. You really think I would send someone into a situation like that because I think it's funny?"

Landon shook his head. "I don't know what you would do."

"Exactly." Paisley shook her head.

You don't know me at all, and you never will.

Chester

I love my cousin, Paisley. She's more than just my family, she's my friend. I remember the day her mother brought her to my house to meet her. I was three years old. I looked into the face of that tiny bundle, dressed in pink and white, and my first thoughts were "I wish I were her. She's sooo pretty," and Paisley looked right back at me and smiled. It was as if she understood what I was thinking and was saying, "I know."

In that instant, our relationship was formed. Growing up, she always had my back. When kids on the street teased me about my femininity or adults gave me those weird looks, Paisley didn't hesitate putting them in their place. She was definitely my she-ro. And to me, everything about her was perfect.

She was beautiful, smart, funny, witty, bold, and she commanded attention without even trying to. And for those same reasons, her mother, my aunt, the evil Emma Jean Lawrence, hated her. It was as if Emma Jean had decided that it was her life's purpose to make Paisley miser-

able in whatever she did. Paisley was an honors student who excelled in track and basketball. But she was also a loner who didn't have many female friends. I believe that was partly due to the relationship she had with her mother. Paisley really didn't like girls at all.

Paisley's relationship with her father, on the other hand, was wonderful. She was truly "Daddy's little girl" and their bond was unbreakable. In that sense, Paisley got along better with guys. The funny thing is that Paisley has trust issues with everyone, including me. The girl can keep secrets from God. That's why she's never gonna get a man, because she has this wall built around her and she won't let anyone in.

Scooter needs to give it up. Anyone who truly knows Paisley knows that he's not the man for her. She needs someone who sees her for who she truly is, and not the woman she thinks she should be.

"So, you think we made the right decision?" Seymone asked Chester as they were preparing to leave. She placed the pictures and resumes of the girls they selected on Paisley's desk.

"Yeah, those girls are gonna be fierce, and I like the thought of hiring a couple of guys, too. That's gonna be hot." Chester nodded. "I can't wait to audition them."

After careful deliberation, they had decided on the six girls who were soon to be known as the "Dream Angels." Diesel, Scooter, and Paisley had come up with the crazy, off-the-wall concept for the club. State Streets, the club they were purchasing, was already one of the hottest nightspots in town. But the changes they were about to make, including renaming the club Street Dreams, were going to make it one of the hottest spots in the nation. They were planning a cross between Jay-Z's 40/40 Club and Coyote Ugly. Chester was glad to be a part of it, and he saw the hard work Seymone had been doing.

"Seymone, you're really doing a good job," Chester told her.

Seymone turned and smiled. "Thanks, Chester. Coming from you that means a lot. We all know how super critical you are."

"I know that was meant to be an insult, but I'm taking it as a compliment," he told her. "Is Bobby coming to the opening?"

"Hell to the naw." Seymone shook her head.

"You didn't invite him?"

"I didn't even mention Diesel and Scooter buying the club. He doesn't even know I'm working here." Seymone sighed. "If he knew I was involved in all of this, Bobby would have a fit."

"Why? It's not like you're doing anything wrong." Chester shrugged.

"You know Bobby wants me out of the spotlight. I think he wants to be the only superstar in the relationship." Seymone laughed.

"That's crazy. Didn't you all meet on the set of a music video? You were already a successful model when he met you."

"But now that we're engaged, Bobby feels that my image should be toned down, and I feel him on that," Seymone explained. "I mean, how would it look to his fans if I'm table dancing in Usher's new video?"

"Chile, please, you know I wouldn't give a damn how it looked to his fans. You're a better one than I am. There's no way his career should come before yours. What about what makes you happy?"

"I am happy, Chester. Bobby makes me happy," Seymone told him.

"This studio was your dream, too, Seymone. Working here, being here, doing this, makes you happy too. And if that nigga is too stuck on himself to see that, then you need to reconsider being with him. How are you gonna marry someone you can't even share your dreams with?" Chester touched Seymone's face. He had wanted to tell her this ever since she had left Paisley high and dry to go and be with Bobby last year. He had noticed the changes in her: the weight gain, the uncomfortable nervousness, the unusual quietness that wasn't really her nature before she left. Now, a month later, the old, familiar Seymone was emerging and he wanted her to remain that way.

"Don't get me wrong, Chester, I can talk to Bobby. It's just complicated. I have to be careful. You know Bobby and Paisley hate each other. That kinda puts me in a difficult situation also." Seymone's cell phone began ringing. She looked down at it and said, "Speak of the devil. Hey, baby."

"I'm gonna wait in the car," Chester said.

"Okay, I'll be right there." Seymone nodded. "Yeah, baby, I'm here. Oh, that was Chester, we are uh, about to, uh, go pick up a prescription for Paisley."

Chester shook his head and headed out to the car. If there was one thing he was grateful for, it was his ability to be honest in every relationship he was involved in.

I am who I am, and there's nothing you can do about it. Hate it or love it, love it or leave it, I keep it real with it, so deal with it.

Chapter 15

"So, what's the difference between the girls you hired to be Dream Angels and strippers?"

"There's a big difference. First of all, these girls are gonna be fully clothed, and they won't have people throwing money at them. Granted, they'll be dancing, but they are there to enhance the atmosphere of the club, not be the sole entertainment for the guests."

"Are they go-go dancers?"

"Well, I guess you could call them that. But, we decided last night to bring some guys in, too. It's gonna be hot. You'll have to just wait and see."

"I don't do the nightclub thing."

"Why not?"

"That's just not my life anymore. I try to stay as far away from that atmosphere as I possibly can."

"Then how the hell you're gonna be security for Paisley Lawrence, I don't know."

Paisley stood at the top of the steps and listened as Seymone and Landon laughed and talked. *She is such a traitor, laughing with him like he's cool. If she only knew he was thinking that she's an immoral slut, she wouldn't be so quick to be his friend. And he's just as bad, fronting like he's interested in what's going on. I hate him.*

"Good morning." Seymone smiled when Paisley entered the kitchen after putting the dog outside. She and Landon were both sitting at the table, drinking coffee. "I went to Java's for you and got your usual."

"Thanks," Paisley said, picking up the lone cup sitting in the middle of the table. Landon had been there two weeks and she didn't like him any more than the day he started. Seymone, on the other hand, acted as if Landon was the greatest thing since sliced bread. Unlike Paisley, she talked to Landon all the time.

"Morning." Landon barely spoke. "What's on your agenda for today?"

"Working, that's all," Paisley said. "I'll just be at the studio all day."

"Paisley, don't forget Dr. Singleton is coming by this morning," Seymone reminded her. She looked down at her watch and said, "He should be here any minute with his sexy self. You should try to holler at him."

"Yeah, right. I don't think so. I hope he'll let me get this cast off," Paisley sighed.

"That reminds me." Seymone reached into her purse and pulled out a set of wooden stirrers, connected together. They were similar to the ones Paisley already had, but these were painted pink and had her initials on them. "Nick told me to give these to you. I don't know what they're for."

Paisley grabbed the stirrers from her and quickly used them to scratch inside the cast. "God, he's a genius. And these are fly."

"That's so gross." Seymone shook her head.

"It's better than a butcher knife," Landon mumbled. Paisley gave him an ugly look.

"A butcher knife? Who used that?" Seymone asked.

The doorbell rang and Paisley rushed to answer it. Dr. Singleton smiled, standing in the doorway with his black bag in hand.

"Well, looks like you're getting around a whole lot better."

"Hey, Evan." Paisley welcomed him inside. "Come on in."

He followed her inside. "How are you feeling?"

"I'm feeling better," she told him. Seymone walked into the foyer, followed by Landon.

"Hi Evan." Seymone smiled.

"How are you doing, Seymone? It's nice to see you again." Evan stretched his hand out toward Seymone and she shook it.

"Evan, this is Landon Malone. He works security for me now." Paisley introduced the two men. "Landon, this is my physician, Evan Singleton."

"Security, huh?" Evan looked surprised.

"Yeah, things got a little rough around here," Paisley explained.

"I guess your being here makes the ladies feel a lot better," Evan said. "That's good."

"If you say so," Paisley commented.

Seymone rolled her eyes at Paisley and replied, "Yeah, Landon being here makes us feel safe."

"Well, let's see how you're doing." Evan nodded at Paisley. "Have you been doing the physical therapy exercises we discussed? And not the retail exercises, either."

"No, none at all, and she's been going to the studio almost every day," Seymone volunteered.

Paisley rolled her eyes at her best friend, thinking how Seymone was a straight tattletale.

"Paisley, I know she has to be exaggerating," Evan said.

Landon shook his head and said, "She hasn't exercised since I've been here and that's been over two weeks."

I know like hell he isn't trying to tell my business, she thought. "I've been really busy catching up on paperwork for The Playground, that's all."

"I understand," Evan told her, "but as a therapist, you should know more than anyone how important getting the proper strengthening activities is."

"I do, and I'm gonna do better," Paisley promised.

"Well, let's head upstairs and make sure you're okay," the doctor said. As she walked toward the staircase, Paisley couldn't help noticing the strange look Landon had on his face.

"Is there a problem?" she snapped at him, knowing he was probably thinking something was up.

Landon shrugged. "I didn't say anything."

The doctor followed Paisley into her room and examined her.

"Can I get this cast off? It itches like hell," she asked when he finished.

"I know it's probably uncomfortable for you. It really needs to stay on for another week or so," he told her.

"I can't take another week or so," she whined. "I swear, I'm gonna use my own damn electric knife and cut it off myself."

Evan's eyes widened in surprise. "Come on now, Paisley. You've lasted this long."

"Don't get it twisted, Dr. Singleton, I'll do it myself, for real, I'm not kidding." She stared at him in a way that let him know she was serious.

"I'll schedule an X-ray this afternoon and if it looks good, we can go ahead and take it off," he told her.

"Great." She smiled.

"But if that bone isn't set and healed, we're gonna have to put another one on there," Dr. Singleton said.

Paisley rolled her eyes to the back of her head. "Fine."

"And since you're being such a good sport about this, how about I take you to dinner to celebrate once the cast is finally off?"

Paisley was shocked by his question. "Are you asking me out?"

"Did I say something wrong?"

"No, it's just . . . you don't want to take me out on a date, really, you don't."

"And why not?" He frowned.

"Dating me is really complicated," she tried to explain. "We couldn't even go anywhere and enjoy ourselves. For real, everywhere I go, cameras are flashing."

"So, that just means my business would increase," he laughed.

"Now you're using our date as free advertisement for your practice?" She faked a gasp.

"Hey, any press is good press, isn't that what they say?"

Paisley realized that she really did want to go out with him, but her life was so complicated right now, and she didn't want to bring all of her current drama into what could possibly be a new relationship. She liked him too much. *He deserves more than what I can give him right now.*

"Maybe, when things calm down a bit, and I'm cast-free, we can do that," she told him.

"I can respect that," he responded.

"Everything good?" Seymone asked when they returned downstairs.

"Cast is coming off today." Paisley winked.

"Maybe," Evan corrected her.

"Today," Paisley said emphatically.

The doorbell rang again. Seymone peeped out the window and said, "It's the UPS man."

"What did you order now?" Paisley asked her.

"I didn't order anything."

Landon opened the door and signed for the large boxes the man was carrying. He brought them inside and said, "They're all for you, Paisley."

"Looks like someone's been doing a lot of shopping." Dr. Singleton pointed to the packages.

"That's crazy. I haven't ordered anything. Besides, when I order things, I have them sent to the studio." Paisley was confused. Landon took the boxes into the den and put them on the floor.

"Open them." Seymone shrugged.

"I'm scared." Paisley hesitated, then turned to Landon and asked, "Can you open them for me?"

He looked at her like she was crazy, but then, seeing her distress, his eyes softened and he nodded. Reaching into his pocket and removing a small knife, he sliced through the tape at the top of the first large box. He looked inside before pulling out four shirt-sized gift boxes. "You want me to open these?"

Paisley nodded and braced herself, afraid to see what was inside. Landon opened the first box, ruffled through the tissue paper inside, and pulled out a pink lace nightie with matching bra and panties.

"Cute," Seymone said, reaching for the garments.

Paisley frowned and said, "Yeah, I was looking at that set the other week."

Landon opened the next box and removed a pair of red satin boxers and a matching tank top.

There was also a black cocktail dress, a pair of 7 jeans, and an Ed Hardy jacket.

"That's cute, too!" Seymone gushed.

As Landon continued opening the boxes and removing items, Paisley felt her stomach begin turning, and became nauseated. Beads of sweat began to form on her forehead, and her lips began to tremble.

"Are you all right, Paisley?" Dr. Singleton rushed beside her.

"Paisley, what's wrong?" Seymone asked.

Landon opened the next box and took out a large Coach duffel bag, a pair of seven-hundred-dollar Giuseppe Zanotti pumps, a bottle of Dolce & Gabbana Light Blue, and finally, a Premiere Chanel diamond watch.

"Wow," Landon said, looking at the watch.

Paisley began rocking back and forth. "This is crazy."

"Paisley, calm down." Seymone rubbed her back.

"I can't calm down!" Paisley snapped.

"You don't know where this stuff came from?" Landon asked.

"Yes, well, no . . . I don't know!"

"What do you mean? Either you know where it came from or you don't!" Landon's voice became loud.

"Why are you yelling at me?" Paisley cried.

"Because, you're sitting here having a nervous breakdown over this stuff and we don't know why!" Landon retorted.

"Okay, let's calm down before things get heated," Dr. Singleton said. "Paisley, do you know anything about these items?"

"Yes," Paisley said. "I know about them. They're all things I wanted to buy. They're all things I looked at online. They're all things that I had 'wish listed' on Web sites on my computer!"

"Then there you go. Someone looked on your computer and sent you some gifts." Dr. Singleton said it like it was as simple as counting to ten.

Seymone shook her head and told him, "You don't understand, someone stole her laptop two weeks ago from out of her bedroom."

"It's gonna be okay, Paisley, I promise." Scooter sat on the side of Paisley's bed. Paisley hadn't left the house in days after receiving the package from UPS. Her bed was the only place she found solace. Her friends had all been trying to coax her out of the obvious funk of a mood she was in, but no one had succeeded. Paisley felt like her every move was being watched and the only place she found that she could relax was in her bed, so that was where she had chosen to stay.

"You can't promise me that." Paisley shook her head. "You know what? I realize now that this person isn't trying to harm me."

"Huh?" Scooter was confused.

"They're not trying to kill me. They're not trying to kidnap me or slice me up and throw my body in the river." Paisley sniffed. "They're trying to get me to lose my mind. They want me to be crazy, and I am."

"I want you to listen to me," Scooter said. "You're not crazy and you're not gonna lose your mind. What you are gonna do is get yourself together and regain control of your life. You're not gonna let this bastard stop you from living."

"I'm trying. I've gone back to work, despite the damn media whores everywhere I go. I still get out and about. Whoever is doing this has all my banking information. There's no telling what they're gonna do next."

"And you're gonna keep doing it." Scooter nodded. "Fallon checked all of your accounts. Nothing was charged to you. Whoever sent all this shit paid for it themselves and we're gonna find out who it was. Come on, get up. Aren't you supposed to be going to get your cast off?"

Paisley stared at him, wondering if he was serious. She had made up her mind that she was going to be confined to the walls of her house, this room even. She was too afraid to go anywhere or do anything.

"I'm not leaving this house," Paisley told him.

"Yes, you are. Get your ass up and let's go." Scooter pulled the comforter off Paisley and tossed it on the foot of the bed. "The grand opening of the club is in a week. Do you even have anything to wear?"

"I'm not going." Paisley sat up. Killa hopped off the sofa in the sitting area where he had been lying and jumped into her lap.

"That's bull. You're going. You're a part of this whole thing; you wouldn't disappoint Diesel by not going nor would you disappoint yourself. Besides, stalker or not, your nosy ass wants to see who's gonna be there. Now get up so we can get that damn cast off and go to the mall."

Paisley stared at Scooter, who was waiting for her to get out of bed. She slowly tossed her legs to the side and stood up. He looked into her eyes and gently pulled her to him. For some strange reason, Paisley became lost in the embrace, the warmth of his body relaxing her. *Damn, this feels nice*, she thought, closing her eyes and inhaling the scent of his cologne. It felt so good that, for a moment, she forgot it was Scooter's arms that were holding her. His fingers caressed the small of her back, causing chills to run up and down her spine.

Reality snapped her back when she heard him whisper, "Damn, Pais, I wanna hold you like this forever."

Paisley's eyes opened and she took a step back and out of his grasp.

"What's wrong?" he asked.

"I . . . I . . . need to make a phone call," Paisley lied. "Go ahead and wait downstairs, I'll be ready in a few minutes."

Scooter walked out of her room, and she sat on the bed. Her body was still warm from the hug. A hug that she didn't want to end, but she didn't want to be hugging Scooter. She thought about Evan, and his offer to take her to dinner. The thought of sitting across from him in a dimly lit restaurant, talking about their lives, excited her. She wanted to share her life with someone, to be loved and connect. *That connection*, it was the one thing that had been missing from her life. She ached for it, and she realized, her heart still ached for him. The connection she shared with Warren had been unlike anything she had ever felt before. It was as if he knew her inside and out; and no one had ever come remotely close to reaching that core of her that he had touched. He was the only one, and as much as she was attracted to Evan, she knew that she would never feel for him the love that she had for Warren.

You'll know you've met the one, when Warren no longer matters.

Chapter 16

"Welcome to the good liiifffe!" Paisley sang along with Kanye West as she stared at her reflection in the full-length mirror. She snapped her fingers in true Chester fashion, complimenting herself out loud. "Girl, you are fierce!"

The black sheer top she wore was tasteful and had just the right touch of sexiness without being slutty; the shirt along with her form-fitting jeans and Manolo Blahnik stilettos was enough to turn heads, exactly what she wanted to happen. Scooter had aided her in picking out her outfit and, she had to admit, she didn't think Chester, in all of his fashionista, could have done a better job. The curly hair extensions she wore fell just right, and reached the center of her back. The diamonds in her hoop earrings, bracelet, and necklace shimmered. Feeling daring and in a playful mood, she reached into her jewelry box, removed her set of platinum fronts, and popped them into her mouth. The teeth were a gift from Nelly from when she starred in his last video. Satisfied with her appearance, she headed downstairs.

"Uh-oh, no you didn't break out the fronts!" Seymone giggled when Paisley smiled. Her friend looked gorgeous in an all black, form-fitting jumpsuit.

"You know that's what's up," Paisley said with attitude.

Landon, looking handsome in a black dress shirt and pants, shook his head at her. "You look like a ghetto super model."

"Haters beware." She crossed her arms across her chest in a hip-hop pose.

The doorbell rang and Chester, Scooter, and Diesel all walked in.

"Wow," Scooter commented, looking Paisley up and down. "You look good as hell. I told you that shirt was gonna fit perfectly."

"Yes, it does," Chester agreed. "I don't think I could've done better myself."

"You look good too." Paisley hugged her cousin, dressed in a vintage white ruffle shirt and black tuxedo jacket. His large fro was wild as ever and he had a large pair of sunglasses on.

"We all look good." Diesel smiled. He held up a bottle of gold foil–wrapped Roederer Cristal. "Y'all know we gotta get our toast on before we leave."

"Where's Yaya?" Paisley asked him.

"She said she was gonna be here when I got here." Diesel shrugged.

Seymone grabbed some flutes from Paisley's china cabinet and passed them out.

"No, thanks," Landon said when she got to him.

"What's wrong?" Chester asked him.

"Landon doesn't drink," Paisley told him.

"What? Say it ain't so." Chester seemed surprised.

"Aw, come on, Landon," Diesel said. "One drink won't hurt you. I know you're gonna help celebrate my moment with me."

"I'm celebrating." Landon smiled. "But, I'm working, what can I say?"

"He doesn't even wanna go tonight, but he has to because I'm going." Paisley smirked.

Landon shook his head at Paisley and was about to say something, but the doorbell rang, stopping him. He walked over and opened the door.

"Where my party people at?" Yaya yelled as she walked inside, followed by her partner, Taryn, and best friend, Camille. The three girls were dressed to impress and in hype mode, and Paisley was glad they were tagging along.

"We were just about to make a toast," Diesel said, pulling Yaya close to him and kissing her on her cheek.

Seymone continued pouring champagne, and even handed Landon a glass of ginger ale. "We still want you to participate in the toast."

"Thanks." He smiled at Seymone.

Diesel raised his glass and said, "To my friends, who are closer to me than my own family. I love and thank each and every one of you. You've been there as I struggled, worked, fought, partied, laughed, cried, was broke, got paid, and you helped me make my dream a reality. To Street Dreams!"

"To Street Dreams!" they all echoed, and tapped glasses in the air.

"All right, let's roll," Chester announced. "Who's riding with who?"

"We're all riding together." Yaya smiled.

"How is that possible?" Landon asked.

Yaya opened the front door. Sitting in front of Paisley's house was a black stretch Hummer.

"Baby, you think of everything, that's why I keep you by my side." Diesel picked Yaya up and twirled her around.

"I'm glad you did think of that," Scooter agreed. "For a minute, I thought you were talking about Paisley's little MDX. I don't know why she didn't go ahead and get a Range Rover like I told her to. That's more her style and she would look hot as hell behind the wheel."

"Let's go," Paisley told him, rolling her eyes.

"I know Dorian Wilson personally; the dude who used to be in the NFL who owns that luxury lot downtown. One phone call and you can be riding in class and style." Scooter winked.

Paisley shook her head and walked out the door. Landon made sure the house was locked up, and they were all on their way.

The line to get into Street Dreams was wrapped around the building. The limo they all rode in pulled right up to the front and they got out. Cameras flashed and the crowd called out their names, everyone hoping to get noticed and allowed to walk in with them. Although she and Seymone were used to the attention, they both smiled as they noticed the pleasure their friends were having. They all posed for pictures and even signed a few autographs before going in. Once inside, Paisley was amazed at the transformation. Before being renovated, the club was already huge, with three floors. It seemed even bigger now, and classier, with the bar extended across the entire back portion of the club and the expanded dance floor. The guys had decided to keep Tobias "Deejay Terror" Sims. He was the best in the business and had been the house deejay for years. As Diesel pointed out in one of their business meetings, not everything needed to be changed. Deejay Terror shouted them out over the microphone when he spotted them enter the club, and they headed to the VIP section.

"This is amazing," Seymone yelled over the music.

Paisley nodded, and watched as the crowd flowed in. In what seemed like seconds, the club was packed and VIP was overflowing with celebrities. Stars from every sports and music genre were everywhere Paisley looked. She greeted familiar faces nonstop, and everyone commented on how sorry they were about the accident and how beautiful she looked. Even Evan showed up, to her surprise.

"I'm going to the bathroom," she said to Seymone after a while, and stood up. Landon didn't hesitate standing and was right behind her. She turned and told him, "I'm just going to the bathroom."

"I know. But if you think I'm gonna have you wandering alone in this crowd, you're crazy. Anything could happen."

Paisley knew there was no arguing with him. "Fine."

"Hi, Paisley," a chipper voice yelled.

She looked over and spotted Nick, her waiter from Java's, and she waved at him, showing him her cast-less arm. Landon stayed close behind her as they made their way through the thick crowd. Guys were trying to get at her from left to right, and she was grateful Landon was there to help her. They walked to the top of the club. Paisley spoke to the security guy guarding the door of the hallway that led to the offices and dressing areas.

"Good evening, Ms. Lawrence." He smiled and opened the door for her. As she passed the dressing rooms, she saw Yaya, Taryn, and Camille hard at work putting makeup on the girls, while Chester assisted with the uniforms he had designed. Everything was coming together as planned. Paisley couldn't wait to see the performance Seymone had choreographed.

She entered Diesel's office and went to his restroom. She was relieved for the moment of quiet. To her surprise, her cell phone rang. She saw that it was Warren and didn't hesitate to answer.

"I need to see you," he said before she could say hello. "I'm at the Seashore Marriott, suite sixteen-forty-two. Be here in an hour."

"Warren, I can't meet you tonight. I'm at the club's grand opening," Paisley whispered into the phone.

"I don't give a damn where you are. Meet me here in an hour, Paisley. I mean it. Alone."

"How am I supposed to do that? Landon is practically glued to my ass and he's everywhere I go," she hissed. "What the hell is going on?"

"You tell me!" he snapped. "I'm not getting into this right now. See you when you get here!"

He hung up the phone and she shook her head. *This man has lost his mind*, she thought. She was about to put the phone back into her purse when it began buzzing again. It was a text from him.

Fake sick . . . do something . . . and get the hell over here . . . we need to talk . . . I'm not playing . . . Suite 1642 . . . W.

Paisley got herself together and returned to the office area where Landon was waiting.

"You all right?" he asked. "You look kinda sick."

"I really don't feel well," she lied. "I'll be fine. Come on."

Seymone was in the hallway when they came out of the office.

"I gotta go give my guys and girls a pep talk." She smiled.

"They'll be fine," Paisley assured her. "You did a great job with them. It's gonna be a smash."

"We'll see," Seymone said. "I'll be back down once they're settled in place."

"Okay." Paisley smiled. She was still trying to figure out if and how she was going to slip out to meet Warren. She could tell by the tone of his voice that something was wrong and he was upset. By the time they made it back to VIP, Diesel was on the stage near the deejay booth and talking into the microphone. Paisley stood at the edge of the balcony so she could get a good view. Scooter came and stood behind her, putting his arms on her shoulders.

"I wanna thank everyone for coming out to Street Dreams. We all loved State Streets for years, but when we bought it, we wanted to bring some new flavor to the place. As you can see, we did a little remodeling and changed things up a bit, and made the bar a little bigger on the first floor." The crowd yelled as Diesel pointed to the bar. "Well, we thought that maybe since we made the bar so big, we could throw in some eye candy for everyone to enjoy while getting their drink on. And so we came up with this!"

The two red velvet curtains hanging on each end of the bar fell, revealing two large glass boxes measuring ten by ten. Inside each one was a girl and a guy, dressed in matching white outfits, dancing precisely to Usher's "Bad Girl," which was blasting. The bass was so loud and deep that Paisley could feel it in her chest. The couples were so intense as they moved in unison to the music, and the dance was so sexy, that Paisley found herself slightly aroused by the time they finished. The crowd went wild and Deejay Terror went into another song. The dance floor became packed and the party went into full swing.

"I knew that shit was gonna be hot," Scooter's voice said in her ear. "Diesel is a crowd pleaser."

"Indeed he is." She eased from his grasp.

Seymone rushed over and squealed, "They liked it."

"They loved it!" Paisley nodded.

"Yo, you worked that." Scooter smiled. "I'm proud of you."

"Seymone, you choreographed that?" someone asked.

"Yeah." Seymone nodded, downing another drink. Paisley counted it as her fourth one, which was unusual because Seymone normally wasn't a drinker.

"I don't believe it. Come over here and let me see if you really got those moves," another guy yelled. Pretty soon, the crowd was chanting Seymone's name and calling for her to dance. Someone helped Seymone on top of the small bar in the VIP area, and she began moving her body seductively to the music.

"Well, she's drunk," Paisley commented.

"She's worked hard, she deserves to unwind. Let her enjoy her moment," Dr. Singleton laughed. She turned and saw that Landon was staring in amazement at her best friend as she danced.

"What the hell do you think you're doing?"

Everyone turned around to see Bobby Taylor frowning.

"Oh, damn," Paisley said, and started easing back a bit. Seymone was so into the song that she didn't even realize her fiancé was there.

"Seymone! Get your ass down!" Bobby yelled. Seymone saw Bobby and stopped dead in her tracks.

"Bobby," she whispered.

Bobby stormed over to the table and just as he reached up to pull Seymone down, Landon was beside him, grabbing his arm. Bobby snatched away and swung his fist toward Landon's face. Landon moved back and collared Bobby, tossing him across the room. Bobby's boys went after Landon but were stopped by both Scooter and Evan. Within seconds, the fight broke out. Paisley continued easing out of the mayhem until she was near the door. People were so caught up in the fight that no one noticed her slip out.

"Paisley, Paisley!"

Paisley turned and saw Nick, the waiter from Java's, waving at her. She beckoned for him to come to her. "Do you have a car?"

"Yeah." He nodded, looking at her strangely. "You need a ride?"

"Please." She smiled. "Can you take me to the Seashore Marriott?"

He shrugged. "No problem."

Warren

Jack Daniels . . . that's my new best friend. It seems to be the only thing that brings me any sort of happiness these days . . . The taste of it brings me back to the days when I would go to the bar and sit and talk to Paisley . . . It was the last thing I remember tasting the night of the accident, when we were together, at Charley's . . . Every time I take a swallow, I'm back with her. I love Paisley Janelle Lawrence more than anything in my life. She is the one person who I can honestly say brings me true happiness.

The biggest mistake I made in my life was walking out that door the night before I got married, and leaving her. What the hell was I thinking? I was thinking that I would marry Kollette, and secure my contract with her un-

cle's music label, make it big, leave her ugly ass, and eventually be with Paisley, my one true love. But things got complicated.

For starters, I didn't realize that Kollette's uncle was only dealing with gospel acts, which meant the R & B career I hoped I would have was gonna have to change. So, all the songs I had written about my love for Paisley I basically changed to be written about my love for God, had a couple of crossover gospel hits, and voila, my career was born. Don't get me wrong, I love God, but this whole gospel thing is getting kind of tired. I have to be this person I'm not, so much so that it's exhausting. No one knows me for real except Paisley. It pisses me off when I think about the night of the accident. I know it wasn't my fault, even though I had a couple of drinks. But somehow, I still feel responsible. If only I hadn't pressured her into coming with me. I got her involved in all this drama, and she doesn't deserve any of it.

That's why I looked out when I found out someone was stalking her. If anything happened to her, I don't know what I would do. So, I had the best in the business, Landon Malone, assigned to her. I know we were both put in a bad situation, and I made it worse by saying I didn't know who she was. But I thought we were moving past that and moving forward.

Since the accident, I have been putting things into perspective and am realizing that I can't keep living like this, in a meaningless marriage with a woman who grates my last nerve. And just when I come to grips about what I need to do and how I need to do it, I gotta deal with this. I thought Paisley and I were on the same page, but it's quite obvious that we're not, and I gotta find out what the hell is going on.

Knock knock knock.

Warren walked over to the door and opened it without even seeing who it was. Paisley stood in the doorway looking fine as hell, dressed in a black shirt and jeans that hugged the contour of her shapely legs. His eyes fell on the high heels she wore, making her appear statuesque, and slowly moved up her body until they rested on her picture perfect face that he thought about nonstop. She stepped into the room without saying a word, and faced him.

"I'm here," she said after a few moments. Warren half expected her to rush in and fall into his arms. It was, after all, the first time they had seen each other since the accident. This definitely wasn't the reaction he expected, confirming what he already expected.

"I see," Warren said, fighting the urge to pull her into his arms and kiss her full lips. "You look good, Paisley."

"You're not so bad yourself." She gave him a half smile, and then said, "So, what's going on?"

"I'm wondering the same thing, Pais." Warren shrugged. "I've been calling and texting you for a few days now, and you've been conveniently unavailable."

"Come on, Warren, you know I've been dealing with a lot." Paisley frowned. "My life is crazy right now."

"And you think mine's not?" Warren asked.

"I'm not saying it isn't. The studio is back open, we got the grand opening of the club, and I'm dealing with this psycho who seems determined to make me lose my mind," Paisley explained. Her cell phone began ringing from her purse and she ignored it.

"Are you trying to ruin me?" Warren added, taking a swig of Jack Daniels.

"What are you talking about?" Paisley gave him a strange look.

"I know that I may have hurt you in the past, and I'm sorry . . ."

"What are you talking about Warren? You're drunk."

"Don't try and play me, Paisley." Warren shook his head. "I thought the one thing that made our relationship work was the fact that we never lied to each other."

"Are you implying that I'm lying to you, Warren?" Paisley asked. "Why would I try to ruin you? Are you crazy?"

"Then why are you doing this to me?" Warren folded his arms.

"What are you talking about?" Paisley shook her head in confusion.

"I got this in an e-mail," Warren huffed. He reached into his back pocket and pulled out a folded picture of her and him taken years ago. Paisley was topless and so was Warren. Her hands caressed his face as she leaned back. He was kissing her neck. Anyone who saw the picture instantly knew that it was an intimate moment between two people who were in love.

"Where did you get this from?" Paisley took it from his hand and stared at it.

"I told you, it came from an e-mail. I thought you had something to do with it."

Paisley shook her head at him. "Warren, you've gotta be kidding me. You think I would do something like this?"

"Well, I tried to call you and talk about it, but your ass was so busy that you couldn't talk," he replied.

"What e-mail address did it come from?"

"I don't remember. Like I said, I thought you had something to do with it."

Warren was relieved to know that the pictures hadn't come from Paisley. He still had to wonder where the picture they had taken more than ten years ago did indeed come from.

"So, where did the picture come from Paisley, if it didn't come from you?"

"I don't know, Warren! The only people in the world that had copies of the pictures were you and me. Where are your copies?" Paisley snapped.

"Locked away! And what the hell is that supposed to mean? You think I would do this to us? This picture is private." Warren's voice softened and he added, "I wouldn't want anyone else seeing it. It's like . . . like invading a private memory."

"Exactly, Warren. We gotta figure out where this came from."

Warren stared at her. He was still in love with her. It killed him that they couldn't be together. His heart ached every time he thought about it. Which is why he kept the pictures locked away; every time he looked at them, they reminded him of a time he could never get back. He had messed up and he knew it. But he still wanted her. He thought about the recent pictures he had seen in the tabloids of her and Python, and couldn't help feeling jealous.

"Are you fucking somebody?" Warren asked.

"You're crazy," Paisley retorted. "Are you still on meds from the accident? Someone is selling private pictures of you and me together . . . provocative pictures I might add, and you're asking me who I'm sleeping with?"

"Forget the damn pictures! I'll take care of that. Just answer the question." Warren took another swig. "I love you and I wanna be with you. Tell me, Paisley. I need to know!"

"Did someone really send you that picture, Warren, or are you making this up?" Paisley frowned. "Is this some kind of game you're playing with me?"

"Answer the damn question, Paisley!" Warren stared at her. "Are you fucking Python? Or maybe you're fucking Landon."

Paisley's phone began ringing and she reached into her purse and stared at it. Shaking her head, she clicked it off. "You've gotta be kidding me, Warren. You really didn't call me all the way over here for this bullshit. I did not leave one of the most important events in my best friend's life to come deal with this bullshit. I'm leaving."

Warren grabbed her by the arm. "You're not going anywhere until I'm done talking to you."

Paisley snatched away from him. "I swear, if I find that you did sell that picture to Bad Babes, you won't have to worry about leaving your bitch-ass wife because she'll be a widow, believe that. I don't know where all this is coming from, but call me when your ass sobers up."

"You know I would never do anything like that to you, Paisley. You're my everything."

Warren pulled her to him and crushed his lips against hers, forcing her mouth open with his tongue. She struggled at first, then relaxed and kissed him back. Just as he felt himself becoming aroused, she pushed him and he stumbled backward.

"No, Warren!" she said. "I'm not doing this."

Her phone began ringing again. She shook her head as she walked past him, heading toward the door.

"Don't," he told her, struggling to get up. "Paisley, I love you."

She turned and stared at him, her eyes filled with tears. "I love you too, Warren. That's the problem."

Kollette

Oh, hell no. This is not happening. I swear to God, I'm gonna kill her. How dare she? I mean, does she really think I'm gonna let her disrespect me and my marriage like this and get away with it? Well, if she does, she has another think coming. I knew I would catch them eventually. Warren has been acting crazy these days. He's so damn somber and sour that no one even enjoys being around him. And it has nothing to do with the accident.

He's been like this for months. He won't talk to me, let alone touch me. I've known for a while that he had something going on but I thought it was with that stuck-up, know-it-all Ebonie. I don't like the way she looks at me. Like she's better than me. Like I'm not Mrs. Warren Cobb. When I got the call that Warren and a woman were involved in a car crash, my first thought was that it was Ebonie. To find out that it was Paisley Lawrence, a video ho of all people, was devastating to me. How could Warren be so stupid? This woman is the epitome of skankness, I don't care how beautiful and sexy she is. Sensual Seductress my ass. She's a disrespectful bitch who needs to be taught a lesson. I'm tired of her, and if she and Warren think that I'm about to just sit back and continue to let them have their little secret rendezvous, they've got another think coming.

"I love you too, Warren. That's the problem." Paisley's voice drifted down the hall.

"Paisley, Paisley, come back!" Warren called out.

Kollette watched as Paisley closed the door of Warren's suite and rushed to the elevator. *This bitch has the nerve to be crying?* Kollette could feel her anger rising and, in a brief moment, thought about walking up to her and punching her in the face. *No,* she told herself, *that would just make me look bad. It's time I show both of them what I'm capable of.* Once Paisley got on the elevator, Kollette grabbed her phone and dialed.

"Ebonie, it's Kollette." She was direct and to the point. "I need you to meet me at the office right now. We need to make some calls and set up a press conference for first thing in the morning. What do you mean? Listen here, sweetie, that's where you're wrong. You don't work for Warren, you work for the Ministry. Now stop what you're doing and get your ass over to the office right now before you don't work for anyone."

Chapter 17

"You a'ight?" Nick asked as Paisley got into the car. She said nothing as she climbed into his awaiting Trooper. Ignoring the tears that were streaming down her face, she pulled the seatbelt across her body, closed her eyes, and leaned back. The SUV jerked as Nick pulled out of the back parking lot of the hotel, where Paisley had specifically told him to wait.

Did Warren actually just come out of his mouth and threaten me? Does he really think he has that much control and power over my life? No way, it had to be the alcohol talking.

"Where to?" Nick's voice seemed to come out of nowhere. Paisley had become so engrossed in her thoughts that she almost forgot where she was and who she was with. Glancing over at the young, handsome driver, she just shrugged. Although she knew that returning to Street Dreams was the obvious choice, Paisley didn't have the energy to face the crowd or her friends, who were probably pissed that she left the way she had.

"Can we just ride around for a while?" she finally answered.

"Sure thing," he replied, reaching into the center console and putting a CD into the dashboard player. The jazz melody of Pharrell and Snoop Dogg's "Beautiful" streamed through the speakers. "You like Hidden Beach music? I love it; makes me relax."

"My life is so fucked up right now that I don't even know what that is anymore," Paisley mumbled, closing her eyes again.

"Huh?" Nick asked, turning the music down a little.

"Nothing," Paisley answered, "I was just thinking out loud. The music is nice."

Paisley's eyes opened for a moment and she saw that they were on the interstate. She wondered if Nick had a specific destination in mind, but she didn't bother to ask. It dawned on her that she really had no idea who Nick was other than the fact that he worked at Java's and was a computer whiz.

What the hell are you doing, Paisley? You're in a strange car with a strange man. No one has a clue where you are or who you're with. What

*if he tries to kidnap you, rape you, or worse, kill
you?*

She glanced over at Nick and saw him nodding along to the music. For some reason, there was something about him that put her at ease. He was so nerdy and quirky, but in a cute way. It was as if there was a familiarity about him that she liked.

He looked over and gave her a half smile and said, "You okay? You want something to eat? Drink? Gotta pee?"

"Pee?" she repeated, smiling.

"Just thought I'd ask," he said. "I gotta get some gas and my ex-girl once commented that I never thought to ask if she had to use the bathroom when I pulled into a gas station. Something about cheap gas means nasty bathrooms or something."

"No, I don't have to use the bathroom." Paisley sighed. "Thanks for asking though."

"No problem. I guess that was the one good thing I got from that relationship," he commented. He got off the next exit and drove past several grungy gas stations, finally pulling into a brightly lit 7-Eleven. As he got out, he told her, "Just in case."

Paisley reached into her purse and took out her cell phone. She cut it on and decided that she should at least let everyone know that she was okay. She sent a text to Fallon and Seymone, simply saying: What's up? Not feeling good, dipped out. Call you later.

Within moments, her cell phone alerted her with messages from both of them, neither one too pleasant. She responded to both with a simple sorry and turned the phone back off.

"I brought you a Slurpee." Nick passed her a cup as he got back in. "Coke-flavored, your favorite."

"Thanks," Paisley said, surprised.

"And guess what else?" he said, reaching into the plastic bag he was holding.

"What?"

"Almond M&M's!"

She looked at him like he was crazy, hesitating to take them until he said, "Um, I read your interview last year in *King* magazine. They asked you what your vices in life were, remember?"

Paisley relaxed, and couldn't help laughing as she thought about the interview in which she admitted that when she was stressed, she would indulge in Coke Slurpees and almond M&Ms. "I forgot. Thanks a lot."

"You look a little stressed so I figured I would help you out," he told her. Soon, they were back on the interstate, headed to their unknown destination. Paisley appreciated the fact that Nick wasn't trying to talk her to death. It was as if he needed this ride as much as she did. They were both in their own little worlds, neither one saying anything, just enjoying the lull of the road and the hip-hop jazz coming from the speakers.

Things seemed to be going well until Paisley noticed Nick speeding up and continually checking his mirrors. "What's wrong?"

He frowned. "I think someone is following us."

"What?" Paisley sat up and turned around. There was a pair of brightly lit headlights riding behind them. "Stop playing."

"I don't know. I could be tripping, but hold tight, because I'm about to find out."

Nick swerved from the far right lane they had been riding in, across two other lanes and into the far left lane. Sure enough, the headlights followed. "I knew it!"

"Who the hell is that?" Paisley's body twisted as she turned around to see if she could make out the car.

"I don't know. They've been behind us for a minute. I thought I was being paranoid when I went to the gas station and they kept going." Nick frowned.

"Why the hell didn't you say something then?" Paisley snapped, now looking into the side mirror.

"I told you, I didn't realize someone was really following us," Nick said.

"I know it's some dumb-ass photographer." Paisley shook her head. "I thought I ditched all of them at the club."

"We're being chased by paparazzi?" Nick's eyes widened. "Aw, hell."

"Calm down," she said. "They—"

"Calm down? Does the name Princess Diana ring a bell?" Nick interrupted her. He increased his speed and changed lanes again. The lights followed, this time even closer.

"Just try to lose them," Paisley told him.

"Uh, duh! What do you think I'm trying to do?" Nick got off at the next exit onto a dark road, and floored it. The faster he went, the closer the lights behind them got.

"Where the hell are the damn state troopers when you need them? If I was going two miles-per-hour over the limit, their asses would be right swarming around me, guns cocked and loaded to take me out. Any other time they would be ready to racially profile my black ass, but nooo, here I am going damn near ninety-six miles-an-hour and not a freakin' blue light in sight. Ain't this a bitch?" Nick seemed to be talking to himself.

Paisley exhaled loudly and braced herself in the speeding vehicle. She reached into her purse and pulled out her phone, quickly dialing 911.

"We're being chased on the interstate!" she yelled into the phone when she heard the operator's voice. "Someone is following us!"

"What is your location, ma'am?" The operator's nonchalance irritated Paisley.

"Um, I don't know . . . Where are we, Nick?"

"We're on route Thirteen! We got off at exit two-forty-one!" Nick answered.

Paisley repeated the information to the operator.

"East or west, ma'am?" the operator asked.

"Hell, I don't know!" Paisley replied. Her heart was pounding as she tried to see some type of landmark. Nick was driving so erratically that everything seemed to whiz past. Frustrated she took a guess. "East!"

"Okay, ma'am, I'm trying to get you some help, but I need to get some information from you. What type of vehicle are you in?"

"We're in a black Isuzu Trooper."

"And what type of car is the person following you driving?"

"I don't know. They're behind us with their high beams on. I can't tell," Paisley spat into the phone.

"Hold on!" Nick yelled, turning the steering wheel hard to the left. Tires screeched and flashbacks of the accident flashed in Paisley's head. She screamed, and she felt Nick's arm holding her back like her mother used to do when she slammed on brakes. Nick's truck spun around and slid, and Paisley heard the squeaking of tires from the vehicle behind them.

God, help us, she prayed silently. Then her eyes opened, and she saw they were now facing the vehicle as it turned to speed away.

"What the hell is going on?" Nick spoke slowly.

Paisley could hear approaching sirens, and in the distance she saw the flashing blue lights Nick was just asking for.

"Ma'am, ma'am!" the operator was yelling from Paisley's phone. "Are you all right?"

Paisley put the phone to her ear. "Yeah, we're fine. The police are coming."

It was as if she was having an out-of-body experience and watching everything happening in slow motion. Nick opened his door and got out, waving at the police cars that were now pulling up to them. Paisley unhooked her seatbelt and opened her door, but she couldn't move. She sat in the truck, stunned beyond belief.

"Paisley." She looked up and saw Nick reaching for her, a state trooper right behind him. "Can you walk?"

Paisley shrugged, not sure if she was stable enough mentally or physically to get out of the truck.

"Just stay right there, ma'am. The medics are on their way." The state trooper nodded reassuringly.

"No, I'm fine," Paisley finally said.

"Are you sure? Maybe we need to get you checked out," Nick suggested.

"I'm sure," she told him. She looked down and saw that her Slurpee was now a melted glob of brown ice, much like how she felt at that moment.

Nick

Now, I have to admit, I have fantasized about being alone with Paisley Lawrence. What African American male between the ages of fifteen and forty-five hasn't? But never in a million years would I have dreamt that we would be alone in my ride, and my fantasies never included us being in a high-speed car chase. That had to be the craziest thing I've ever experienced, and I don't think any of my boys would believe me if I told them, so I'm not even gonna bother. Hell, they hardly believe me when I tell them she comes into the coffee shop almost every day, and they think I'm lying when I try to tell them how cool and down-to-earth she truly is.

I ain't gonna front. I was kinda psyched when she ran up on me at Street Dreams and asked me for a ride. I ain't know what the hell was going on. Then, when she had me take her to the hotel and park around back, a brother was kinda hoping she was gonna turn and say that she had been secretly wanting me from the moment we met, and had been planning this night for weeks. Then, she would invite me upstairs where she would slowly undress me and ravish my body. Needless to say, that shit didn't happen. The only thing she turned to me and said (after removing her fronts which, for some reason, made her even sexier to me) was, "Stay here, and don't move. I will be back in a few." She was so adamant that in the back of my mind, I had to wonder if she was going to kill or rob someone and I would be charged as her accomplice. But I waited, and low and behold, she returns twenty minutes later, tears falling, and telling me to drive. So, I drive. For the life of me, I am trying to recall if maybe I saw someone waiting or lingering in the parking lot while I was sitting there.

I really didn't say much to Paisley during the ride after she got into my truck. I could tell she had a lot on her mind and I could relate. Sometimes, all you need is a nice long drive to process everything going on in your life. Hell, I have a lot going on myself. And there are times when you just need someone on the ride with you to keep you company. I'm glad I was able to be that person for Paisley Lawrence. It had to be one of the greatest rides of my life.

Chapter 18

"Where the hell are you now?" Fallon screamed through the phone. "I'm on my way home." Paisley tried to ignore the frustration in her friend's voice. "Are you at the police station?"

"No, we filed a report and we left already."

"Who the hell is 'we'? You know what, never mind. We'll meet you there!" Fallon hung up before Paisley had a chance to say anything else.

"Turn here," Paisley said to Nick as he approached her street.

"Wow." Nick whistled. "Wellington Estates. I'm impressed. All the houses out here are hella big. I figured you would have a pimped-out condo or a spot in one of the high-rises. You live in a mansion. You got servants, too? A maid, a butler?"

"You're not funny." She gave him a sarcastic look, directing him to her home.

"Seriously, what made you buy a crib out here?" he asked.

Paisley looked at the humongous homes that lined the streets as they drove by. Even in the darkness, you could still make out the perfectly manicured lawns. She smiled, and for the first time in her life, she confessed the reason she had bought the huge house. "Because I wanted to make my mother look stupid."

"Huh?" He looked at her strangely.

"My teenage years were kinda crazy," she sighed.

"Whose weren't?"

"No, I mean, my mother was really strict. She was an assistant principal at the high school I attended. I was an honor roll student, active in sports, dance, and church. But she didn't allow me any freedom whatsoever. I couldn't talk on the phone, have people come over to the house, no guy friends at all. And I was sixteen."

"Damn, Moms was strict." Nick nodded.

"My house was like a prison and she was the warden."

"Where was your dad?"

"He was there, and he constantly told my mother she was being ridiculous, but she wasn't trying to hear that. She reminded him that she was an educator who dealt with teenagers and their issues on a daily basis, whereas he was a steel worker with a high school diploma. Needless to say, he got tired of arguing with her and so did I. I dipped out during my junior year of high school." Paisley recalled packing up her clothes and things she thought she would need, including her bedroom furniture, one afternoon when no one was home and moving into the home of one of her basketball teammates. Her mother quickly came looking for her and threatened to have the girl's mother arrested for not only allowing Paisley to stay there, but because Paisley had moved her bedroom set into the woman's home, she threatened to file a theft report as well.

"Damn, I bet your mother was even harder on you when you came back home." Nick laughed. "She probably ain't even let you sleep back in your own bed for a minute."

"I never went back home."

"Huh?"

"I took the furniture back, but I didn't go. I dropped out of school and kept moving. There was no way I could live there again."

"Where did you live?"

"With boyfriends, mostly. I was young and cute," she laughed. "I lied about my age and I learned how to tend bar. Got a job at a strip club, Diesel came in one night and decided I was the next big music video star, and the rest is history," she told him, purposely leaving out the part where she met and fell in love with Warren Cobb along the way.

"So, how does buying the house make your mother look stupid?"

"When I ran away from home and dropped out of school, my mother said that I would never be anything; that I would never achieve anything. She expected me to come crawling back, begging her for a handout. It pushed me to be the best, to work harder, and to make it. I only did the video vixen thing to put myself through school; it isn't exactly what I strived to be in life. But I did get a little satisfaction knowing that every time my mother saw me on that TV screen, scantily dressed in a bikini, grinding on a guy, she would cringe. And this is the house she said I would never be able to afford. When I saw it, I knew that I was going to decorate it perfectly, and I was going to have a fabulous housewarming and invite her, so that when she pulled into my driveway—which is the third one on the right, by the way—she would have the stupidest look on her face and I would have, as they say, arrived."

Nick slowed down and pulled into the circular driveway. "Home sweet home."

"Yes, indeed." Paisley nodded.

"You need me to help you inside?" Nick asked.

"I think I got it," Paisley said, opening her door. Her back was already stiffening and she grimaced in pain.

Paisley's front door quickly opened and Fallon, Landon, and Chester rushed toward her. The evil look Landon gave her did not go unnoticed.

"Oh my God! Paisley, what the hell happened?" Fallon called out. "Are you all right?"

"I'm a little achy, but I'm fine," Paisley told her.

"Let me carry you inside." Nick went to pick Paisley up but Landon stopped him.

"I got her." Landon put his arm around her waist and lifted her off the ground. Nick, Chester, and Fallon followed him as he carried Paisley inside and laid her on the sofa.

"I'm gonna call Dr. Singleton," Fallon said. "You probably need to get checked out."

"I'm fine," Paisley told her. "I just need a hot bath and to stretch my back out before it tightens."

"I know you from somewhere." Chester peered at Nick.

"Aren't you the dude from the Java's?" Landon frowned.

"Yeah, Nick," Nick answered.

"How the hell did you end up with the guy from the Java's?" Fallon asked.

"He gave me a ride home from the club," Paisley told her.

"But you didn't come home, Paisley. Your house is twenty minutes from the club. You left there damn near three hours ago and this high-speed chase took place on the opposite side of town, nowhere near here. You didn't go straight home when you left." Landon stared at her, waiting for her answer.

"We rode around for a while, listening to jazz," Nick offered. "It seemed to relax her after all the heat and excitement of the club."

"Yeah, right," Landon said sarcastically.

"What's your problem?" Nick questioned.

"He's pissed." Chester glared at Paisley. "And so am I. We all are, but I'll address that issue another time."

"I didn't think it would be that big of a deal." Paisley's jaw tightened. "I'm sorry."

"You obviously didn't think at all," Landon answered. "Well, I take that back, you probably did think, but you only thought of yourself. You didn't think about your family or friends who may have been worried. You also didn't think about putting anyone else in danger, or you wouldn't have involved this young man."

Landon's words both stunned and stung Paisley. She knew what he was saying was right, but she didn't appreciate his chastising her in front of everyone. She looked over to Chester for some support, but when her eyes met his, she could see that he agreed with Landon.

"I wasn't feeling well and I needed to leave. It was crowded and I just got overwhelmed. I ran into Nick, and he offered to give me a ride home," Paisley lied. "Everyone was having a great time and I didn't want to be a burden, so I left."

"But do you see the predicament you put us in when you disappeared? You're not even thinking rationally, Paisley. Do you know how worried we were about you?"

"I know." Paisley began to feel worse and worse about her impulsive decision to leave the club to go see Warren. "I just didn't want to interrupt anyone's good time."

"Well, guess what, Paisley? You did. You messed up everybody's good time."

"I'm sorry, really, Fallon," Paisley started.

"That's some straight bullshit and you know it!"

It was the first time Paisley had heard Landon curse and it took her by surprise.

"Yeah, that's what I said, bullshit! You're not sorry, you're selfish, that's what you are. I don't know why you pulled this little disappearing act tonight, and I really don't care. What I do know is that you have no regard for your life or mine and I'm tired of your little games. I'm not one of your little flunkies, believe it or not. My purpose for being here is to keep you safe. If something worse had happened to you tonight, my ass would've been on the line. How do you think I felt when you were missing and everyone was looking at me? No one cared about the fact that I had just kept Bobby's drunk ass from yoking Seymone up like he had lost his mind. Not to mention I did it without beating the hell out of him, which is really what I wanted to do, but I didn't. All that was irrelevant once we realized that you were missing and no one could get in contact with you; all that mattered to everyone at that point was that you were my responsibility, and I didn't know where you were. It was all *my* fault. And you know what, they were right. Your safety and well being *are* the only things I should've been concerned with. I will be the first one to admit that I looked like a total asshole, but believe me, it won't happen again. I promise." With that said, and everyone staring, Landon walked out of the house, slamming the front door behind him.

"What is he talking about? Where is Sey-mone?"

"She went with Bobby to the hospital," Fallon told her.

"Hospital? For what?" Paisley was confused.

"Well, I guess you dipped out before the fireworks erupted. Your personal security guard knocked Bobby the hell out," Fallon said matter-of-factly.

"You're lying." Paisley's eyes widened.

"No, I'm not. Things got really ugly and the press was front and center. Took a minute, but things calmed down and then we realized that you were nowhere to be found. That started a whole other scene . . ."

Paisley began to realize that running off to see Warren wasn't worth the chaos that she'd caused. The house phone began ringing and Paisley grabbed it, thinking that it was Seymone or Diesel.

"Hello," she said.

"You're playing a dangerous game and you betta stop before someone gets hurt!"

A chill ran down Paisley's spine and her heart began racing. "What are you talking about? Who is this?"

"Let's call it a friendly warning. I hate women like you, you and your little damsel-in-distress act, putting people's lives in danger just for kicks. Well, you better get ready," the voice said. "Game over!"

Kenya

The time has come for me to finally put my foot down. It's as simple as this: Landon has to quit. There's no reason for him to be working for this chick and there's no way I'm gonna allow this nonsense to continue, especially after last night. I've put up with it for this long and I'm not dealing with it anymore. It's bad enough that he's sleeping at her house, following her around looking more like a sick puppy than a body-guard in the tabloid pictures. And I'm beginning to think that this is more of an opportunity for him to hobnob with the ghetto celebs than providing the supposed protection that she needs. Why does he need to be around her twenty, four, seven? So she can feel special? She's a video ho for God's sake, not Condoleeza freakin' Rice. I can't believe Landon's dumb self doesn't see that this is all part of her little stunt. Well, it's about to stop. This whole ordeal regarding Paisley Lawrence has been nothing but a distraction from what we need to be doing. We have a wedding to plan, a house to buy, and a future to prepare for.

Landon is out playing rent-a-cop for a high-class whore; he needs to be getting a real job. I mean, it's ridiculous for a man his age to be working as someone's "personal security" anyway. Working for Warren Cobb is one thing. I mean, after all, not only is he world-famous, but he's a man of God. But this chick is a straight-up nobody. I'm sure they could easily hire one of the young thugs who worship the magazine covers she graces to walk beside her into a nightclub and block the one or two photographers that are trying to take her picture. Landon needs to man up and realize that he needs to get it together. Paisley Lawrence has no regard for her own safety or privacy, while he's trying to protect her. How can you save someone who doesn't want to be saved? He needs an eye opener and he's about to get one. That's for sure.

"Kenya, what are you doing here?"

Kenya was doubly surprised. One, she was expecting a maid or butler to answer the door, not Landon. And two, she thought he would be a little more happy to see her. He looked as if he had been up all night and his face was bruised.

"Well, that's not the reaction I expected," Kenya commented as she reached out to touch his face. "What happened to you? Did you get into a fight?"

Landon grabbed her wrist and pushed her away. "I'm fine. What are you doing here?"

"I came to see you," she told him.

"Why? What was so important that you had to drive all the way over here without calling first?" Landon asked.

"Why should I have to call, Landon? Is there some reason I can't come by to check on you? Are you doing something that you don't want me to see you doing?" Kenya folded her arms and stood back, waiting for Landon to answer.

He closed his eyes and rubbed his temples. "Yeah, Kenya, it's called working. I don't come popping up at the high school checking up on you, do I?"

"I don't work as a live-in bodyguard for a famous whore who's known for trying to take what isn't hers," Kenya snapped at him.

"Don't do that," Landon warned. "Don't start tripping. I'm not even in the mood right now."

"Listen, Landon," Kenya's voice softened, "you can't keep doing this. It's stressing you out and it's affecting on our relationship. Can't you see that? You're staying out all night, hanging with these demonic people. That's not you. You left that lifestyle a long time ago. You're better than this and you know it."

"I can handle this, Kenya, and you know that. I've been doing this long enough to know what I'm doing."

"You're right, you've been doing this long enough. Maybe it's time . . ."

Kenya was interrupted by a black Range Rover pulling into the driveway. The passenger door opened and a beautiful woman hopped out, dressed in a form-fitting black jumpsuit and the baddest black stiletto heels Kenya had ever seen. She was draped in diamonds, and although it wasn't even nine in the morning, her makeup and hair were flawless. She was so stunning that Kenya had to wonder if she woke up looking that damn perfect. *There's no way, she probably has to get up at like four in the morning to get herself together.* The woman was thick, but she was shapely in all the right places, and Kenya watched the long, perfect strides along the driveway as she walked toward them. She noticed that the man driving the truck was also staring at the woman, and so was Landon. Kenya was suddenly conscious of her own attire consisting of a pair of Old Navy jeans and a baby tee; she ran her fingers through her short but neat bob. Seconds later, the truck backed out the driveway and pulled off.

"Good morning." The woman smiled, showing off her perfect teeth and deeply set dimples.

There was something inviting and genuine about her, causing Kenya to feel threatened because not only was she beautiful, she was probably a nice person, something Kenya wasn't.

"Good morning, Seymone," Landon said. "This is Kenya."

"Nice to meet you, Kenya. That's a beautiful name," Seymone said.

"Thanks," Kenya said in an overly nice tone, giving her a half smile.

"Landon, thanks again for last night," Seymone told him.

"No need to thank me," he said, "it's all good."

"Is Paisley up yet?" Seymone paused before going inside the house.

"I think I heard her fumbling around upstairs." Landon nodded. "You okay?"

"I'm fine," Seymone said. "Nice to meet you."

"Well, I can see why you're so dedicated to your job here, Landon," Kenya said when the door closed behind Seymone. "Beautiful women coming in and out of the house all the time."

"You're not funny," Landon said. "She lives here."

Kenya frowned. "What do you mean she lives here? I thought the whole purpose of your being here was because Paisley lived alone and her life was in so much danger, Landon?"

"Seymone is just staying here temporarily. And I'm here because it's my job. Paisley is in danger. Why don't you believe that? Someone just tried to run her off the road last night."

"That's a damn lie!" Kenya hissed. "Paisley snuck her ass out of the club and went to be with Warren Cobb. They got a suite on the top floor. I didn't want to believe it myself, Landon, but it's true."

"How do you know this? Where is this info coming from?" Landon demanded.

"I saw it with my own eyes," Kenya said smugly. She watched as frowns formed across Landon's forehead and his anger began to rise. It was just the reaction she wanted, and she knew that he would be coming home to her tonight.

Chapter 19

"Paisley, we need to talk," Seymone announced as she walked into Paisley's room.

Paisley was sitting in the middle of her bed, staring at the crumpled photo she had gotten from Warren. She stared at it, wondering if someone had indeed sold it to Bad Babes. She tried to decide whether or not to tell Fallon.

"You leaving?" Paisley murmured, still staring at the picture.

"What's wrong?" Seymone walked over and sat beside her. "Paisley? Why are you crying?"

"Nothing, I'm good. What's up?" Paisley wiped the tears from her face. "How's Bobby?"

"He's pissed, but he'll be all right," Seymone told her.

"What do you wanna talk to me about?"

Moments later, Landon was standing in Paisley's doorway.

"Landon, what's wrong?" Seymone asked.

Paisley looked up and saw the anger in his eyes. "What?"

"Where did you go last night, Paisley?" he growled.

"I told you, I was riding with Nick."

"You really are a self-centered, conceited piece of work, you know that? You think my being here is some kind of joke? You're sitting there lying to my face, acting like you're some kind of victim. You think that's cute?"

"What's going on?" Seymone asked.

"Your life is in danger, huh, Paisley? Someone is out to get you, huh? Someone is stalking you? This whole thing has been a game between you and that lowlife, Warren. To hell with both of you, I'm outta here!"

"What the hell is that all about, Paisley? What was he talking about?"

Paisley stared out of her window and saw that there was a woman parked outside of her house. She frowned as she saw the woman looking up at her, and their eyes met. The woman smiled wickedly and Paisley realized it was the same woman who had tried to run her and Nick off the road.

Paisley turned and looked at Seymone. The reality of everything that was happening seemed to overwhelm her. *Warren, leaving the club, the hotel, the pictures, the woman*. It was all too much.

"I don't even want to know," Seymone told her. "This entire time, all I've asked you to be was honest with me, Paisley. I've been right here with you, put my life on hold to be by your side as your friend. More like a sister, because you know you're the only family I have, to be honest."

"Seymone, I swear, it's not like it seems," Paisley cried, walking over to her best friend.

"It's never what it seems when it comes to you. It's all about who you want, what you want, and when you want it." Seymone shook her head. A car horn blared and Seymone's cell phone rang at the same time. She looked at it and headed for the door.

"You're leaving me, Seymone? By myself?" Paisley sniffed.

Seymone didn't say a word as she walked out of Paisley's room. Paisley listened until she heard the front door slam. She flung herself across the bed and cried. Throwing the crumpled picture she still held on the floor, she knew that she was indeed all alone, and something told her things were about to get worse.

"Paisley, wake up!"

Paisley's eyes fluttered open and she blinked to focus. Chester was standing beside her bed, his arms folded. She could tell by the wrinkles in his forehead that he was angry. She closed her eyes again.

"Get up, now!" His voice got louder.

"What do you want, Chester?"

"I want you to get up and tell me what the hell is going on," Chester replied.

"I'm sleeping, that's what's going on," she told him. "I'm tired."

"I don't care. Hell, I'm tired too. I would love to be home in my three-thousand-dollar Ethan Allen California king bed with my eight-hundred-dollar duvet where I was happily curled up after leaving here this morning at four-thirty. But, I can't, no, I can't. Why not? Because *your* best friend is calling me at nine this morning, in tears, mind you, telling me how someone needs to come and be here with you, because both she and your personal security guard left after finding out that you caused all that damn drama in the club because you wanted to sneak off and be with Warren Cobb!" Chester said in one breath.

Paisley swallowed hard. "I'm sorry. I don't know . . . Landon . . . This woman . . . Last night—"

"Yeah, let's talk about last night," Chester said. "What the hell happened? Did you really leave the club to go and be with him, Paisley?"

Paisley simply nodded. *Just tell the truth. Get it over with. It's time.* She sat up and wiped her face, preparing to open up to her cousin. Just as she was about to speak, the doorbell rang.

"I'll get it." Chester shook his head.

Paisley walked into the bathroom and washed her face. She looked at her reflection in the mirror and for a moment, she didn't recognize herself. *What are you doing, Paisley? Why are you putting your family and friends through all this drama? For Warren?*

Chester returned a few moments later, wearing a strange look on her face. "Paisley."

"Who is it? What's wrong?" Paisley asked.

"It's Bishop Arnold," he told her. "He wants to talk to you."

Paisley frowned. "I don't want to talk to him. For what?"

"I don't know." Chester shrugged.

"I don't have anything to talk to him about," Paisley said.

"He's a *bishop,* Paisley. What do you want me to do, tell him no?" Chester asked.

"Tell him I'm not home. Tell him I'm asleep." Paisley shrugged.

"I'm not lying to a man of *God!* Are you crazy?" Chester shook his head. "I'm gonna be right here with you. I will be a witness to anything that is said."

Paisley stared at her cousin, and then said, "Fine."

As she walked down the steps, she became nervous. *Whatever this is, it can't be good.*

"Ms. Lawrence, I'm Bishop Julian Arnold. This is my armor bearer, Neil." He gestured toward the man with him. "How are you?"

"I'm fine, thank you," Paisley replied.

"I won't take up too much of your time. I just wanted to stop by and see and talk to you for a few minutes."

"About?" Paisley asked, wanting to get to the bottom of his being there.

The bishop smiled at her. He was a handsome man, in his mid-sixties. He was a bit taller than Paisley thought he would be, with a nice build. Dressed in a gray pinstriped suit and yellow tie, he looked very much like the prestigious man he was on television. Paisley couldn't help but feel a bit intimidated by his presence.

"About the unfortunate situation you and the leader of my music ministry are involved in," he said.

"The accident?" Paisley stared at him. "Is that what you're referring to?"

"Yes, the accident," the Bishop answered, "among other things."

"What other things are you referring to, Bishop Arnold," Paisley asked him.

"It's my understanding that you and Warren ran into each other last night at the Marriott."

Paisley slowly nodded. "We did."

"Ms. Lawrence, can you explain the nature of your friendship with Warren?"

Paisley glanced over at Chester, who was beginning to look uncomfortable, and cleared her throat. "I'm not trying to be funny, Bishop. But I believe these are questions you should be asking Warren."

"I did ask him," the Bishop told her. "As a matter of fact, I just had a conversation with him regarding you."

Paisley was surprised to hear that. "Then why are you questioning me, Bishop?"

"Let me be honest with you, Ms. Lawrence, there are really only two reasons I'm questioning you. The first is that I love my niece, Kollette, very much, and I refuse to see her hurt by a man who wouldn't be anything if it weren't for her. The second is that I love my ministry very much, and I refuse to have its reputation tarnished by anyone, be it the Prince of Praise or whomever he's chosen to become involved with. I've worked too hard and achieved too much. So, you take this any way you wish."

"Oh, really?" Paisley looked the bishop in the eye. "Well, Bishop Arnold, I appreciate your concern regarding the situation, but I feel the need to tell you that as far as your niece is concerned, I don't have anything to do with her insecurities. She's Mrs. Warren Cobb, and she needs to realize that fact herself, instead of trying to prove to everyone that she is. Warren Cobb has what he has and is a successful musician because of God's favor, not because of you or Kollette. I would think you, of all people, would realize that. And regarding your ministry, I have nothing but the utmost respect for it and what you're doing. That's why I've been a faithful tither and supporter for the past four years. Check your books."

The tension between them was so thick that Paisley thought they were about to square off and start taking blows at each other.

"I see," the bishop said. He continued to stare at her as if he was trying to detect some gesture of deception from her.

"I don't have a need to lie to you, Bishop Arnold. I have too much respect for you as a man of God to lie to your face," Paisley told him. "Warren and I are just friends, nothing more, nothing less. I have nothing to hide regarding our relationship. He is the one who feels the need to be dishonest with you, not me."

"I appreciate your honesty, if that's what it truly is." The bishop nodded.

"That's what it is," Paisley replied.

"Bishop, I can see you to the door." Chester's voice finally broke the silence.

"Well, thank you for your time." The bishop extended his hand and Paisley shook it.

"Have a blessed day." She smiled at him.

As they were leaving, Neil, who had remained quiet the entire time she and the bishop were talking, stared back at her.

"Do I know you?" Paisley frowned at him. He didn't respond as he followed the bishop out of her front door.

Paisley inhaled deeply, her heart pounding in her chest as the aroma of the stale cologne filled her nostrils. It was a scent she had become familiar with, causing chills to form on her arms. It was the same scent she smelled every time the stalker had been in her house. Flustered, Paisley rushed over to the window just in time to see the two men climb into a black Jaguar.

Chapter 20

"I'm not crazy." Paisley began pacing back and forth. "No one said you're crazy," Chester replied. "You need to calm down."

"How the hell can I calm down? Look at all the stuff this man had done to me! He's been in my house, stood over me while I was asleep, and invaded my privacy! It's him, Chester, I know it is! It's the same damn Jaguar that's been following me!"

"Okay, I'm not saying it's not him, Paisley. I'm just saying we have to be a little rational and think all this through."

"I've thought it through." Paisley snatched the phone off the nearby coffee table. "I'm calling the police and I'm having him picked up."

"Put the phone down," Chester told her. "What do you think the police are gonna say when you call them and tell them that Bishop Julian Arnold has been stalking you? Do you have any solid proof of it?"

"I know that scent, Chester! Don't you smell it? It's the same one that was in my hospital room, in my bedroom. Every time he's been near me, I could smell it! It's the same scent that's on the notes he leaves." Paisley was becoming frustrated. She knew it had to be Bishop Arnold.

"It's just cologne, Paisley, that's it." Chester sniffed the air. "Cheap cologne, no doubt, but a million men wear it."

"Okay, explain this then, how the hell did he know where I lived? How did he get my address?" Paisley asked.

"I don't know. He's a bishop. He probably has access to a whole lot of information. His church has what, a billion members. I'm sure he called someone who knows someone that works somewhere that has access to classified information and they gave it to him," Chester told her.

Feeling hopeless, Paisley said, "You're right, the police are probably on the board of deacons."

"I'm not saying that. I'm just saying that we are gonna have to come up with something a little more concrete than his popping up at your house and wearing the same cologne that crazy man does."

"So, now what?" Paisley asked, putting the phone back down on the table and flopping back on the sofa.

"If he comes back—"

"If? What's stopping him from coming back? Landon?" Paisley faked a laugh. "Hell, Landon was hired by the Ministry, remember? He's probably been reporting my whereabouts to the bishop this entire time. God, please help me. You said in your Word that anything done in the dark will come to light!"

"That ain't nowhere in the Bible, Paisley. Oh my gosh, you may be a tithing member of the Bishop's church, but you certainly don't attend." Chester shook his head at her.

"Shut up," Paisley told him. "God knows my heart and you can't critique someone while they're praying!"

Again, the doorbell rang, causing Paisley to jump. She looked over at Chester. "He's back. He's coming back to kill me."

"Shut up, Paisley," Chester told her. He walked over and looked out the window. "It's the police."

"The police?" Paisley asked. "They caught him. I knew God wouldn't fail me."

"Whatever." Chester went and opened the door. "Can I help you?"

"We're looking for Paisley Lawrence," the officer said.

"Right this way." Chester lead them into the living room. Paisley immediately recognized Officers Bell and Jenson, and she was relieved.

"Thank God you're here. I know who my stalker is. I figured it out," she told them. "He was just here in my living room. I was just about to call you. Wait, why are you here?"

"Ms. Lawrence, we're here to give you this." Officer Bell passed her a set of folded papers. "It's a restraining order."

"A restraining order?" Paisley and Chester spoke at the same time.

"Yes, ma'am." Officer Jenson nodded.

"From who?" Chester asked.

Paisley scanned the papers and her mouth fell open. She couldn't believe she was reading correctly, and she felt her anger rising. "That bitch!"

Chester reached over and took the papers from her. Soon, he wore the same shocked look as his cousin. "How can she take a restraining order out?"

"Well, it's for both of them. Mr. and Mrs. Cobb," Officer Bell sighed.

"And Warren let her?" Paisley asked, becoming upset because she knew Warren wouldn't stand for Kollette's craziness. "How? Why?"

"Have you made any type of threats against them? In person or by phone?" Officer Jenson asked.

"No, I haven't." Paisley shook her head. "This is crazy! I'm the one being stalked!"

"We know, Ms. Lawrence. And believe me, we pointed that out when we were told to serve you," Officer Bell told her. "I'm actually stunned because in this state, usually a restraining order isn't even issued without an arrest warrant being issued. I don't understand it either."

"This is some straight bull," Chester said.

"Listen, just stay as far away from both of them as possible. Don't contact either one of them in any fashion," Officer Jenson suggested. "This is probably just her way of getting back at you. You know how the jealous wife can be."

Paisley glared at Officer Jenson, but before she could say what she was thinking, Officer Bell asked, "Now, what were you talking about when we first got here? You believe you know who your stalker is?"

Paisley nodded. "Yes, I do."

"She suspects," Chester corrected her. "She doesn't know."

"I do know." Paisley looked Officer Bell in the eye. She knew that the female officer liked her and felt confident that she would believe her. "Remember you told me to remember the little things, even things that seem insignificant can be the biggest clues?"

"Yeah," Officer Bell said. "Do you remember something?"

"His scent. The smell each time he was near me. That lingering muskiness," Paisley told her. "Today, Bishop Arnold just shows up at my home to talk to me. He's never been here before and I've never met him until today. And when he left, I could smell it. It's him."

Officer Jenson looked at her like she was telling a joke, and Chester gave her a look that clearly read, *I told you so!*

"That's it?" Officer Jenson asked.

"Yes." Paisley nodded. "You don't think it's strange that all of a sudden this man I don't even know shows up at my house?"

"Well, considering his niece just took out a restraining order against you and had you served at your address, he probably got the address from her."

"Whatever," Paisley snapped at him, then turned to Officer Bell. "You have to believe me. I know it's him. I could feel it. I want him arrested."

"I'm not saying I don't believe you, Paisley. But we can't go and arrest someone without having a little more concrete evidence that he's done what you're accusing him of," Officer Bell told her.

"Oh, I get it. The bishop's niece can come to the station and make up lies about me stalking her and her husband and take out a restraining order, but there's nothing I can do about my being stalked because I'm a whore, right?" Paisley could feel the tears stinging her eyes.

"That's not what I'm saying at all," Officer Bell replied. "Let me check into this and I promise I'll let you know what I find. I told you we're gonna catch him, whether it's the bishop or not."

"In the meantime, stay away from the Cobbs," Officer Jenson reminded her.

"I'll make sure she does," Chester assured him.

"You have my number," Officer Bell told her. "Call me if you remember anything else. Anything."

"Thanks," Paisley mumbled. *I need a damn drink,* she thought, craving the taste of Jack and Coke from Warren's mouth.

Emma Jean

"Good evening. I'm your host, Leslie Dickey and tonight on Gospel Central we have with us the Prince of Praise, the unconquerable Warren Cobb, and his wife, Kollette. Welcome, we are so happy to have you here with us," the reporter said. The sound of Warren Cobb's name caused

Emma Jean to look up from her sudoku puzzle. Warren Cobb was dressed in a crisp white shirt, jeans, and a brown blazer, looking just as handsome as ever, although a bit uncomfortable. *He is fine. I can see why Paisley was with him.* It was the first time Emma Jean had seen his wife, who was sitting next to him, her arm possessively wrapped around his. *She looks nothing like I pictured her to look like. I would have never put the two of them together.* She reached for the remote, not interested in anything he or his wife had to say, but her curiosity got the best of her, and she continued to watch.

"It's so nice to be here," Kollette gushed, smiling a little too hard.

"Warren, congratulations on your accomplishments this year: an American Music Award, two Grammys, three Stellar Awards, three Essence Awards, three from the NAACP. Other than an Oscar and an Emmy, is there anything you didn't win this year?" The pretty brown TV host's voice was rich and her smile was warm. Her natural hair was worn neatly in small twists. Emma Jean could see why she was on television; there was something inviting about her, like you wanted to be her friend. It would have made more sense for her to be married to Warren Cobb, rather than the unattractive woman beside him.

Warren laughed, "What can I say, Leslie, it's been a good year. God is good and I thank Him continually for His favor."

"I know that's right," Leslie said, "but there have been some hardships for you the past few months. You were seriously injured in a car accident and were in a coma for some days."

"Yes, he was, Leslie," Kollette spoke before Warren could respond. "It was touch and go, girl. My husband almost died!"

"It was a bit of a setback." Warren tried to ease his arm from her grasp, but Kollette held on. "But, you know, I believe that setbacks are just setups for even greater comebacks, Leslie, and after coming back from being in a coma, there's no telling what God has in store."

"I know that's right, Warren. Maybe even that Oscar or Emmy that's missing off your shelf," Leslie laughed. "Are you going back in the studio soon?"

"Most definitely. The accident has certainly caused me to put a lot of things into perspective that will be reflected on the new album," Warren told her.

"This near-death experience has brought Warren and me closer as husband and wife. We have a newfound appreciation for each other, and there are some people out there who truly don't want to see us happy, mainly Paisley Lawrence, who caused the accident. The devil is always so busy. Just this morning, we had to file a restraining order against her," Kollette announced. The look on Warren's face was horrific and even the host was stunned.

"Oh my," Leslie said. "That was the young woman who was in the car with you during the accident, right?"

"Yes, that's her!" Kollette said. "Since this horrible incident occurred, she continues to harass my husband. She calls, sends text messages, Paisley Lawrence is stalking my husband. And now, in retaliation, she's posting these pictures of her and my husband on her Web site. Just disrespectful."

Emma Jean watched in devastation as photos of her daughter's blurred, partially nude body posed with Warren Cobb appeared on the television screen. *She's lying*, Emma Jean instinctively thought, *Paisley wouldn't do anything so desperate. That's not even her style.* It was as if some mysterious maternal sense kicked in and assured her that Paisley hadn't done any of the things this woman was saying that she did.

"I'm so sorry you all have to go through all of this," Leslie said sympathetically.

"Warren and I would just like to ask the fans to keep us in prayer because on top of his still going through all of this, we have another setback in our lives." Kollette's eyes welled up with tears and she spoke directly into the camera. "I've been diagnosed with cancer."

"Oh my." Leslie reached over and grabbed Kollette's hand. She began tearing up as well. "Kollette, I had no idea."

"This is just such a difficult time for my husband and our family. My uncle, Bishop Julian Arnold, has been our spiritual rock and we are claiming victory over all of this," Kollette said.

Unable to take any more, Emma Jean turned the television off. At that moment, her husband, Gordon, walked into their bedroom.

"You turned the TV off, EJ? Umph, baby, I wasn't expecting *it*, not on a Sunday night." He began taking his shirt off and smiling.

"Gordon, leave your shirt on," she told him.

Ignoring his own slight disappointment and noticing the worried look on his wife's face, he asked, "What's wrong?"

Emma Jean shook her head. "Warren Cobb and his wife were just on television giving an interview. They said that Paisley is stalking him and they've taken out a restraining order on her. And now there's some picture of Warren and Paisley from some magazine."

"Stalking? Paisley wouldn't do anything like that," he said, sitting beside his wife.

"I know she wouldn't. Paisley's too classy to be that desperate," Emma Jean told him. "I'm not worried about that."

"What are you worried about then, EJ?"

"The repercussions this is gonna have and the fallout this is going to cause. This woman just announced to the world that not only has our daughter been stalking her husband, but also that she has cancer. It's not gonna be pretty and I wonder if Paisley is gonna be able to handle all of this, Gordon."

"You know Paisley's a strong woman, Emma Jean. She's smart, beautiful, and talented, just like her mother. We raised her that way." He put his arm around her.

We raised her that way. If we did such a great job raising her, then why did she leave when she was seventeen? If we were such great parents, then why did our daughter become a video vixen rather than a pediatrician or a teacher? If I'm such a great mother, then why, when my friends talk about their daughters getting married and having kids, do I feel like I will never be given that opportunity? I know that I was hard on Paisley growing up. But it was as if all anyone wanted to talk about was how pretty or beautiful she was, and I didn't want her to grow up thinking that because she had been blessed with good looks, she was entitled to any more than anyone else. The beautiful people are what I call them. My sister and her son, Chester, were beautiful people. And so was Paisley, but I wanted her to value hard work and education. I wanted her to see that life wasn't easy. So I critiqued and criticized, the same way my mother did me, so that when life became hard, she would know how to succeed in the face of adversity. And for a while, it worked. Paisley excelled academically, athletically, and socially. And just when I began seeing the fruits of my labor, I came home to find that Paisley and her bedroom set were gone. Our relationship had worsened over the years, eventually turning into forced conversations lasting a few minutes when Paisley called to talk to Gordon. It was as if she didn't know what to say. Paisley has become this person that I no longer know. But as much as I tried to give up, that maternal instinct wouldn't leave. I still hold a longing and love for my daughter, and want to be there for her, I just don't know how. Even after the accident, Paisley pushed me away.

"I don't know how she's gonna handle this, Gordon." She leaned into her husband's strong body. She envied that he was still able to hold on to his relationship with Paisley after all this time.

"Why don't you call her and ask?" he suggested.

Emma Jean looked into her husband's eyes. *He's always such an optimist.* It was as if he still believed that they were a happy family. She smiled and said, "The TV's off. Why do you still have your shirt on?"

"Like I always said, like mother, like daughter," Gordon teased.

Chapter 21

"This is bad, really bad," Fallon said, sitting in Paisley's office. She flipped through the stack of newspapers she'd picked up on her way to the studio. News of Warren and Paisley had made several of them and the Internet was swarming with the picture and it wasn't even eight in the morning. Fallon had picked her up before dawn from Chester's house, where she had spent the night. Knowing the press would be hot on their heels, they decided to get an early start.

"I know, it can't get any worse," Paisley agreed. She had been in a state of shock from the moment she had gotten the call telling her to turn to the weekly gospel show.

"Jamison Grossman is on his way over here." Fallon referred to her friend, who had been their longtime attorney.

"What are we gonna do?" Paisley asked. "This is unbelievable."

"We're gonna come up with a game plan, for starters."

Paisley and Fallon both looked up to see Ebonie Monroe, Warren's publicist, standing in the doorway.

"What the hell are you doing here?" Paisley stood up. "You need to get the hell out right now!"

"Wait, Paisley. I swear, I didn't have anything to do with any of this. I didn't even have a clue," Ebonie told her.

"How did you even get in here?" Paisley asked, knowing that she locked all the doors after they came in.

"Some guy with an orange afro," Ebonie told them.

I thought Chester was lying when he said he would be here in a few minutes.

"What do you want? Why are you here?" Fallon demanded. "Shouldn't you be with your client scheduling more interviews between his wife's chemo?"

"I no longer work for Warren, his wife fired me," Ebonie told them.

"What?" Fallon asked, looking at her suspiciously.

"Kollette fired me. She fired me Saturday night, before any of this took place."

"Why? What did you do?" Paisley sat back down in her chair. "I guess you can come in and have a seat."

Ebonie walked into the office, briefcase in hand, neatly dressed in a brown and white silk top, pair of brown pants, and matching heels. She took a seat beside Fallon and told them, "She called me late Saturday night demanding that I meet her at the office to help her 'strategize.' I got out of bed and went to meet her and she was livid; going on and on about how you keep disrespecting her and her marriage and she was going to make you pay. She had come up with some of the craziest schemes I have ever heard. When I refused to go along with them, she fired me."

"What did Warren have to say about her firing you?" Fallon asked. "Isn't he the one you work for?"

"Well, technically, I work for the Ministry. I was just assigned to Warren. And when it comes to Kollette, Julian Arnold does whatever she tells him to do. If she wanted to, she could have Warren fired!" Ebonie told them.

"That's crazy." Paisley shook her head. "Poor Warren."

"You shouldn't feel bad for Warren, Paisley." Ebonie sighed. "He knows that he is the money-maker for the Ministry and he could have a lot more control if he wanted to. This situation over the past few months has made me realize that Warren Cobb doesn't have backbone."

"I've been saying that for a while now," Fallon agreed.

"Paisley, I know more than you think I know. I know that Warren knows you and has known you for some time. I know that most of the songs that he writes, he writes for you. I know that he was in love with you but through the years, you all have remained just friends. I know that he was drinking the night of the accident. And I know that he didn't have the balls to even stand up to his wife or anyone else and tell them that despite your career differences, you are his friend."

As Ebonie spoke, Paisley felt the burden she had been carrying for years begin to lighten. It was as if someone finally knew and understood what she had been going through and dealing with. Someone finally knew the truth and she didn't have to sell anyone out.

"Oh my God," Fallon said. "Paisley, is that true?"

Paisley nodded. "Yeah."

"I also know that you love him, Paisley. I understand why because I loved him too," Ebonie confessed.

"Were you . . . Did you," Paisley couldn't help asking.

Ebonie quickly said, "No, we were never together, not at all. I will admit that I was plotting for a while. Anyone who knows Warren knows that he really doesn't love his wife, so I thought I had a chance. I even tried a few times, and he rejected me. I thought it was because he was having an affair with someone else. But I couldn't figure out with whom and how. I made Warren's schedule and I knew his whereabouts at all times. So there was no way it was anyone visible."

"So, how did you find out about Paisley?" Fallon turned and asked.

"The accident," Ebonie sighed. "I figured something was up. And when I mentioned the problems Paisley was having with the constant paparazzi and the stalker, Warren was adamant about having Landon, who has been his personal security for the past two years, leave his side to be with you. Landon wasn't happy at all, but Warren insisted. I think knowing that Landon was there gave him a bit of relief. I realized then that there was more to you than he cared to share and I wasn't the only one." Ebonie sat back and crossed her legs.

Paisley stared at her suspiciously, wondering if she should trust this woman who, until a few hours ago, worked for the people who were attempting to slander her and make her life miserable.

"I assume you're talking about Kollette," Fallon commented.

"Yes, Kollette, and Bishop Arnold had his concerns as well," Ebonie answered.

At the mention of the bishop's name, Paisley stood up. "I'll bet! That bastard probably had a lot to say about me."

"Here we go." Fallon shook her head.

Ebonie gave her a strange look. "Did I miss something?"

"Let's just say the bishop is at the top of Paisley's suspect list of possible stalkers," Fallon sighed.

"The bishop?" Ebonie asked. "Bishop Julian Arnold?"

"I know, you think that's ridiculous, right? Everyone does. No one thinks that he's capable of doing something like that, so that makes me crazy." Paisley began ruffling through a stack of papers on her desk. "Go ahead, say it."

"I'm not saying you're crazy," Ebonie told her. "I wouldn't put anything past anyone. One thing I've learned in this business is that people are capable of anything. Christian or not, people are human."

"You're right about that," Fallon said.

"I will say that stalking you is not something that Bishop Arnold is likely to do." Ebonie shrugged. "I just don't see that happening. What makes you think that it's him?"

A knock on the door stopped Paisley from answering Ebonie's question. They looked up to see Paisley's attorney, Jamison Grossman, standing in the doorway. Paisley couldn't help smiling when she saw the look on Ebonie's face. It was the same reaction most women had when they saw him. *Lust at first sight.* And rightly so. To say that Jamison, who they affectionately called 'Jimmy Jam,' was handsome, would be like saying Jill Scott could sing. It was a true understatement at least. Jimmy stood six foot tall and his well-built frame carried his two hundred ten pounds perfectly. His neatly trimmed beard and long eyelashes accented the smoothness of his dark chocolate skin. He was what Paisley considered the epitome of the perfect black man: attractive, smart, funny, well built, educated, successful, and charming. The kind of man who lit up a room when he walked in and commanded attention; women wanted him and men wanted to be him. But the gold band he wore on his left hand stopped Paisley, and a lot of others, from taking their lust at first sight any further.

"Good morning, ladies. Am I interrupting?" Jimmy asked.

Paisley walked around her desk and gave Jimmy a big hug. "Jimmy, I'm glad to see you!"

Fallon also didn't hesitate in getting up and hugging him. "Me too!"

"Now that's the kind of welcome I like to get from my favorite clients." Jimmy smiled.

"That's the kind of welcome you probably get from all your clients." Fallon playfully hit his shoulder.

"OK, well, you're the sexiest." He winked.

"That I definitely agree with." Paisley nodded.

"And who is this lovely young lady?" Jimmy gestured toward Ebonie.

Paisley shook her head at Ebonie, who was now blushing. "Guess what, Jimmy? This is Warren Cobb's publicist, Ebonie Monroe."

The smile that Jimmy wore quickly faded into a look of concern. "Warren Cobb's publicist."

"Ex-publicist," Ebonie corrected him as she stood up. "I was graciously fired Saturday night. Nice to meet you."

Jimmy shook Ebonie's extended hand. "Likewise. In my client's best interest, I do need to know your reason for being *here*."

"I don't really know." Ebonie shrugged as she sat back down. "I guess I'm here to help her."

"Help in what capacity?" Jimmy asked. "And don't get me wrong, I'm not trying to be facetious in any way. But you have to realize my skepticism. You're sitting here in Paisley's office offering to help when, up until forty-eight hours ago, you worked for the man who is publicly attacking her with malicious allegations."

"I understand, and that's why I am here. The reason I was fired was due to the fact that I refused to assist Warren's crazy wife, Kollette, with her plans to publicly humiliate Paisley," Ebonie said matter-of-factly.

Paisley looked at Fallon, who was looking at Jimmy. She cleared her throat and shook her head at her friend, and wondered if she had heard anything Ebonie had just said. "Ebonie, can you please excuse us for a minute?"

"Sure," Ebonie said.

Just as she was about to walk out of Paisley's office, Landon walked in.

"Ebonie, what are you doing here?" he asked.

"I could ask you the same question," Paisley quickly answered. "I thought you quit."

"I didn't say I quit, did I?" he replied, and then asked, "Where's Seymone?"

"You left," Paisley snapped, "and so did she!"

"And when I came back, you were gone. As a matter of fact, you didn't come home at all.

And when I tried to call you, you didn't answer." Landon walked closer to Paisley. "I shouldn't be surprised, though. I think we all are pretty used to your not answering your phone when you're too busy. We all learned that Saturday night."

Although Landon was right and she had ignored all of his calls and text messages, it didn't make her any less angry that he had left her house with no explanation. She really did think that he had quit, and not only was she afraid because that meant that she would be alone at home, but she was hurt because she thought he had honestly cared about her well-being. But, obviously not, because she and Killa had spent the night with Chester.

"What is that supposed to mean? I don't care . . ." Paisley began yelling. *How dare this fool come in here and try to clown me like this. I will go off up in here! I'm already one palm away from slapping someone and he just stepped up to volunteer!*

"Okay, why don't we all calm down," Fallon suggested.

"That's a good idea," Jimmy agreed. "Ebonie, go ahead and wait outside. Landon come on in."

Landon closed the door, and and Fallon introduced him to Jimmy as he took the seat Ebonie left vacant.

"All right, so what's going on with you? We got too many other issues to deal with right now than dealing with you and Paisley going back and forth," Fallon spoke.

"I'm not going back and forth." Paisley sat on the edge of her desk. "Landon left by choice and he's free to do so now. According to him, I don't even need security because Warren and I were just using him as part of some kind of game we were playing. Isn't that what you said, Landon? I don't even know why he's here now."

"Obviously he's here because he cares," Jimmy said, "and it doesn't matter why. The press is gonna be hounding you in the next few hours and his being here is probably a good thing."

There was a knock on the door and Seymone's head came peeking in. "Paisley?"

"Well, well, well, look who else—" Paisley started, but was interrupted.

"Don't," Fallon warned, giving Paisley an ugly look. She beckoned for Seymone to come in. "Hey, Seymone."

"Good morning," Seymone greeted them. "What's up, Jimmy?"

Jimmy didn't hesitate giving Seymone a big hug. "Man, you look good!"

"Whatever, Jimmy. I know I'm fat," Seymone laughed.

"Yeah, p-h-a-t!" Jimmy told her.

Paisley glanced over at Landon and saw a strange look on his face as he watched Seymone and Jimmy. He looked as if he wanted to stand up and come between them. *I know he's not jealous*, Paisley thought. *Why would he be jealous of Jimmy? Oh my God, he's feeling Seymone! He didn't come back here for me; he came back here for her!*

"Did you all know the photogs are out front already?" Seymone asked. "There were a couple snapping away when I was coming in."

"I didn't think you'd show, either," Paisley said.

"Anyway, I got a class to get ready for." Seymone glared. "Nice to see you again, Jimmy."

"I'll go make sure everything's secure," Landon hopped up and said, following Seymone out the door.

I'll bet, Paisley thought.

"So, what's the deal with Ms. Monroe?" Jimmy asked.

"I don't know." Fallon shrugged. "She seems sincere, I guess."

"Exactly what does she know? She mentioned Warren's wife planning something. What did she mean by that?" Jimmy sat down.

"Jimmy, you're asking us questions we really don't know the answer to." Paisley was becoming frustrated. "You should be asking Ebonie Monroe that."

"You're right, and I'll do just that. Let me ask you something that I'm sure you know the answer to. The picture of you and Warren, is it real?"

"Yeah," Paisley admitted, "but it's so old. It's from like ninety-seven."

"Where did this picture come from?" Fallon asked her.

"I don't know." Paisley shrugged. "I swear."

"Did Warren have a copy?" Jimmy asked.

Paisley tried to remember if he did. "I don't know. But even if he does, why would he do this? It's more harmful to him than it is me."

Fallon's and Jimmy's phones began ringing at the same time. They both looked down at them.

"It's a text," Fallon said, looking at Paisley, "from you."

"What?" Paisley grabbed the phone from her. She opened the text message and, to her horror, there was another picture of her and Warren, taken the same night as the one that was shown on television the night before. This one was even more revealing than the first. *Oh my God, this can't be happening*, Paisley thought. The memory of that night came flooding back to her. It was his birthday. Before she was the Sensual Seductress and he was the Prince of Praise. A night when she was Paisley, a dancer at the club trying to figure out how to pay for college, and he was Warren, a struggling singer trying to catch a break in the music industry . . .

Warren was the one and only man she had met at the club she had ever let into the tiny apartment she called home. She had cooked dinner for him and even bought a small cake. After dinner, they sat in the middle of her bed, as she was helping him write lyrics for a new song.

"How about I can't do anything without thinking about you-*I yearn for you, yes I do," Paisley suggested.*

"You know that's kinda corny, Pais. But I like it." He shrugged. "What about My every thought is filled with you-my love for you is strong and true."

Warren's melodic voice caused chill bumps on her arms. She stared at him and smiled. "Yeah, that's what I meant."

"I meant that too." Warren put his guitar down beside him and pulled her to him. "I think about you all the time, and I love you."

His sudden confession made Paisley's heart beat fast. Although it wasn't the first time a man

*had said those words to her, it was the first time
she knew that he meant it. She could see it in
his eyes and hear it in his voice; she could feel
it in his touch and taste it in his kiss. She had
no doubt in her mind that Warren loved her.
She put her forehead against his and kissed him
tenderly.*

"Tell me your fantasy," she whispered.

*He brushed the hair out of her face and smiled.
"You're my fantasy."*

*"Don't even try it. You're not getting off that
easy." She slowly kissed all over his face. "Tell
me."*

"I'm thinking."

*Paisley began licking his neck. "Tell me. I
want to know. Close your eyes and tell me what
you see."*

*Warren's breathing became heavy, and he
finally said, "Janet, the cover of Rolling Stone."*

Paisley laughed, "Really?"

*"Yes, really." He nodded. "But instead of Ja-
net's face, it's yours."*

*"Interesting." Paisley winked. "You know I
have a camera and a tripod."*

*Warren looked at her seductively. "I can have
my own private photo shoot for my birthday?"*

Paisley nodded. "Give me twenty minutes."

She set up the camera in her living room and changed into a worn pair of Guess jeans and a bra. She unloosed her curly hair and put a small mole on her face, a la Janet Jackson.

"OK, Rene, you can come out now," she called to him.

Warren walked out of the bedroom, asking, "Rene?"

"Rene Elizondo, Janet's ex. Those are his hands covering her breasts in the photo," Paisley informed him.

"Well, I don't wanna be your ex, but Lord knows I want my hands covering these in our photo." Warren cupped Paisley's breasts and sucked her neck.

"Let's get started then, Birthday Boy!"

The Bishop

I'm trying to not become frustrated and do anything that will possibly jeopardize my position, my ministry, and most of all, my place in heaven, but at this point, I'm on the brink. I've sat back and said nothing for too long and this entire situation has gotten out of hand. If I don't step in and do something, everything I've worked hard for will be gone, and I refuse to let the fruits of my labor be destroyed. No way, no how. The years I've spent working, preaching, teaching, building, and establishing is just a foundation for the goals I have planned. This is just the beginning and I don't care how much devotion Kollette has to her successful husband, the future of this ministry will not be jeopardized by his inability to sever his ties with some random video chick from his past. I don't care how sexy she is. And Lord knows, that woman is sexy. The tabloids certainly weren't lying when they called her breathtaking because I had to catch my breath when I came face to face with her. Nonetheless, she ain't worth my losing everything over. This situation has gotten out of hand and this was not how things were supposed to turn out, not by a long shot.

"Well, Sister Ebonie, how are you today?" The bishop's voice boomed across the parking lot of the building where he knew she lived. From the way she jumped, he knew he had startled the attractive woman with whom he had worked closely over the past few years.

"Bishop Arnold." She smiled nervously. "I . . . How . . . I'm fine."

"That's good to hear," the bishop smiled as he stepped closer to her. "Can I speak with you a few minutes?"

Ebonie hesitated for a few moments, and then said, "Yes, sir. What can I help you with?"

"I just have a few concerns. It's been brought to my attention that you've decided to resign." The bishop casually leaned on the sleek, silver Infinity M35 that Ebonie drove. *A classy car for a classy woman.*

"And who told you that, Bishop? Let me guess, Kollette, right?"

Bishop Arnold shook his head. "No, it wasn't Kollette at all. Neil was the one who delivered the disappointing news to me."

"Neil," Ebonie sighed. "And he said that I resigned? OK."

"Was Neil wrong in telling me that?"

"Yes, he was wrong. I didn't resign, I was fired," Ebonie told him.

"Fired? By whom?" The bishop frowned as he loosened the knot of his tie.

"Bishop, let me ask you a question. Who hired me to work for the ministry?" Ebonie asked.

"I did," he said matter-of-factly.

"And who gave me the assignment to personally handle Warren Cobb when they realized the potential that his future held?" Ebonie continued.

"That was me." The bishop nodded.

"Whenever there was an issue or concern regarding a situation or project that would directly affect the Ministry, who did I address those concerns with?"

"Again, me."

"Now, Bishop, considering the fact that I've been a member of your staff for the past seven-and-a-half years, and we've never uttered a cross word to each other, do you think that I would resign and not have enough respect for you to give proper notice?"

The bishop considered what Ebonie was asking and slowly answered, "I would think not. But a lot has transpired in the past few days, and I don't know what to think. I believe we are all being tested in some way, and some of us have been placed in some uncomfortable situations that we have to deal with. Jumping ship because it looks like it's sinking may be your reaction. And I understand that."

"Be real, Bishop Arnold, if I was gonna run from this situation, I would've done so the night that Warren was in the accident," Ebonie told him. "That makes no sense."

"Neither does your going to Paisley Lawrence's studio either, but isn't that where you're coming from?" The bishop stood back and waited for Ebonie to answer.

Ebonie's eyes widened in surprise. "Were you following me, Bishop?"

"Not at all, I happened to notice your car in the parking lot." He shrugged.

"I don't believe you." Ebonie shook her head. "Paisley's studio is all the way on the other side of town, past the warehouse district."

"I know where her studio is located. What I don't know is why you were there."

"I was there meeting with Paisley and her publicist," Ebonie answered.

"There was no need for you to meet with them, especially now. I hope you're not trying to, how should I put this, *switch teams*, Ebonie. That wouldn't be a wise move on your part at all," he warned her. "You're a smart girl, and I know you remember that when you were hired, you signed a confidentiality agreement. Anything regarding Warren Cobb or the Ministry that conveniently gets 'leaked' and traced back to you would be detrimental."

"For who?" Ebonie asked, staring the bishop down.

"Anyone involved," the bishop answered.

"Bishop Arnold, you're right, I am a smart girl. You know why? Because when you said you wanted to speak to me for a few minutes, I thought it was to apologize on behalf of the

Ministry for the unwarranted dismissal I was given Saturday night, and to tell me it was all a misunderstanding. You know that I was fired, and you know who fired me.

"My reason for going over to Paisley's studio to meet with her and her publicist this morning was to see if I could possibly deter them from seeking legal action against Kollette for slander and defamation of character which, by the way, if they don't, they'd be crazy. I'm well aware of the confidentiality statement I signed and don't worry, I don't plan on saying a word. Even though she suspects that you're the one stalking her, and I'm inclined to believe the same thing, I won't say a word about the items that were charged to the Ministry that were sent to her house, I won't dare say anything about the background check that was done on her by the Ministry and the 'dirt' you tried to find. And most of all, I won't mention the sad fact that while you're worried about Warren causing damage to the Ministry, the reality is that you don't have the balls to be honest and stand up to Kollette, who's causing all of this. She and Neil, screwing and scheming."

"What are you talking about?" The bishop raised his voice in distress, shocked by everything Ebonie said.

"Kollete, your niece, is sleeping with your so-called 'beloved son' and has been for years. She's evil and insecure, and because of her, the Ministry is gonna fester from the inside out. Lying on national television about having *cancer*, of all things, and you're just gonna stand by and watch. She's such a waste on so many levels, but that's no longer my issue."

"Ebonie," the Bishop said as he looked around the parking lot, "maybe we need to go in and discuss this further."

"We don't need to discuss anything, Bishop. Your secrets are safe with me, it's the others you need to worry about because they're the ones who are gonna bring you down."

Bishop Arnold watched as Ebonie Monroe walked away. Anger and confusion engulfed him as he reached into his suit pocket and took out his cell phone. *How could Kollette do a thing like this after all I've done for her? And Neil, who I opened my heart and my home to when he was just a boy living on the streets. Have I really been that naïve that this has been going on and I haven't realized it?*

"Hey, Dad."

"Meet me at my office," the bishop said into the phone.

"I have some things going on right now. Can it be later?" Neil asked. The bishop heard Kollette laughing in the background and it angered him even more.

"Thirty minutes!" he yelled, and hung up.

The confidence he'd had when he pulled into the parking lot behind Ebonie was now gone, replaced by disgust and doubt. He was all set to handle the situation, but now realized that it was so out of control, this one would definitely be left up to God.

Chapter 22

Paisley turned over in her bed for the hundredth time. She was exhausted and had been in bed for hours, but had yet to fall asleep. It was as if her body wanted to rest, but her mind wouldn't allow it to happen. There was so much going on in her head that she figured she would be tired of thinking, wondering, worrying, and imagining; she was already on edge and her lack of sleep was making it worse. It was as if she could hear every sound in the house; from the water dripping in the kitchen sink to the *whish* of the air coming through the vents.

Climbing out of bed, she decided that maybe a cup of tea would help rest her nerves. She was careful not to wake the dog, sleeping in the sitting area of her bedroom, as she closed the door behind her. Landon's loud snoring could be heard as she passed his bedroom door. *He sounds like a bear*, she thought as she slipped down the steps. The coolness of the kitchen floor surprised her and caused a chill to go up her body. *I shoulda put on some socks.* She reached into the cabinet and removed her silver "The Playground" mug with the pink logo and put it on the counter as she waited for her water to heat up on the stove. She went to the food closet and sorted through her vast array of teabags until she located a chamomile one and prepared her drink. The warm liquid burned her lips as she took the first sip.

As she drank, Paisley walked into the living room of her home—a room she rarely entered. Her attention was drawn to the large picture window, and she peeked through the venetian blinds. When she first saw the shadowy figure standing across the street, she began to panic. As she realized who it was standing in the darkness staring back at her, she thought she was dreaming, or seeing a mirage, at best. She opened the blinds further, and saw that indeed, the man was real. He saw her staring back and started to walk away. Ignoring that she only wore a tank top and a thong, Paisley didn't hesitate disarming her alarm, and slowly opened her front door, ready to chase after him. She didn't have to, because he was now standing in the doorway.

"Warren," she gasped. Before she had the chance to say anything else, his mouth covered hers and his tongue danced with hers. As much as she wanted to pull away, she couldn't. She kissed him back with as much fullness and intensity as he had. She put her arms around his head and he lifted her up, her legs wrapped around his body as he carried her into the house. Within minutes, she was fumbling with the buttons of his shirt and he was taking off her tank top, licking her neck and rubbing her nipples.

Paisley unfastened his belt and pushed down his pants in one motion, and they fell on the thick carpet. Her fingers ran along the thickness of his manhood and she arched her back as he removed her lacy thong. Neither one said a word, knowing that if they spoke, the magic of the moment may be broken. The heat between her legs intensified as she felt his tongue tasting her. She wanted to moan, but she couldn't. Instead, she grabbed his head and held on as he sent her into a state of oblivion.

When she felt that she could take it no more, he entered her, slowly, intensely, as if he wanted to savor each moment, each second, each plunge. They stared at one another in silence, holding on to their passion, neither one wanting it to end. The rhythm of their bodies increased, faster and faster; she lifted her body to meet his with each thrust, clawing into his shoulders as they approached the point of ecstasy they both needed. The core of her body seemed to erupt as she climaxed along with him.

When it was over, they both lay intertwined in the middle of her living room floor, bodies wet with perspiration, neither one daring to move. *Exhausted.* He was hers, she was his in that very moment and nothing else mattered. Theirs was a forbidden love, a love that could never be, they both knew it. Their lovemaking had been wrong on so many levels, but to them, it was the most right thing in the world. She was content, and so was he. The much needed sleep she desired soon arrived.

"Paisley . . . Paisley . . ."

Paisley's eyes fluttered open and she felt a hand under her chin. As she looked up to stare into her lover's eyes, she realized that it wasn't Warren at all, it was Scooter. She sat up.

"Baby, are you okay?" he asked, touching her face softly.

"I'm fine," she said slowly, realizing that she had been dreaming. She glanced around, trying to figure out where she was and exactly what she had done. *Oh shit, did I sleep with Scooter?* Looking down, she was relieved to see that she was still fully dressed and lying on Chester's sofa. "What are you doing here?"

"I came by to check on you," he told her.

"I guess you got the text message, too, huh?" Paisley asked.

"Yeah, I did." Scooter nodded.

"And the e-mail?"

"Yeah, the e-mail too," he admitted.

Paisley shook her head in disbelief. Whoever was out to get her was doing a damn good job. Not only had they hacked into her Web site and posted the pictures of her and Warren, they also sent the pictures to everyone in her cell phone, and everyone in her e-mail address book. Her life had turned even more upside down than after the accident. She knew her parents were pissed. In an effort to avoid her mother, she hadn't called them with her new cell number.

I can't deal with Mama's yelling and lecturing in addition to everything else that's going on around here. Reporters and photographers were everywhere; once again she had to change her cell phone number, and she was considering closing The Playground until things died down again. One thing her clients appreciated was that they could come to class inconspicuously, secretly embrace that sexy diva within, get their workouts on, and leave, no questions asked. Now, with everything going on, her clients pulled out of the parking lot once they saw the paparazzi crowded out front.

Her only saving grace was Miriam "Magic" Johnson, one of the dancers they just hired for the club. Magic was the spitting image of Paisley; from their coloring to their build. Chester had begun teasing and calling her PJ or Paisley Jr. in rehearsals. When they called and asked if she could be Paisley's decoy for a couple of days, which included staying at Paisley's house, the young girl was ecstatic and didn't hesitate to say yes.

"Life's a bitch, ain't it?" she asked Scooter. "The moment I decide to hang up my hat as the Sensual Seductress and get out of the spotlight, this happens."

"Look at it as a sign that maybe you don't need to hang up your hat," Scooter teased.

She shook her head. "OK, He couldn't give me some other sign, like maybe a part in a Spike Lee movie or something?"

"Come on, now how boring and obvious would that be? And you know better than anyone that God has a sense of humor," Scooter told her.

"Don't bring God into this, Scooter. That's blasphemous."

"You don't know why this is happening. Maybe this situation will be the door that leads you and Warren back to one another." He shrugged.

Paisley couldn't help laughing at her friend's sincerity. "But I thought you wanted the door to lead me to you."

"I want the door to lead you to happiness." Scooter sighed. "I don't want you to be with me knowing that I can't make you happy."

"I don't think a person's happiness lies in another person, Scooter, you know that. Happiness is within one's self. Only I can make me happy."

"You know what I mean, Paisley."

"I do," she told him, then added, "I owe you an apology for my little disappearing stunt the other night. I'm sorry."

"You did what you had to do. I admit I was pissed, but I know you and I know you did what you felt you had to do."

"Paisley, I have to run out for a bit, but I'll be right back." Chester poked his head in the room. "Oh, and Dr. Singleton is here."

She glanced up and saw Evan standing in the doorway behind her cousin, medical bag in hand. She smiled weakly. "Hello."

"Hello, yourself. I allow you to get your cast off and this is what happens." He shook his head at her. "I have to track you down for my house calls."

"I'll leave you two alone." Scooter excused himself.

"I told you a long time ago that you didn't have to make house calls," she told him, sitting up.

"Yeah, but it's doctor's orders, not patient's orders. Remember that."

"I'm fine, Evan." She blinked, looking down.

"I'm not worried about the physical, Paisley, I'm worried about your overall well-being."

"I guess you heard about what happened. I told you my life was chaotic as hell, aren't you glad I won't go out with you?"

"No, that's why I keep asking you out," he replied. "And, no, I don't know what happened. Why don't you tell me?"

She paused and stared into his handsome face, and suddenly, she realized that she wanted to tell him everything, and she did. She told him all about how she and Warren were the best of friends and how they eventually became lovers, about how his marriage to Kollette led to his success and how she loved him. And as she talked, she shared with him that seeing Warren on television beside Kollette had been the eye-opener that indeed, no matter how much she loved Warren and he claimed to love her, Kollette was the one who wore the ring and had his last name, not her. Paisley cried as she shared with Evan that she felt betrayed not by Warren, but by herself for allowing her heart to hold on to the feelings that she had for him, even after all these years.

"I've got to be the dumbest woman ever, huh?" She wiped away the tears that fell down her cheek. "Is dumbness a medical diagnosis?"

"If it were, it would be a worldwide epidemic." Evan smiled. "And I would definitely be a survivor. You're not dumb, Paisley, you're just heartbroken and have been for a while. The good thing is, there's a cure for it."

"And what's that?" she asked.

"Love," he replied. "You have to open yourself up and allow someone to love you. You're worth it."

"Easier said than done." She shrugged her shoulders.

"Doctor's orders." He leaned over and kissed her gently. The softness of his lips touching hers was just as enjoyable as she had imagined. Their mouths parted and his tongue sensually danced with hers. They tasted each other for what seemed like endless moments. And when they finally broke apart, she realized that not Warren, nor Kollette, nor anyone else mattered.

"Scooter and I are about to order some food from Ochie's," Landon came in and announced.

Paisley had forgotten that he was there. After hashing it out in her office, she conceded that she did indeed need him. There was still some slight tension between them, but she realized he had a genuine concern for her safety and well-being. *In addition to his feeling some type of way for my best friend. He acted like he hated to leave her at the studio when I told him I was ready to leave.*

"No, I'm good," Paisley told him.

"You haven't eaten all day, Paisley," Landon told her, "you're getting something. If you don't want Ochie's that's fine, I'll get something else."

"Would you like to stay for dinner?" Paisley asked Evan.

"Anything for my patient." He grinned. "Besides, I need to be here to make sure you eat."

"Ochie's is fine. Get me the stewed chicken."

"I'll order something for Seymone, too. She's stopping by when she leaves the studio. What do you think she wants?" Landon asked.

"You can get her the same thing." Paisley tried not to laugh. Landon's crush on her best friend was funny.

"Man, order me the curry," Evan told him.

"Cool," Landon said and went to place their order. An hour later, just as their food arrived, Seymone and Chester walked through the door. Paisley was relieved neither one commented on Evan being there beside her, but she knew she would hear about it later.

"Oh my God, is that Ochie's?" she asked.

"Yep." Paisley nodded.

"Thank God, I'm starving." Chester began rummaging through the bags sitting in the middle of his dining room table.

Paisley looked at Scooter, who looked at Landon, who turned to Evan, who looked back at Paisley, and then all eyes fell on Chester.

"Oh," Paisley mumbled.

"Oh, what?" Chester asked. "Say it ain't so. I know y'all ain't order Ochie's, had it delivered to my house, and ain't get me *nothing!*"

"Of course we got you something, Chester, calm down!" Paisley lied.

"We got you stewed chicken." Landon reached into the bag, pulled out a greasy Styrofoam container, and passed it to him.

"I was about to say." Chester smiled and they all breathed a sigh of relief. "Hold up, let me take that food in the kitchen and put it on some real plates. Just because the food came from the hood doesn't mean we can't eat off china, sweeties."

"I'll do it," Paisley said and grabbed the bags. "Seymone, you can come and help."

The two women walked into the kitchen and Paisley took plates from the cabinet.

"We're gonna have to share one of those stewed chickens," Paisley told her.

"I take it you didn't order Chester anything?" Seymone laughed.

"Girl, I forgot about Chester to tell the truth," Paisley told her.

"Did you forget me, too?" Seymone asked.

"Yep, but you know Landon remembered you," Paisley teased. "I swear, sometimes I think he forgets that both of you are engaged."

"No, he doesn't. You need to quit, Paisley." Seymone rolled her eyes as she gathered eating utensils out of the drawer.

"Whatever," Paisley told her. "Was it a madhouse at the studio when you left?"

"It was until Magic left. It's amazing how much she looks like you, especially when she put on those sunglasses and a hat. She walked out and got into the SUV and they were all over her. She even had the nerve to wave as she pulled off," Seymone laughed. "She said she was going straight to the club."

"I hope she's okay," Paisley commented. "I don't want some fool harming her thinking that she's me."

"I think she'll be good. Diesel is gonna have security meet her outside."

"That's good." Paisley nodded, grateful that her friends seemed to have everything under control.

"What's taking so long?" Chester called out. "I'm hungry!"

"We're coming," Paisley replied. Soon, they were all seated around the table cracking open a bottle of white zinfandel, and eating like one big family. They laughed and joked, and Paisley felt better than she had in weeks. Despite all the continual and constant drama, everyone at this table, along with Diesel and Fallon, had her back. For the first time in a long time, she felt like she had someone she could confide in, without being judged. "When I went to see Warren the other night, he told me that someone had e-mailed him the picture. It was the first time I had seen that picture in years."

"Do you believe he did this?" Evan asked.

"I don't know. I don't think he did."

"But then again, you don't know," Seymone said. "Do you have copies of the pictures?"

"I have a few." Paisley thought about the pictures that she had tucked under her mattress along with the negatives. She was actually surprised that Warren still had his set.

"Are you sure no one took yours and made copies?" Chester suggested.

"No one even knew that I had the pictures." Paisley glanced over at her best friend who was shaking her head. "And I'm sure Warren didn't tell anyone that he had pictures of us. That would be crazy."

"What is he saying about all of this?" Seymone asked.

"I don't know. I swear, I know you all don't believe me, but I haven't talked to him since Saturday night."

"Well, according to Ebonie, no one has seen or heard from him since Kollette's grandstand announcement about your stalking him and her having cancer," Landon told her.

"Hmm, if I were married and still had sexy pictures of me and my ex, where would I keep them?" Seymone inquired, rubbing her chin as if she was deep in thought.

"Well, I'm not married, but I know where I keep mine," Chester cackled.

"But what I don't get is if I'm married, why would I keep sexy pictures of me and my ex?" Seymone shrugged. "Aren't you supposed to get rid of stuff like that before you say 'I do'?"

"Not if you're still in love with the person in the pictures." Scooter stared at Paisley. "You hold on to them. You hold on to all the memories."

"But where would you keep them?" Seymone asked again. "In a shoe box? In your desk? It has to be somewhere inconspicuous. Come on, you all are men . . . Well, you're excused, Chester."

"Go to hell." Chester cut his eyes at Seymone as they all laughed. "Now, if I were a married man—"

"A straight, married man," Seymone corrected him.

"A straight, unhappily married man," Paisley volunteered, swallowing the last of her wine and refilling her glass.

"A world-famous, straight, unhappily married man," Scooter added to the list.

"Okay, if I were a world-famous, straight, unhappily married man who had sexy pics of me and my ex—" Chester began again.

"Your ex who was a world-famous video-vixen-slash-model with a successful business . . ." Seymone stated.

"We get the picture." Paisley shushed her.

"Yes, we do," Chester said. "I would probably keep the pictures locked away."

"Now that makes sense." Paisley nodded. "But what would you do with the key?"

"Hmm . . ." Chester frowned. "Scooter, what would you do with the key?"

"I would probably give it to Diesel and tell him if anything happened to me, take care of this." Scooter shrugged.

"Why would you give the key to Diesel?" Seymone asked.

"How could you look at the pictures whenever you wanted to if Diesel has the key?" Paisley questioned.

"I wouldn't have to look at them. If I'm still in love with my ex, she's in my mind and I know what she looks like. I think about her all the time. Her image is etched in my mind. The pictures are just a bonus for every now and then."

"Damn, now that makes sense," Chester agreed.

Landon, who had been quiet the entire time, suddenly stood up. "I got a run to make. Can you guys stick around until I get back?"

"What's wrong?" Seymone looked disappointed.

"I just gotta go handle something right quick." Landon looked over at her and touched her hand. The gesture didn't go unnoticed by Paisley.

"Go ahead, man. We ain't going nowhere and we'll make sure Paisley doesn't, either," Scooter assured him.

"Thanks." Landon nodded.

"Landon, you think I can get a ride to the hotel?" Seymone asked.

"Sure, you ready?" Landon turned around.

"Let me just grab my bag," Seymone said.

"OK." Paisley gave her a hug. *I wonder if Seymone is just trying to get some alone time with Landon?* She started to ask her if there was some sort of ulterior motive to asking him for a ride, but she didn't.

"Paisley, I need to leave, too. I'll call you later and check on you." Evan said.

"I'd like that." Paisley walked him to the door and kissed him good-bye. When she returned into the kitchen, Scooter was sitting alone.

"So," Scooter asked when they were alone, "what's up with you and the doctor, Paisley?"

"What? There *you* go." Paisley rolled her eyes at him. "Nothing."

"Okay, nothing," Scooter said sarcastically.

"We're just friends," Paisley said.

"For now." Scooter shook his head. "I knew I shoulda gone to medical school."

The doorbell rang and Chester's voice sang, "I'll get it. Feel free to clear the table and do the dishes."

Paisley picked up some of the plates and walked into the kitchen. Her thoughts turned to Evan as she began running a sink of warm dishwater.

"Paisley, someone's here to see you," Chester said as he walked into the kitchen.

"Mama," she said slowly, seeing her mother standing beside Chester, impeccably dressed in a dark gray pantsuit and black heels. *I wonder if that's how I'll look in twenty-five years?*

"Hey, Paisley," her mother said.

"What are you doing here? Where's Daddy?" Paisley asked.

"I came alone. He's at home," her mother told her. Paisley glanced over at Chester, hoping he would say something, but he remained silent.

"Oh." Paisley became nervous. "I guess you're here . . . because . . ."

"I'm here because you need me," her mother sighed. "I'm here because I'm your mother and despite everything that's gone on between us, I'm here because I love you, Paisley."

"Huh?" Paisley looked at her strangely. This wasn't like Emma Jean at all, and she had to wonder if it was some sort of practical joke.

"She's here to support her daughter," Chester said matterof-factly.

Paisley looked at her mother, who gave her a smile.

What the hell, Paisley thought. *OK, I know I'm tripping because Emma Jean Lawrence hasn't smiled at me since I was fifteen and won an award at the Rotary Club luncheon.* She looked into her mother's eyes and saw something that she hadn't seen in years . . . *love.*

Neil

A'ight. I'll be the first to admit that I fucked up. I mean, I fucked up big time. I don't know what I was thinking agreeing to even be a part of this shit. At first, when Kollette called me and told me about Warren being in an accident and in a coma and shit, I was afraid he was gonna die, just like everyone else. I mean, Warren is my nigga. He's a cool dude and I like him. I was just as surprised as everyone else that he was driving a car with fine-ass Paisley Lawrence inside.

Believe it or not, that brought me a little bit of relief due to the fact that I'd been fucking Kollette for the past eight years. Well, to be honest, we started fucking back in high school and we've never stopped. The whole reason she married Warren all those years ago was to make me jealous, but it didn't work. How could I be jealous when, number one, I knew he didn't love her and he married her out of need, and number two, she was still sleeping with me whenever I wanted it.

Kollette ain't the best looking broad on the block, but believe me, she gives the greatest head a man could ever want. Her nickname in high school was "Slurpee" because those huge lips can slurp around a man's Johnson like no one else. She's also dumb as a damn brick, which is why I convinced her to talk my beloved father into backing Warren's singing career. He's always had a soft spot for her ugly ass, and

I often wondered if she was sucking him off, too. Sure enough, the bishop obliged, Warren blew up, we all got paid, and life was pretty damn sweet until the damn accident.

When Kollette found out about it, she was pissed. Her dumb ass actually thought about leaving Warren until I reminded her that he was the bread and butter we were living off of. Instead, I told her to think before doing something irrational. Kollette was the typical woman scorned and she wasn't even concerned with whether Warren was having an affair.

All her dumb ass was worried about was retaliation against Paisley Lawrence. So, one night, she convinced me to sneak into Paisley's hospital room and check her out. Fine with me, I wanted to see Paisley's fine ass anyway. So I headed down to her floor, grabbed a face mask off a nearby cart, and went into her room. Damn, she was so beautiful. I stared at her for what seemed like hours; until she woke up.

She started panicking and I hauled ass outta there. I told Kollette how scared Paisley was when she woke up and saw me standing at the end of her bed, and she thought it was hilarious. So much so that she wanted to scare her even more. Imagine my surprise when she reached into her purse and pulled out a BlackBerry and a set of keys and told me that the police recovered them from the accident scene and gave them to her thinking that they were Warren's. They were, in fact, Paisley's.

At that moment, it became Kollette's goal in life to make Paisley Lawrence go crazy. I don't know why I agreed to go along with the plan, other than the fact that it was kind of a turn on to think that I had access to Paisley's private life. I wanted to see more of her. I thought of her lying in bed, looking like a chocolate Sleeping Beauty and I wanted to see more. Kollette's goal was to somehow drive Paisley crazy, my goal was to watch her, be near her. It became a fundamental desire for me. I can't explain it. To me, it wasn't stalking; it was fulfilling a request given by a friend in need. In a way, I was saving Warren's marriage. I was making his wife happy.

The first time I slipped into Paisley's house, no one was home. She hadn't even been released from the hospital. I used her key and let myself in. Her immaculate home was so huge that it took me nearly three hours to explore it. Each time I went, I took a memento: a Juicy Couture bracelet—which would come in handy when I dropped off the dog exactly like the one in a picture with Paisley when she was little, that I came across in her desk drawer, a rhinestone studded tank top with the logo from her studio, a silver business card holder, and of course, a pair of lacy underwear from her drawer; little things that wouldn't be obvious.

Finding out that Warren hired Landon Malone to act as Paisley's personal security was a surprise of sorts. When I asked him about his decision, he brushed me off, telling me I was getting a little too personal. He was so cavalier and condescending when he said it that I didn't know whether to be pissed or hurt. Granted, I was fucking his wife, but I still felt like we were friends. How could he treat me like I was a member of his random entourage?

Warren Malone had gotten above himself and he needed to be taken down a notch or two. I convinced Kollette that we could take Warren's apparent relationship with Paisley to a whole other level, exposing it as an affair, presenting her as the betrayed wife, and putting him in a position where he couldn't leave her. It was brilliant, so much so that Warren had basically vanished after his and Kollette's appearance on Gospel Today. No one has seen or heard from him. Kollette has the nerve to be worried about her missing husband, but I know she'll be back soon to handle her business as usual—slurp, slurp!

"You bastard!"

Neil turned to see Landon, Warren and Bishop Arnold standing in the doorway of his office.

"Landon, what the hell has gotten into you, man?" Neil looked at him like he was crazy.

"Where the hell are the pictures?" Landon demanded.

"What are you talking about?" Neil feigned a look of confusion.

"Warren's safety deposit box, the key. You stole the pictures and used them, you shiesty little—"

"Landon, you're tripping." Neil took a step back. The way Warren was looking at him made him uneasy.

"No I'm not. I was there that night Warren came to for that brief moment and told you to 'give P the key' in his top drawer. I thought he was delusional, but I get it now. Where the hell are the pictures?" Landon ran over to Neil and started choking him. Neil began clawing at Landon's hands, but they tightened around his neck. He gasped as he tried to breathe, his eyes watering. Landon shook him slightly and repeated, "Where are they? Tell me!"

"Landon, let him go," Warren's voice screamed.

For a slight second, Neil felt a bit of relief, thinking that Landon would obey the instructions, but his grip remained tight.

"You low-down conniving snake, how could you do this?" Warren growled.

Sinking under Landon's grip, Neil tried unsuccessfully to get away. Warren walked behind Landon and grabbed him by the shoulders. Landon jerked away, continuing to choke Neil.

"Landon, you're gonna hurt him!" Warren warned.

"No, I'm gonna kill him!" Landon replied.

"No, you're not. Let him go!" the bishop yelled. Landon loosened his grip and Neil began coughing as he rubbed his neck. The bishop glared at him and commanded, "Start talking!"

"I don't have the pictures," Neil lied.

Landon lunged at him and he moved quickly. Neil looked over at the bishop. "He's crazy!"

To Neil's surprise, the bishop shook his head. "He's not crazy. I know all about you and Kollette's little schemes. I can't believe the two of you! After all I've done to support you both, you turn around and do something like this to me? Do you realize the damage that the two of you have caused my ministry?"

"Bishop, you know I would never—"

SLAP! The sound of the bishop's palm against Neil's face echoed in the office. The sting on his cheek was nothing compared to the anger Neil felt. The natural reaction to hit the bishop back was immediately interrupted by the bishop's fist into his gut, causing him to fall backward. As he tried to sit up, the bishop's foot pushed him back down.

"Bishop!" The tables were now turned, and Landon was trying to subdue the bishop.

"Landon, get out. I will handle this!" the bishop told him.

"Naw, Bishop." Landon glared. "This fool . . ."

Neil watched as the two men looked each other in the eye. Finally, the bishop said, "I got this! I know everything this *fool* has done and I'm telling you I got this! The pictures, the break-ins into Paisley's home, *everything!* It will be dealt with, trust me. Now, I need you to just leave and let me handle this."

Landon hesitated. "Fine, Bishop. I trust you." He walked out.

As the door slammed, Neil began to panic, knowing that there would be no witnesses to whatever wrath the bishop was about to bestow upon him.

Epilogue

Listen, Mama, Seymone and I have to do this party at the studio tonight. Do you want to go over to Chester's and spend the night because it's probably gonna be kind of late when I get back?" Paisley asked, feeling guilty. Her mother's visits the past few weeks had been pleasant and, to her surprise, she really didn't want to leave her.

"Girl, don't be trying to dump me off on Chester. I can stay right at your house." Her mother laughed.

The paparazzi had finally moved on to the next big story and Paisley had returned to her own home. With the exception of the typical photographer every now and then when they went out to eat, or the frequent fans they ran into every now and then with a cell phone camera, Paisley's life was back to normal.

"You don't need to be here by yourself. I'll ask Landon if he can stay with you instead of coming to the studio," Paisley suggested.

"Or, she can come to the studio with us." Seymone shrugged.

Paisley stared at her best friend and stopped herself before asking if she was on crack.

"I don't mind tagging along," Emma Jean replied.

"She was just joking, Mama," Paisley quickly said.

"What kind of party is it? Do I need to dress up?" Emma Jean asked. "I don't think I brought anything really dressy."

Seymone started giggling. "No, it's not a party like that."

"Mama, really, I don't think you want to come. Seymone and I will be working." Paisley tried to think of something to deter her mother from coming with them.

"Well, I think I would like to see you girls working. Maybe I can get a better understanding of what you do," Emma Jean told them. "Now, tell me what I need to wear because I'm going."

Paisley shook her head, knowing that her mother would be joining them along with the other twenty women at The Playground for the private Girls Night Out they had scheduled.

"Just wear some workout clothes, Mama," Paisley sighed.

"I don't even think I have any with me." Her mother began digging in her suitcase.

"Don't worry, Ms. EJ, we have a salon full of gear at the studio that you can choose from. But do you have any stilettos?" Seymone asked.

Emma Jean's eyes widened and she shook her head. "No, I only have pumps."

"And you need to be thinking about your 'play name'," Seymone told her.

"What is a 'play name'?" Emma Jean looked at the girls suspiciously.

"Whatever name you think personafies the sexy diva within."

Paisley could not believe Seymone was having this conversation with her mother of all people. A couple of months ago, she would never had thought her mother would be stepping foot into The Playground, and now she was trying to think of her "play name."

"Hmm," Emma Jean said, "what about Siren? You know that's what Gordon calls me sometimes when . . ."

"Oh God," Paisley groaned, not wanting to think about why her mother picked that name. "Mama, please."

"All right now, Siren," Seymone laughed. "That's *hot!*"

The dog began barking uncontrollably, alerting Paisley that something was not right outside.

"What in the world?" Seymone frowned.

"Someone must be outside." Paisley tried not to panic. Paisley's heart began to pound as she got up and walked into the hallway. The dog continued to bark at the door and Paisley headed down the steps.

"Paisley, where are you going?" Seymone frowned.

"To see what Killa is barking at," Paisley told her. She went into the living room and looked out the window. Standing on her porch was a UPS delivery man. Relieved, she yelled, "It's just the UPS man. Killa shut up!"

Paisley picked her small dog up into her arms as she opened the door.

"How you doing, ma'am?" the delivery man smiled.

"I'm good." She tried to hold on to the wiggling animal.

"I have a delivery for Paisley Lawrence," he told her.

"That's me," Paisley said and signed the electronic clipboard.

"The box is fairly heavy. You want me to bring it in for you?" the man offered.

"I can get it," Seymone said as she walked down the steps and joined her best friend in the doorway. She reached down and pulled the box into the foyer.

"Oh." The deliveryman sounded disappointed. He looked at the two women and said, "I'm not gonna front. I'm a big fan of both of you. Can a brother get a pic with you?"

Paisley shook her head. "Sorry, friend, no pics, and if you're a fan, you know why."

"I know. I just thought I would give it a shot." The man grinned.

"It's all good," she told him.

"I gotta say it was nice to meet you in person, though." He nodded, then walked away. Paisley watched until he got into his truck and pulled off. By the time Paisley closed the door, Seymone had carried the box into the kitchen and placed it on Paisley's large marble table. "I don't even know if I wanna open this."

"Maybe you should wait until Landon gets out of the shower," Seymone suggested.

Paisley put the dog down on the floor and grabbed a knife out of a nearby drawer. She placed the tip of the blade against the brown tape and slit the box open. Nervously, she closed her eyes and lifted the top. It was filled with white Styrofoam peanuts. She put her hand inside and began pulling them out, not caring that they fell to the floor. Killa began playing with them as she continued her search.

"What's that?" Landon asked, walking into the kitchen.

"The UPS man just dropped it off," Seymone told him. "I told her to wait for you before she opened it, but you know how hardheaded she is."

"What? Move, Paisley." Landon slid the box from in front of her. "You don't know what could be in here."

"That's what I was trying to see," she told him, waiting as he now pulled out handfuls of Styrofoam and dropped them. He frowned as he said, "Are you sure there's anything even in here?"

"That box has some weight to it," Seymone replied. "It's not empty at all. Something's in there."

"Wait, I feel something," he said, and pulled out a Styrofoam-wrapped item. He removed the coating to reveal a rhinestone studded Black-Berry.

"That's my phone!" Paisley took it from him. "The one I thought I lost!"

"Wait, there's something else," Landon said. He pulled out a larger wrapped item, which turned out to be Paisley's laptop.

"Oh, my God," Paisley gasped.

Landon continued as he pulled out another envelope holding something else. He opened it and poured out Paisley's missing keys.

"This is crazy." Seymone stood and watched in amazement. "Is that everything?" Paisley asked. "I think so," Landon told her. He flipped the box over and the remaining Styrofoam fell out, along with a small envelope with Paisley's name on it. "Wait, there's a note or a letter or something," Seymone said, picking it up off the table and passing it to Paisley.

Paisley took it from her and hesitated as she opened it, afraid of what it may say. She blinked as she read handwritten words on the paper:

Ms. Lawrence,

Let me begin by apologizing for everything that you've been through these past few weeks. The harrowing, traumatic chain of events that you've endured is unimaginable, but your strength and versatility prevailed and one can't help but admire the class with which you have handled the situation. You are truly a lady, if nothing else, and I am humbled by your grace. Those who doubt you obviously do not know you. I was one of those doubters. And for that, I also apologize.

Enclosed, you will find the personal effects that were stolen from you. Let me assure you that those responsible have been dealt with accordingly. The blatant disrespect that was shown to you, the mental anguish they caused, and the attack on your reputation will not go unpunished. I personally have dealt with them and no court system anywhere can inflict any greater punishment on the guilty parties than I can. It's over, Ms. Lawrence. You

*are free to continue the successful journey
that you were travelling on before the accident.*

*We all know that everything happens
for a reason, and there is a lesson in everything. This experience has enlightened me
to the fact that every saint has a past, and
every sinner has a future. So many times,
we run from the mistakes that we've made
and the judgments that come along with
them. You, my dear, have embraced all
that you are and what becomes you. I will
continue to pray for you as I hope you will
do the same for me. Blessings,*

J. A.

Paisley folded the letter and placed it back in
the envelope. "Who is it from?" Seymone asked.
"It doesn't matter." Paisley sighed, reflecting
on everything she had just read. She knew that
it had come from the bishop, but there was no
need to tell that to anyone. It was finally over and
she was ready to move on. "Go tell Emma Jean
the Siren we gotta go before we're late."